Powderhouse

Powderhouse
Scientific Postscript and Last Protocol

Jens Bjørneboe

Translated from the Norwegian by
Esther Greenleaf Mürer

Dufour Editions

First published in the United States of America, 2000
by Dufour Editions Inc., Chester Springs, Pennsylvania 19425

Original title: Kruttårnet. (1969). © Gyldendal norsk forlag
© Esther Greenleaf Mürer 2000: English translation
of Jens Bjørneboe: *Powderhouse*

Publication of this volume has been aided by
a grant from the Norwegian Ministry of Culture.

Powderhouse is the second volume in a trilogy which
also includes *Moment of Freedom* and *The Silence*.

Cover design by James B. Elliott

Cover illustration: Frans Widerberg: Beherskeren gjennom ilden
(The Conqueror Through Fire), 1976. 140 x 105 cms., oil on canvas.
Property of Bergen Art Museum. Photographer Geir S. Johannessen.
Copyright DACS 1999

Dufour ISBN 0-8023-1331-0

Library of Congress Cataloging-in-Publication Data

Bjørneboe, Jens, 1920-1976.
    [Kruttårnet. English]
    Powderhouse : Scientific postscript and last protocol / Jens
Bjørneboe ; translated from the Norwegian by Esther
Greenleaf Mürer.
        p.   cm.
    ISBN 0-8023-1331-0 (pbk.)
    I. Mürer, Esther Greenleaf. II. Title.
PT8950.B528K713   1999
839.8'2374--dc21   99-39925
                                                         CIP

Printed and bound in the United States of America

Contents

Ewig jung ist nur die Sonne
Sie allein ist ewig schön

CFM

[C.F. Meyer]

Translator's Introduction

Powderhouse was my introduction to the writings of Jens Bjørneboe. It is the second volume in his trilogy of experimental novels, following *Moment of Freedom* (1966). However, I first read it without realizing that it was a sequel to anything. My husband, Erik, is Norwegian, and we had been living in Norway since 1965. Being an American abroad during the Vietnam War was for me an increasingly conflicted and isolating experience. Evil though I felt my country's actions to be, I could not deny my own complicity in them, witting or not. A single incident will illustrate: Early in our stay we encountered an antiwar procession in downtown Oslo. My first impulse was to join them. But then I saw a sign, "U-ᛏ-A," and thought, "No, it's *me* you're protesting against." So I stood there and looked as many of the marchers in the eye as I could.

For Christmas 1969 Erik gave me a newly-published novel, *Powderhouse* by Jens Bjørneboe. With my still-rudimentary Norwegian it took me two or three weeks to plough through it, but I felt I was in the presence of someone who shared my experience of being (in Pogo's words) "in the extreme middle." The swings between graphic violence and intense lyricism, the whole tempered by what the narrator of *Moment of Freedom* calls "Florentine laughter," mirrored my inner state wonderfully. As I finished the book I had only one thought: "I have to translate this." The next day I telephoned the author.

As things worked out I did not start translating until we

had returned to the U.S. in 1972, and I began with *Moment of Freedom*. Bjørneboe showed hardly any interest in that project; I don't know whether he read the finished translation or not. On the other hand, he did respond to my questions about *Powderhouse*, read the translation in manuscript and offered suggestions. The difference is doubtless due to several factors, but this excerpt from a 1974 letter is revealing:

> A strange side of *Powderhouse* is that it's the one of my books that I sometimes open and read. That may mean that I haven't fully understood it myself, or that I'm not finished with it. I am still in love with this particular book, but also a little confused, I don't completely see through it. And after all, it's precisely when we don't wholly understand a person, when we feel that we're up against something mysterious which we don't comprehend—that we fall in love. . . . *The Silence* (the third volume of the trilogy, 1973) and *Moment of Freedom* I've almost forgotten . . .

If the form of *Moment of Freedom* is a painting or collage, *Powderhouse* defies genre boundaries in a different way. Bjørneboe wrote in the same letter,

> I don't know myself what genre it belongs to. You yourself once characterized it as an "essay," and I agree with that—also in the true sense of the word,—an "attempt". . . Strictly speaking everything I write is both essay and attempt, experiment. I think it has to be that way, so that I don't get into a rut, don't stagnate. At the same time *Powder* is also decidedly a piece of polemics. But it has its very strong, purely poetic element. But there is one thing it is *not*, namely a psychological novel about the middle class's daily (and nightly) problems. The book is quite certainly not entirely successful from a literary standpoint,—*but:* should it really be judged as literature? And what does "literary" really mean?—Me, I only judge a book by

one single yardstick: Have I learnt something from it? Have I become wiser, older, do I know more than before—about myself, about the world, about people? Therefore I don't distinguish between "belles lettres" and "nonfiction." The most correct term for *Powderhouse* may be simply "book."

And so to the book itself, which takes the form of a journal. The scene has shifted from *Moment of Freedom*'s Alpine principality of Heiligenberg to La Poudrière, a private and highly unorthodox asylum for the criminally insane in Alsace. The narrator now lives in a small cottage on the hospital grounds, where he functions as groundskeeper and general odd-job man while continuing work on his monumental opus, "The History of Bestiality."[1]

As in *Moment of Freedom*, the ambiguity of the narrator's position is indicated by a pun. In the previous book he was a *rettstjener* (courthouse factotum/Servant of Justice); here he describes himself as a *renovasjonsarbeider* ("renovation worker"), a Norwegian euphemism for garbage collector (the dual meaning is underscored in several places). He claims that Dr. Lefèvre, the head of the institute, calls him "combination caretaker and physician-in-chief," meaning "chief ideologist and father-confessor to nearly everybody." Given the free-wheeling nature of Lefèvre's therapeutic methods, however, the narrator may well be a patient.

Once again, not much happens. Dr. Lefèvre and the narrator go on an LSD trip. One of the inmates attempts suicide. The asylum cat and a hedgehog are important characters. The narrator has conversations with various people, and lyrical erotic interludes with the nurse Christine. He reminisces and ruminates. A wispy plot strand concerns the murder of another of the inmates, a former interrogator for the French in Algeria.

All this serves as counterpoint to a harrowing lecture series which, we are told, is part of Lefèvre's therapeutic method. The narrator leads off with a long and graphic lecture entitled "The Witches' Revolution," in which he describes the Church's persecution of heretics and witches during the Reformation as part of a "permanent witchhunt" which he sees as characteristic of Western culture, and attempts to get at its metaphysical roots. The second lecture, by Lacroix, a former executioner, concerns the public executioner's lot and examines various methods of execution in gruesome detail to show that there is no such thing as a humane, fast and painless method of capital punishment. Lefèvre's concluding talk, "The Culture of the Stake," centers on what motivates the heretic to risk such persecution.

Bjørneboe's early experience as a teacher in a Waldorf school, where myths and legends form the basis of the curriculum, had a lasting effect on his writing. His tendency to think in mythological terms often causes his work to lack nuance; his characters tend to be types rather than people.

The interplay between the gruesome passages and the lyrical ones likewise harks back to his early pedagogical experience. In a 1953 essay, "Two Years at a Rudolf Steiner School," he writes of the necessity for finding the right balance between telling the children pious legends (e.g. Francis of Assisi) and animal fables (Reynard the Fox).

It's downright refreshing for a teacher to see how the children become wild and unruly when they've heard a sufficient number of pious legends. As saints they become totally unusable. If you want children to be nice and placid, you must resort to the exact opposite of the legends.

And the opposite is the animal fables. . . . When the children have heard about Reynard long enough, they don't want any more. They're tired of cowardice, mendacity, hypocrisy, and deviltry. They become strikingly docile. . . .

But the fox would be impossible without Francis. The children have become acquainted with the extremes of human possibility: the beast and the saint. People need them both.[2]

Little has been written about *Powderhouse* as a novel in its own right; most commentators treat it, if at all, as an adjunct to *Moment of Freedom*. However, the book went through a long period of independent gestation. In a note apparently written in 1959, Bjørneboe sketched his ideas for a "NEW, MAJOR WORK" which would "collect the whole content and aim" of his previous novels of social criticism in one big book, "the Book about Our Time."[3] It would not only document the atrocities of the twentieth century but would include "a look back on history, all the way back to the Inquisition, the heretic burnings and witch trials, a comprehensive, large-scale treatment of the history of atrocity."

He envisioned the action as taking place "in a sanatorium in the Alps—with a doctor—The Great Doctor—as central figure. Here at the sanatorium are gathered representatives from all the calamities, the victims—but also the *guilty!*" He noted further that "This sanatorium is actually a state after death . . . a clinic for healing the aftereffects of the meeting with Evil." Mention is made of a lecture about the Inquisition by one of the doctors.

In the novel as we have it, the "state after death" has become a kind of anarchist utopia. Anarchism is a thread which runs through Bjørneboe's work; he sees it first and foremost as a creative impulse which is eternally at war with the inherent entropy of institutional forms. This creative impulse is basic to both Christianity and socialism, "the two most important ideas about freedom which the human race has had"—which, however, have been "twisted around into their absolute opposites":

> Equality and propertylessness have been totally abolished in both ideas; in both, enmity toward the state—which was one of the most important points of all—has been changed into devoted worship of power and of the state; the original emphasis on peace, pacifism, has in both cases been transformed into a wild

cult of weapons and military power. The fundamental idea of love, which can be summed up as a belief in equality, liberty and fraternity, has been transformed into hatred of everyone who desires or believes in equality, liberty and fraternity; love is transformed into violence and brotherhood into oppression. [91f]

Amid his characters' bitter diatribes against the institutional church and Leninist communism, Bjørneboe pays homage to the original ideals of which they are perversions by such means as character names suggesting Christianity—Christine, Lefèvre (maker), Lacroix (cross), Jean/Ivan (John, the writer of the Apocalypse)—and chapter dates using the French revolutionary calendar.

The embattled creative impulse must be constantly brought to bear on society; freedom of information and the ever-vigilant exercise of the critical intelligence are essential to counteract stagnation. In a 1971 essay he writes, *"A society is a healthy society only to the degree that it exhibits anarchistic traits"* (italics his), but adds that he does not "believe in perfection where anarchism is concerned. It is quite certain that anarchism today can only exist as a leaven, as an adjective if you will. . . ."[4]

In *Powderhouse* that leaven is seen, not only in the direct references to Haymarket and to Sacco and Vanzetti, but in the encouragement of social criticism and analysis via lectures which may be given by anyone, patients as well as staff; and in the free-wheeling way in which the doctors, as Janet Garton puts it, "cheerfully transgress the professional code of ethics whenever it suits them to do so; yet their treatment of the patients in their care is skillful and effective. . . . For all their cynicism and irregular conduct, [they] have retained their essential humanity and are able to see what needs to be done rather than what the rules say."[5]

Bjørneboe was wont to say that when he was finished with "The History of Bestiality" he was going to devote "the next 24 years" to writing a "History of Freedom." He intended

Semmelweis (1968) to be the first of a projected cycle of plays on this theme; the next was to be a play about Emma Goldmann, which he never finished. Although the novel's subtitle, "Scientific Postscript and Concluding Protocol," indicates that Bjørneboe saw it as an addendum to the "History of Bestiality," *Powderhouse* clearly contains elements of the "History of Freedom." Lefèvre's lecture in the last chapter of *Powderhouse* sets forth the theme of this unrealized project:

> Thousands and thousands have given their lives for freedom of human thought, for freedom of conscience, and for the freedom of future generations—this freedom which we treat so badly today.
> The bloodbaths aren't the main thing; the main thing is the *heretic.*
> What is it that gives a person such strength?
> Greater than the problem of evil is the problem of good. [194f]

In sum, *Powderhouse* may be viewed not merely as an adjunct to *Moment of Freedom,* but as an explosive (if flawed) novel in its own right, a twin star which converged with *Moment of Freedom* after a long independent genesis. The Norwegian literary scholar Leif Longum wrote of *Moment of Freedom*: "'The History of Bestiality'. . . could stand to be supplemented by a 'History of Goodness, Generosity and Love.'"[6] For all its surface cynicism, *Powderhouse* contains many indications that writing such a supplement was the direction in which Bjørneboe was hoping to move.

Bjørneboe wrote me in 1974: "I'm beginning to get used to the fact that my books are understood only after ca. 15-20 years, that's true of a number of my books by now. In other words: One has to have patience. I'm anxious about *Moment of Freedom*'s fate in the U.S., but I'm sure that *Powder* will also finally be published there, even if it may take time." Yes indeed. Words cannot express my gratitude to Norvik Press and Dufour Editions, and to my editors, Janet Garton at Norvik and Tom Lavoie at Dufour, for undertaking its publication after all these years.

Esther Greenleaf Mürer
April 1999

For more information about Jens Bjørneboe and his work, visit the "Jens Bjørneboe in English" online archive at http://home.att.net/~emurer

NOTES

1. The relation between the narrators of the three novels is so tenuous that not all commentators believe they are the same person. In her critical study *Jens Bjørneboe: Prophet Without Honor* (Westport, CT: Greenwood Publishing Group, 1985), Janet Garton takes the position that they are three different narrators. Among Norwegian critics, his biographer, Fredrik Wandrup, regards them as the same; Inge S. Kristiansen takes great care to marshall the evidence to that effect; and Steinar Lem leaves the question open. My own view is that the few scattered references back to *Moment of Freedom* (e.g., "My walls no longer bleed in here") justify regarding the narrator of all three books as the same person.

2. Jens Bjørneboe, "To år ved en Rudolf Steinerskole," *Ny skole* No. 3-4 (1953); *Under en Mykere Himmel* (Oslo: Gyldendal, 1976), 50f, 56.

3. Published posthumously in *Gyldendals aktuelle magasin*, no. 1 (1977):9. Quoted in Fredrik Wandrup, *Jens Bjørneboe: mannen, myten og kunsten* (Oslo: Gyldendal, 1984), 273f.

4. "Anarkismen... idag" in *Politi og anarki* (Oslo: Pax, 1973); *Samlede Essays: Politikk* (Oslo: Pax, 1996), 209f. English translation: "Anarchism–today?" in *Degrees of Freedom* (Philadelphia: Protocol Press, 1997), 5.

5. Garton, 95.

6. Leif Longum, *Et speil for oss selv: Menneskesyn og virkelighetsoppfatning i norsk etterkrigsprosa* (Oslo: Aschehoug, 1968), 238.

Author's Foreword

In this genre, poetic naturalism, it is not usual to include references with one's record-keeping. However, considering the fact that the reality is for most people totally improbable—and that many a precise iteration of the same reality has so often publicly been labeled as "exaggerated," "untrue," "tendentious," etc., etc., I find it appropriate to refer to the following more scientific record-keepers, all of international stature:

Christopher Hibbert, *The Roots of Evil*
Walter Nigg, *Das Buch der Ketzer Symbolum Athanasii*
Kurt Rossa, *Todestrafen*
H. R. Trevor-Roper, *Witches and Witchcraft*
Karlheinz Deschner, *Abermals krähte der Hahn*; *Christliches Vorspiel; Mit Gott und den Faschisten*

These are mentioned as easily accessible summaries, which together contain several thousand references to original sources.

LA POUDRIÈRE

Whitsunday morning, Prairial 6, the year 176

This morning the hospital cat piddled on the Minister of Finance. The paper lay folded with His Excellency's portrait turned upward. Whether the occurrence has a deeper or a higher significance is not easy for a layman to determine. Yet it is remarkable that this desecration of the worthy economist took place on the morning of Pentecost, the very feast of the Holy Spirit, and that it was a French puss which relieved itself on Franz-Josef Strauss's visage—in other words a cat which, as compatriot of Stendhal and La Rochefoucauld, must already be accorded a far more intimate bond with the Paraclete than most cats. One is thus tempted to conclude that the urination has a *higher* significance.

Even if the newspaper is now too wet to be read with edification, I can nonetheless state that henceforth the creature has my permission to leave its wee-wee on every single one of our contemporary politicians.

It is a beautiful, sun-drenched, quiet Sunday morning. There is a smell of dew, grass, manure, and damp earth. There is no wind, not a leaf is stirring in the vineyard around the house where I have lived alone for. . . many months, perhaps a year or more. It is the first day of Whitsuntide.

✧

The chief physician, Professor Dr. Lefèvre, was already down at my place before eight o'clock. He brought the medicaments with him; as usual, neither of us had touched food or drink beforehand—not even smoked a morning cigarette; the effect is cleaner and surer that way. "Greetings, great clinician," I said; "what a splendid morning!" He smiled and raised his large, heavy head—looked out over the garden, off toward the woods, and finally toward the sparkling cobalt-blue mountains far away. They seemed to be made of glass, floating above the earth.

"And what a country!" he replied. "Do you know what France's last great cultural contribution was?"

"No."

"It happened in Africa," continued the doctor, "during the wars down there. It was the invention of the electro-method. Since then France has been silent.

"The exploitation of the field telephone's political potential was an intellectual achievement of the first order. Thousands and thousands of military men had been dragging the apparatuses around without an inkling of what they could be used for; then one day—in Africa, or perhaps in the Indochinese jungle— there's a scholarly dispute on the point—then one day an ordinary French junior officer and breadwinner, a simple, ordinary, dutiful chief of interrogation, is sitting there with his cognac or his pernod, and all at once he sees the possibilities of the field telephone. It facilitated things enormously for the interrogators. You simply couple one electrode to the subject's rectum or his glans penis, and the other to his nostrils. Then you turn the crank, and depending on the speed and energy you put into the cranking, you send a suitable voltage through the patient, so that he dances a regular St. Vitus's dance of glee. He'll confess anything you want. It takes a people with culture to invent something like that. Only *we* have such sergeants and lieutenants. The invention was a feat of genius, and the Americans have inherited it from us. But it required the last powers of the nation's spirit, the last resources of the national soul. Since then France has been resting. The country is exhausted."

"The contribution was unique," I replied; "the Krauts never thought of anything like it. And neither the cowboys nor the Russians managed it."

Lefèvre shook his head:

"Culture is culture and always will be," he replied; "you have it or you don't."

"For centuries we've disseminated our culture in Africa and Asia, and today it has become the colonial peoples' most precious heritage. There's not a single one of our former colonies where we haven't left behind at least ten million empty wine bottles and six million empty tin cans. Come, let's make our witch's brew!"

We went into the house, and at the kitchen counter he mixed us each a portion of LSD, in fresh, ice-cold water which I'd fetched from the brook beside the house. We raised our glasses in a toast before downing the limpid magic potion.

Afterwards we went out to the grape and tomato arbor, where everything is trained up onto espaliers taller than a man, so that we could stroll around between them as in a labyrinth with a hundred passageways, with sun and shadows in the foliage and the blue sky above us. The earth is moist and snails crawl about between the stakes, right up until they're big enough to eat. Straight through the garden runs the brook from Les Vosges in a channel a few yards wide, built up along the sides with ancient blocks of gray stone. Now and then a dark and soundless fish glides through the cold, clear water, in which stripes of sun at times press through the treetops and draw the trout's shadow on the bottom of the brook.

I was wearing pajamas and sneakers, a bathrobe and a soft silk scarf knotted under my beard, which has gone rather gray. Dr. Lefèvre was in his usual off-duty costume—khakis, a summer shirt and sandals, surmounted by a large Arab headdress. Thus he had come down from La Poudrière on his day off, leaving Dr. al Assadun in charge of the whole Institute.

al Assadun is our assistant doctor; Lefèvre brought him from Algeria, where the professor too may have been born.

They speak Arabic together for the most part, and to judge
from the frequent bursts of laughter they carry on a continual
banter of unheard-of cynicisms and obscenities. The two of
them present a remarkably suspect and frivolous picture
when speaking Arabic together: the middling-tall, slender,
golden-brown assistant doctor and the huge Frenchman, over
six feet and of uncommonly heavy build—with his large, yellowed, dirty mustache drooping over the eternal cigarette.
Always the same laughter which follows Lefèvre's words!
Always the same atmosphere of unmentionable secrets.

What I know about them isn't so unmentionable; Lefèvre
once found the fourteen- or fifteen-year-old Arab boy on the
street or in some alley in the slums, and—lecher that he's
always been—took the pretty boy home and installed him in
his household. Later he discovered al Assadun's uncommon
talent and paid for his medical studies at the Sorbonne. The
more intimate side of the relation has cooled long since, the
professor being over sixty and the Arab boy nearing forty—
but they've remained friends, and work splendidly together.

We strolled among the grape vines and the tomato plants
for just a few minutes, then seated ourselves in the weathered
old garden chairs outside my house. Dazzling spots of sun-
light danced on the whitewashed wall, and the light dripped
down between the leaves.

"Actually I like only the sun," said Lefèvre. "Only the sun
is good."

I looked at him.

"Only the sun," he repeated.

I felt a faint dizziness and a slight chill down my back. The
light and the colors and the sun and the shadows around me
intensified. I lit a cigarette and saw that the smoke was filled
with the colors of the sun. The tabletop shone gold and a
strange, color-saturated white. Lefèvre's large, ever-brown
hands and sunburned face shone like copper now; his face
was golden, and the huge mustache was of ivory. The whole
garden was filled with the red color of the sunrise, but it also
glittered orange and violet. The sky was of gold, a kind of

seething, boiling gold in which the blue was moving in stripes and lines, lines which were soft and snaky and full of life.

"The sun," repeated Lefèvre, "it's the only thing which is true."

I understood at once what he meant, and noticed that above me the sun had now spread out over the whole sky—all was gold and sunshine, gold and sunshine. Everything was itself and its own explanation—the cascades of color in the foliage, the spurting fire in the brook, it all overflowed in a waterfall of color.

Then came the sea, the endless, dark blue, golden sea, the foam and the gleam, and the whole was embraced by the sun, the earth was borne by unending arms of flame, entwining and sustaining it. At the same time a stream ran out of the sun, a cascading, gushing flood of gold and sunshine. An endless yellowed and noble parchment poured out over the world, a document from Columbus's ship, stamped, sealed and inscribed in an old, old script. The truncated pyramids were of gold where they rose from the golden sand. The sky above them was of gold, and all the while the same flood of gold continued to stream from the sun. Once more all was gold and sunshine, gold and sunshine. Everything, everything in the world was gold and sunshine, billowing, flaming, liquid gold.

Mexico was sand and the sand was gold and the gold was sun and truth and there was nothing in the world but sun and gold, gold and sun, and truth was truth and there was no more falsehood left in the world. And the sun was everything.

Lefèvre was talking, but I couldn't hear the words, and when I looked at him I understood what he meant, and he saw by looking at me that I understood what he meant and that everything was its own meaning and explanation.

Then the sun overpowered me again, in a whirling porridge of flame, a wheel which turned from horizon to horizon, and the sea and the ship and the sails and the document and the pyramids and the desert and the sky and Mexico and the earth all turned to gold and sunshine, gold and sunshine, gold and sunshine. And I was in the house of the sun for three hours.

I saw Dr. Lefèvre lie down on the grass and stay there, but he was far away. Only the colors remained, and I was moving through space on a long, long journey, I was on the way toward the earth, and I was tired, exhausted.

A while later the great journey was over; I sat clear and tired in my chair and looked at Lefèvre, who was still in the midst of his visions, repeating over and over some very simple words which for him still contained the whole meaning and aim of the universe, the irrefutable explanation of things-in-themselves. For me there remained—aside from the tiredness, which was not a feeling of abnormal fatigue, but a healthy exhaustion after violent exertion of nerves, brain and senses—there remained a fierce intensification of color in all things, stones, plants, the table and the chairs around me. In form and outline the objects were as usual, but their colors had an incomprehensible harmony and strength, with a clear, logical correspondence between them. It was like being inside a picture by one of the great impressionists whom this remarkable, brutal, swinish and wonderful land has fostered—this greedy, avaricious peasant nation of coarse exploiters, oppressors, and soldiers, of pimps, painters, and whores, saints and sodomites, but above all of painters. The colors filled me with a faint and peaceful sensuality; they ran through my body and surrounded me at the same time.

Lefèvre sat up; he too was back again now.

"Are you hungry?" he said.

We were both hungry, and we knew that now we could eat and drink again without interrupting the visions.

The resonance of our Pentecostal ascension would last for several hours yet—simply as a boundless increase in the beauty of this world, of this garden of Eden which we have been given to dwell in.

I brought out bread, dark and moist; meat, fish, and cheese. Butter, oil, lemon, salt, pepper. A bottle of apéritif and a big bottle of the local wine. Glasses.

We ate as if we had never eaten before. The same enhancement of the sensory faculties which made the colors around us visible as they *really are*, applied also to the taste buds. Just bread and butter, with a mouthful of wine to go with it, contained the whole world's wealth of taste, of sun, earth, and rain, of wheat and of the milk the butter came from. It was afternoon.

The brook lay in shadows again.

We began talking about wars and revolutions. That's the usual topic here.

"The most bothersome thing," he said suddenly, looking up at the unbroken blue plane above us, "at bottom the most bothersome thing is to think how, while the planets follow their feeble-minded, fantastic, pedantically ordered paths around the sun—round and round and round—it's in the midst of all this idiotic precision that the slaughters go on. The bloodbaths—in what ever form you prefer them—bombing, shooting, poisoning, burning—the bloodbaths take place in the midst of a cosmos which is ordered with mathematical pedantry. So far as we've been able to tell, the heavenly bodies are forced to go on and on repeating their circles, ellipses or whatever—apparently they have no freedom. It's a consolation that there's no discernible life on other planets. . . .

"Naturally there's much to indicate that not only we, but Nature too is mad. Or at least strongly neurotic."

We talk a lot about this at La Poudrière.

I accompanied him partway up the road to the main buildings, through the big park, until we could see the old stone wall around the oldest building of all, the tower with its wings in the same stone, in other words the real *poudrière*—which is rightly named, since it was in fact built as a munitions tower, or powder magazine. It's still the center of the complex, in that it houses both the archives of sexual pathology and the chief physician's office and private quarters.

The wall around this holy of holies, as well as the wings and the round tower, are overgrown with ivy, but there are fruit trees too, both in the garden and outside.

Next to this very old nucleus, the real La Poudrière, stand

the newer buildings, which are very large. They make up the
clinic. And around it all lies the park, which covers about fifty
acres, including the "kitchen garden"—but not the vineyards.
This is our world.
Behind it all lie the mountains—to the south.
When we'd come in sight of the wall we parted and went
each to his own; he to rest awhile, and then to work in his
office—I to... yes, actually... to do what?

It's late afternoon, and begins to smell of evening; the
landscape stretches and yawns after the mighty day of sunshine, the air is cooler, the leaves on the trees hang lifelessly.
This hour before sundown is full of odors, of ants and of
mould. The honeybees and the bumblebees are gone. The
flowers are closing. In a little while everything will take on
that wondrous good blue cast. All is peace. And night is coming on.
It is absolutely necessary to take this question seriously—
the one Lefèvre mentioned: the fantastic sense of order, the
monstrous pedantry—the absurd, petty-bourgeois exactitude
which marks the cosmos. The worst, of course, is the solar
system—it's governed by the same finickiness, the same petty
niggling, as the bookkeeping department in the office behind
Monsieur Anatole's secondhand store—but with what a difference in dimensions! And yet pedantry in used goods—small
change, buttons, ribbons, and safety pins—has a clear and
unambiguous, albeit a rather idiotic, *meaning*. And it's this
which is lacking in the solar system. The contrast between the
total meaninglessness of the whole enterprise and the elabo-
rate, foolish mathematical pedantic logic in the enormous cal-
culation—all this is pure and undiluted, unqualified lunacy.
It's well known that madness doesn't always express itself
in a lack of logic, but just as often in the fact that logic is all
that remains of reason; counting and ordering is all that's left
of the lunatic's consciousness. The meaningless screams, but
the pedantry is perfect. Everything is made by a mad school-
master.

Justice, or injustice, which has occupied so much of my life, is one of the plainest examples of this—and it follows its course, like seasons and planets, like banking and theology.

Yet there's this difference, that the solar system has a kind of authority, because *it was there first.* That's the heart of the matter.

Besides, the solar system has authority because it doesn't *defend itself.* While war profiteers, theologians, politicians and judges defend themselves, venture to claim that they have a justification, the solar system has never said a word to apologize for its existence.

It's compellingly necessary to declare that nature—or "God," as some people call it—it's compellingly necessary to declare that "nature" is mad. We can't avoid declaring God to be just as insane as we ourselves. Otherwise nothing is left but metaphysics.

The discrepancy between the gigantic compulsion neurosis in the "natural laws" on the one hand, and their lack of content and meaning on the other, is the fatal, damning proof of insanity.

With humankind it's different; we've tried to imitate this ordered, pedantic and idiotically meaningless cosmos for thousands of years—from Paul to Lenin (a juxtaposition I'll return to later) we've done nothing but try to overcome our dread of freedom by making "laws"; and to strengthen the authoritarian power of the "laws" we've even invented such a phenomenally idiotic expression as "laws of nature"—as if "nature" were some kind of criminal being which must be enjoined to obey "laws"!

But nature has no such core of wild, capricious freedom; only we have that.

So I hereby declare "nature" or "God" or what you will, to be totally insane, even an idiot.

It has grown dark around me in my grape and tomato arbor. The shadows between the trellises are coal-black. All is stillness. But I can hear the brook running. Someone howls up at the clinic. Then it's still again.

I bring out a kerosene lamp and a pitcher of wine and a beaker, and set them on the table. Despite the evening coolness it's warm enough to sit comfortably outside in the pitch-darkness.

I can't get rid of the thought of seeing my own tiny little life against the background of this mechanical, pedantically ordered watchmaker's shop of a universe. Our "culture" complains about rebellions and revolutions which break everything down, overturn everything.

Why in the world *shouldn't* everything be broken down, overturned? We *can* break the "laws." The planets can't.

And my own, teeny weeny little life—and my tiny little consciousness which embraces everything!

Again I think about this one single life, which is still the only one I really know.

For a resident of such a distinguished and well-known madhouse as La Poudrière I must admit that I feel fine, and enjoy a bewildering degree of freedom of thought, expression and movement. At any rate greater than the stars'. And then there's my own highly ambiguous position at the hospital. As caretaker and a kind of jack-of-all-trades (including that of observer) I have at my disposal one of the gardeners' cottages, along with the abovementioned grape and tomato arbor: they lie at the park's outer edge and are surrounded by a high, palisade-like fence with a heavy, lockable gate, so that when I wish, I can be wholly isolated in my own world. For example, I can get drunk in peace, though that happens very seldom now. And I can smoke hashish with al Assadun, though we usually do that up in the tower at Lefèvre's, where he has installed a first-class hi-fi set—since music is an almost indispensable part of the hash. Likewise, Dr. Lefèvre and I can travel to the sun as often as we wish; this always happens at my house.

But that isn't the most important thing; most important are the mornings and the nights, when I can be utterly undisturbed in my work, and can sit in the garden with my break-

fast before proceeding up to the Institute or the clinic to dis-
charge my more routine duties.

The grape and tomato arbor I've described, but the house
is just as important; it's old, whitewashed and very simple,
like the oldest peasant houses in this district: dirt floor, open
fireplace, heavy ceiling beams and a very small sleeping
alcove. Outside: the brook, some leafy trees and the plants.
Best of all are the mornings, going out barefoot and almost
naked right after sunrise, feeling the spicy, fresh scent, the
cool morning air, and looking at the light in the treetops or
the espaliers. I get a boundless pleasure from these simple
things; strictly speaking it's the only happiness I have. I prefer
each day to be exactly like the one before.

This has brought me complete clarity of soul, the old
man's peace, a quiet heart. Perhaps I miss the sea at times, I
don't know.

I said "as caretaker." Of course it's not that simple. It turns
out that nothing, absolutely nothing, is simple when you look
a bit more closely. Now, for example, there's someone howling up in the clinic again; it's probably the Russian ambassador's wife. She cries like a wolf. In the soundless night this
lonely wolf-howl from the ward cuts loose like a stripe on the
black night sky, like the trail of a shooting star. The ululating,
drawn-out cry is repeated a couple of times. Why do the
wolves in the forest also howl thus? For all its wolfishness it's
still first and foremost a human howl. She's probably up there
hanging onto the window bars while she howls, as she usually
does during attacks. If it continues Dr. Lefèvre will have to
leave his desk and his work and go over to the ward to take
care of her. al Assadun can't do it because she always tries to
rape him. It's very clear that at a Soviet embassy in a
Christian country this is not compatible with diplomatic dignity and etiquette. And it's evident that for the wife herself
these diplomatic years beside her silent, flawless ambassador-
husband were pure purgatory, before she finally said to hell
with it and took to howling and raping freely. That's how she
came here. Nothing is simple.

Of course I'm not a "caretaker," but—as Lefèvre puts it—
"combination caretaker and physician-in-chief of the
Institute," and as such I naturally have a radical insight into
all that goes on here, into everything that happens. Now
when I say "physician-in-chief," that's of course to be understood in a higher, so to speak purely spiritual sense—as chief
ideologist and father-confessor to nearly everybody. From the
viewpoint of the employment roster I'm a caretaker. Janitor.
Cleaning man.

This last point in particular—my being the place's trusted
renovation worker*—must not be underestimated from an
epistemological standpoint. How else, for example, would I
have had any awareness of the stupendous quantities of prophylactics with which the diplomat's wife fills her wastebasket
between attacks? What, indeed, would I have understood of
anything at all without access to wastebaskets and garbage
pails?

Another side of the matter is that I have full opportunity
to pursue my studies and my research here. My interests are
the same as before,** even though I've acquired an ice-cold
scientific attitude to reality. Of course, while collecting my
documents I had to come sooner or later to one of the central points in our Christian culture—possibly to its heart, to
the matter's core. It's natural too that I began on the topic in
just the geographic situation in which I now find myself: in a
landscape which has been the historic arena for our culture's
very innermost concerns. One is located even more cen-
trally if one travels some miles further to the northeast, up
to Trier. It was impossible to continue with *The History of
Bestiality* without taking up the Christian churches' heretic
and witch trials.

I must add at once that this isn't a theological matter alone,
but to just as great a degree a secular, judicial problem—one
dear to the hearts not only of theologians, but of jurists as well.
The two disciplines must not be separated too strictly. What
would the church's power have been without support from the

---

*"renovation worker": Norwegian euphemism for "garbage collector." –Tr.
**In *Moment of Freedom* the narrator is working on "an enormous, colossal
twelve-volume work," *The History of Bestiality*. –Tr.

legal profession? It would have been built on sand. But it happened, and it *had* to happen, that love and justice, those two main pillars of good, united in the great crusade against Evil.

Theologians and jurists shrouded themselves in their black robes, in the color of love and justice, and they were victorious in the fight.

As I said, for a man in my field—bestiality and demonology—making the connection was inevitable, though I postponed it as long as I could. A tempting theme it wasn't. But it illuminates a great deal.

Now I'm getting off the track; for now I only mention the matter to illustrate how my position as chief ideologist and head physician at La Poudrière may develop. It's not enough that I can pursue my studies here, and my record keeping; but when I outlined my plan of work for Lefèvre he reacted with enthusiasm, and asked me to prepare a couple of lectures on the subject—lectures which will be given at the Institute, both for staff members and for that part of the clientele which isn't (with a couple of exceptions) domiciled in the security ward.

Part of Lefèvre's therapeutic method consists of regular evening lectures of this sort.

I'm as good as finished with lecture number one, and not many days are left before I give it. It will contain certain insights into the history of both the church and the legal community—a topic in which, above all, the *coupling* of the two orientations is my own idea. Later I also want to deal with the relation between the servants of righteousness and the world's profane masters and rulers after the church had lost its untrammeled power.

But the first lecture will deal with the Christian heretic and witch trials, under the title:

THE WITCHES' REVOLUTION
Satan's seizure of power in Europe
A prelude to Satan's world empire

She just howled again up in the ward. The long, lonesome wolf howl. I could almost answer her by howling back.

But a renovation worker doesn't do such things.

A couple of centuries ago the diplomat's wife wouldn't have been able to sit in a fashionable luxury madhouse and fill her wastebasket with prophylactics; she would have been burned like other witches, since it would hardly have been possible to drive the wolves from the soul of a woman who was still alive.

Many have tried it, but few were chosen.

By the way, plenty of men were burned too.

It goes without saying that in my lectures the Inquisition won't be treated in a moralizing or hostile manner, but from a purely medico-philosophical, psychiatric point of view—as an important piece in a pattern. As a stone in a mosaic about our culture, which can help to portray its true face and to explain why it has brought us where we are today.

Can a nobler motive be imagined?

About "nature" we know a great deal, thanks to its being subject to "laws." About humankind we know almost nothing, for we are not subject to "laws." We've made only scattered observations, among them an overriding human need for two things: bestiality and falsehood. Cruelty and hypocrisy are almost the only things all races, colors and nations have in common—but we've found no law of gravity in the circus which would make these traits wholly necessary and inevitable, like for instance the madness in outer space. There is no necessity in our mental illness.

Again, I think of the apostles Paul and Lenin, the two holy men in the theologies of love and brotherhood.

And then we have a few examples in God's own France, too.

Of La Poudrière it must further be told that it is truly an asylum on earth, an advanced and fashionable place of refuge for the privileged of every land. One can mention our American general, or our magnificent little sex murderer from Belgium; both would have been under lock and key within the confines of the criminal law had they been in less comfortable economic circumstances. The young lust-murderer has his millionaire papa behind him, and the American is backed by the prestige of his by no means indigent fatherland. We also have old M. Lacroix, who despite his Gallic name is of foreign origin, and who in his homeland practices a profession of a highly distinctive sort. I've talked with all three often, and they're unquestionably hospital cases, albeit choice morsels for the criminal law as well.

I shall further mention—this time a pure case of illness with no criminal ingredient—the government prosecutor Dr. Marescot, formerly an outstanding official and a highly educated and cultured personality.

Why I've come to be so sought after as a curator of souls I'm not clear about—but I think it's because I have gradually, and in my own way, acquired the ability to forgive sins. This was a gift which appeared very late in my life. Later I may be able to explain why it appeared at all.

It has something to do with the lecture I'm going to give.

Here I'll briefly mention yet another of the patients with whom I've often conversed. He's an engineer, Dr. Stephan Báthory—Hungarian by birth, but today a French citizen. Báthory is a man of somewhat less than my own age, still in his mid-forties, with an unusually powerful build, so muscular that you can see his arm and shoulder muscles clearly through his clothes. His face is brown and gaunt but at the same time round, with sandy hair and very blue eyes. In Hungary his father was killed by the Communists; Báthory joined the Waffen SS and fought long on the Eastern Front. After the defeat he fled through Germany, sneaked across the border into France and reported to the French Foreign Legion. At different times he fought both in Africa and in "Indochina," and had spent eight years as a legionnaire by the time he retired with a long list of decorations, French citizenship, and a pension for life. In a short time he finished his doctorate in engineering; got an excellent, highly-paid position with the

Americans as an advisor in the Corps of Engineers; and married the daughter of a nationally known, extremely wealthy French industrialist.

His face has a sullen and antagonistic expression, and the whole man is stamped by the fact that he spent so many years as a professional soldier in active combat. He's still a whole-hearted fascist, and not shy about saying so. Dr. Báthory is very attractive and very repulsive. His breakdown came a couple of years ago, in the form first of protracted crying jags, and then of total apathy. He has made significant progress under Lefèvre's treatment and will probably be entirely "well" again, provided that the word means nothing more than being able socially and economically to take care of one-self. The healthiest thing he could do would doubtless be to go on crying as long as possible. He hates al Assadun with a pure passion.

By contrast our other warrior, the general from Texas or Ohio or whatever it's called, is a thoroughly pleasant and amiable person. *"Le général,"* as he's called here, is quiet, introspective and polite unto meekness. You wouldn't see that he has the Pentagon behind him. The only thing about him which might give a military impression is his haircut; he's as closecropped as can be—an upright, wiry man of medium height in his late fifties, very slender and very well-dressed. For awhile it was the hospital's duty to keep him in the security ward because of the deeds he committed in his homeland, but he was transferred months ago to the open part of the Institute. You often see him strolling around in the park—quiet, alone and rather melancholy.

It had grown late in the evening, and I took the lamp, glass, and jug indoors, where I began to undress. All was still now; there was just the night.

A while after I'd gone to bed the alarm bell rang.

It's very loud and is used only in case of dire emergency. It would be utterly impossible to sleep through it. The signal calls for the immediate attendance of the whole staff, because a situation has arisen which those on duty can't handle alone. I relit the lamp and dressed hurriedly. The most likely bet was fire in the hospital building, and that was the first thing I looked for when I came out into the night.

But there was nothing to see, and when I'd come a ways up into the park the buildings were standing as usual—with only a few windows lit, and with the searchlights on as always.

I walked on rapidly, in through the kitchen entrance and over to the duty room.

It was empty.

I went on, and on the second floor the hall was soiled with blood. As expected, the trail led to the operating, or first-aid room, as it's called.

When I entered the blindingly lit room, al Assadun and two nurses were bent over something which lay unconscious on the operating table. They were hard at work. You could see only their eyes and a bit of the assistant doctor's brown, hairy arms. A group of male nurses stood over by the far wall. In the middle of the floor stood Lefèvre with his white smock open, a cigarette in his mouth and his huge arms akimbo. He turned his head toward me and said amiably:

"Bonjour, mon cher enculé!"

This base and untranslatably vulgar word, which designates the passive partner in male intercourse per anum, caused both the male nurses and al Assadun to roar with laughter.

"What's happened?" I said.

"Nothing," replied the chief physician; "practically speaking, nothing at all. It's only that old corpse-fucker Lacroix, who has made a new suicide attempt. In some shitty way he got hold of a gardener's saw, and had almost cut off his head before he was discovered. It looked awfully bloody for a minute; the wound was uncommonly large and dirty, to be made by a man of his former profession, and he was bleeding a great deal. At first we thought we'd have to drive the remains to the slaughterhouse in the district hospital, and so we rang for you—as chauffeur.

"But then it was nothing after all, nothing; and now our little sodomite of a *sal arabe*—the anarcho-surgeon Harun al-Rashid—is in the process of basting him together again."

Le sal arabe—"the dirty Arab," which is one of Lefèvre's pet names for the assistant doctor—raised his head and repaid the notice with an expression so untranslatable that a man in my modest position can't allow himself to quote it—but only to hint that it implied that the senior physician was troubled by gonorrhea in a place where it isn't *comme il faut*. The male nurses laughed again.

The Arab bent over old Lacroix's earthly and mortal parts, but went on talking.

"Now his block will soon be firmly back on," he said. "But this is the first time I've seen anyone do anything like this with a saw. It reminds me a bit of the grenade splinters in the old days."

This last was directed at Dr. Lefèvre. The two of them worked together as doctors during the battles in Africa—on the Arab side, of course.

"Okay," said the doctor, "the rest I leave to you. Good night." He took my arm, and we went out into the hall. He padded straight through the pool of blood outside the door, leaving a line of huge bloody footprints down the corridor behind him. He wears at least a size 14 shoe.

"How's the ambassadress?" I asked. "She was howling some toward sunset this evening, but then she quieted down."

"I went over there myself."

"What did you do with her?"

He laughed:

"If the police knew that, I'd be sitting behind bars in a couple of days. But now she's quiet."

He was still holding my arm as we walked over to his tower.

"So you gave her some pictures?"

"Oh, yes. The most advanced, the rawest I could find in the Institute. Now she's lying there eating them up. It helps."

A faint breeze had begun to blow, and we could hear the

rustling in the treetops. There were stars in the sky.

He looked up, then he said:

"Blood and shit and wind and stars!"

Up in his study we drank a couple of glasses of cognac. He was clearly tired, and used the smock which he now stood holding in his hand to wipe the sweat from his brow. Then he put it down.

"Oh Lord!" he said slowly. "Oh Lord! They howl and masturbate and copulate and saw off their heads, and around it all go Jupiter and Saturn and Uranus and Pluto and the whole heavenly madhouse. Tell something! Tell me a story about something else."

And I thought of a story I hadn't told him yet, from Russia a long time ago. The windows stood open to the garden and the stars, and a faint breeze came in to us, a breath of the wind outside.

"All right," I said, "but I want wine, not cognac. I don't like liquor. Get a couple of bottles of wine, and then I'll tell you a story."

He brought out the wine and opened two bottles. It was an excellent wine—humane, round, and soft. Then he lowered himself into the big armchair and sat there looking at me. Now Lefèvre was just a tired old man. The big, strong, vital body had shrunk into itself, the face was sunken, and the huge shoulders, the thick arms, the hands and the big head all seemed like a heavy, heavy burden to bear.

"Please," he said, "tell!"

A new breath of wind from the starry sky brought the night and the garden into the room, and along with the wine there arose in me pictures from another night, from another life, a night alone in Russia, in a large city, a night in a sick-room in a polyclinic, where I lay awake in the darkness and talked with a stranger—with a young man crippled for life. There too we had wine, several bottles, on the nightstand between us, and we lay in the half-darkness and talked together softly as the dawn began to lighten in the pale Leningrad night. . . .

It began with my coming to the city on a ship, and I had alcohol poisoning as I've hardly had it before or since. Crossing the sea, the Baltic, I'd been drinking day after day, with anyone who could spare the time. One night I fell down all those steep steps to the hold, and I fell as softly and unresistingly as a wet towel. I didn't break anything, but my body was like a Chagall painting the next day, full of violet and red, green and blue bruises from my knees to my neck, and I stood on deck and looked out over the sea before I went on drinking. When we arrived in Leningrad I was found in my bunk with blood all over my face and the bedclothes. I must have been bleeding for several hours, perhaps most of the night. What's more, I had pissed on myself. I couldn't sit up, and they came with the ship's doctor, and he thought it was a bleeding stomach ulcer, for around my mouth there were thick crusts of congealed blood. He laid an icebag over my midriff and prescribed ice-cold milk for me to drink, but I couldn't get anything down but cognac. And I lay there thinking, "Oh Lord, just let me croak soon now, just let me croak, then all this will be over!" But at the same time I was immensely afraid of dying, yes I was terribly afraid of dying. But I got down a little more cognac and everything was better.

A bit later they came with a stretcher which they laid me on, and brought me safely ashore on Russia's holy earth. Precisely thus did I make my entry into the Holy Land, full of blood and cognac and piss, borne by four men clad in white as if I'd been a long-lost son.

With wailing sirens and whistling tires the triumphal procession conquered Leningrad.

Never have I my made my entrance into a strange land in such a fashion, and around me there was not one person who spoke a word of anything but Russian. Everything was soft and friendly, and it sounded as if they were whispering to me inside the ambulance.

When the car stopped I was borne across a cement-paved square, past a reception desk and through a large hall, full of stalls with upholstered benches inside. Between the benches were partitions about six feet high. On one of these benches they laid me, and I felt tired and calm and content, and I said *"Papyros!"* to one of the stretcher bearers, who took a pack out of his smock and laid it on the nightstand beside me. Then they got me some tea, a large glass of it, and I smoked and strewed the ashes on the floor.

Everyone who came past me smiled and nodded, and there was no doubt that I'd been awaited and missed. But now I was come. Beside me, in the next stall, a man lay dying and dying; his throat rattled and he wheezed for awhile and then he was still.

A nurse gave me an injection and lifted my head so that it was easier to drink from the tea glass. My body had gotten all warm and soft and I felt good, despite the fact that I was sober. I lay still with open eyes and looked around me, for everything was different from all the clinics and hospitals I'd been in before. It was like coming far back in time, and the room here had no plastic or glass bricks or steel; it was brown and rather in need of paint, more or less like the schools, like old schools looked in my childhood, and it wouldn't have surprised me if I'd met my old gym teacher in here. All other clinics remind me of La Morgue in Paris, which I once visited out of pure vulgarity, just to see how I would look someday. But I didn't get far before I turned back; the smell of the well-greased, sterilized cadavers from the Seine or the alleys was such that along with the glass bricks they drove me to the door again. Here, in the polyclinic in Leningrad, there was no odor of corpses and chemistry, but only the good healthy smell of tobacco and people. In my Baedeker of Europe's polyclinics it will be the only one to get three stars. . . .

While I lay there I may have slept a little with my eyes open, for all at once a band of angels stood before me, a group of white-clad Samaritans, doctors and nurses of both sexes, with a large, stout man as the center. He had a huge apron tied up around his chest and a white skullcap on his head, so that he was dressed like a butcher. He stood smiling with one arm around the shoulders of a female angel, holding a male angel by the hand with the other. He said some gentle words with a lot of z's in them, and everyone broke out into uncontrollable mirth. Then he bent over me and smiled:

"I speak a leetle Jairman," he said; "a meeligram of bet Jairman!"

That consoled me, and I understood that he was the archangel at the polyclinic. I smiled and answered that he spoke a Jairman that Goethe could have been immensely proud of. He turned beaming to the assistants, of whom there must have been about fifteen, and translated my reply. They all cheered. Then he pulled off my shirt and undershirt and felt my shoulders and torso with large, powerful hands. He smiled again:

"How old are you?"

"Forty-three."

He laid his hand heavily on my chest and tried to press it inward, again with the same beaming, fatherly smile:

"You are very young for your age. You are a strong young man, you will never die, you will live to be a hundred!"

"Jesus!" I said.

He examined me for a moment, especially in the mouth.

"Have any of your relatives had difficulty stanching blood . . . perhaps after shaving . . . from small wounds . . . . And you yourself, does it ever happen that you have small cuts that don't stop bleeding?"

I understood what he was driving at, and I opened my eyes wide and stared at him, a wild, Russian, gloomy stare:

"All we Romanovs," I said, "nearly all we Romanovs have had that morbid trait, it's a family thing. . . ."

He leaned back his head and laughed so that it echoed all over the hall, a high, resounding, cheery laughter through the whole polyclinic. The flock of angels crowded expectantly around him, and while he sat beside me, still with his hand on my shoulder, he translated my remark. It hit like a bomb among the doctors, and for a moment the laughter was deafening. Then he stood up and bowed in my direction:

"Welcome!" he said. "We haven't seen a Romanov in

almost fifty years! We wish you a hearty welcome!"

While the laughter continued he let the doctors examine me one by one, and it was clear that I was a cherished collective possession. When they were finished, he held them in turn by the hand or around the shoulders and let them propose their diagnoses without interruption. Afterwards he waved his hand in an ineffably friendly gesture which said that everything was wrong, but not despicable or inferior. Then softly and quickly he spoke a few sentences, and at once it seemed as if they all understood. He put his arm around one of the youngest male doctors and added a few more words. It all happened with a humanity, an egalitarianism, a humor and a kindness I had never seen before.

When he had explained his diagnosis he looked at me, and once more began to laugh. He sat down beside me again.

"My dear Romanov," he said, "you're an unusually sound and healthy young man, but you lack vitamin K, owing to a way of life unworthy of a Romanov. We'll give you a shot of vitamin K every two hours, and tomorrow you'll be well. We often give vitamin K to pregnant women, too, to strengthen blood-clotting ability before the birth.

"Thanks," I said. "When's the baby due?"

"But you mustn't drink vodka or beer," he added, shaking his head while he translated this into Russian.

Then he stood up and embraced a couple of the angels, and the company moved on to the next patient.

By now it was evening, and I was very weak when they wheeled me up to the room. There it had begun to get dark, and the others were already asleep—or lying completely still. Someone undressed me and disappeared with my clothes. I lay awhile in the twilight, and noticed that one of the patients was lying not in a bed, but on a kind of high table with a rack above him. He was sleeping on his stomach, with his hands above his head, and then I was gone. . . it all flowed away in the half-light. A couple of times I woke up and received an injection, after which I went back to sleep. But around two or three o'clock I awoke fully and my head was sparklingly

clear, entirely clear for the first time in weeks. I was somewhat weak but not unwell. By now I had a certain impression
of the clinic, of the halls and the room, and it all had something of the Left Bank about it, something of my beloved
Quartier Latin. . . . I was continually reminded of France or
Italy. When I turned on my side, facing the window and the
gray dawn outside, I thought I was delirious: on the win-
dowsill stood four bottles of Beaujolais, four familiar bottles of
a well-known sort. Beside them a pile of cigarette packs:
Gauloises. It was all totally unreal to me, and I looked at the
light in the green bottle glass, at the almost black contents. I
understood nothing, and turned on my back again to consider
it more closely.

The man beside me groaned. He'd done so once before
tonight, and had gotten an injection, probably morphine, for
he had quieted down afterwards. But now he'd begun again,
and I could hear his breathing clearly. It seemed that he was
in great pain, and on the point of being awakened by it. He
was also moving his head slightly, back and forth, the way
one does when one is in pain. Now I could clearly see the
structure over him; it was a steel frame with a container
above, from which a tube ran down and in under the featherbed. Right next to it another tube came out and hung down
to a kind of bottle which stood on the floor. It was clear that
he was seriously ill, and that it was the depth of sleep, in other
words the morphine, which determined whether he felt pain
or not. He moaned yet a couple of times, then he was still.
Thus one could hear whether he slept deeply or not, and how
severe his pain was. Now he was utterly still, and I couldn't
even hear his breathing. I turned over again and looked
toward the window and the light, which was gradually growing whiter. I lay thus for a good while, and when I turned
over again I suddenly discovered that he'd raised his head
and was lying with his open eyes turned toward me. He had
black, bushy hair and had propped his chin on the backs of
his hands. He was biting his lower lip, but was no longer
groaning. He was awake.

"Bonjour, monsieur," I said.

"Are you French?" he replied, bewildered. Then he smiled.

I answered that I wasn't, but that I was a stranger in Russia.

After awhile I asked if he were in great pain.

"Yes," he said. He fumbled for the clock on the nightstand and stared at it for a moment, as if with great effort: "But in half an hour the nurse will bring some morphine."

He clenched his teeth and was silent for a moment, then softly mumbled something about a car crash and a crushed pelvis. He moved his head backward toward the apparatus with the rubber tube and said:

"That's why I have this laboratory hanging up there."

He fell silent and smiled again, his lips pinched, and immediately afterwards he nodded toward the window:

"Can you manage to get a bottle?" he said.

I sat up and found that I was able to get out of bed. I placed the bottle and a pack of cigarettes on the nightstand, and lit a cigarette for him.

"Take one yourself," he said, "and have some wine if you like." I got a glass from the sink, and on the way back I glanced at the other two patients, who were still asleep. Two more black heads. They seemed very young. The Frenchman was probably something over thirty. I poured some wine for us both and lay down again under the featherbed. As we drank up the bottle I told him about my arrival and about the doctor in the polyclinic. He too laughed at the Romanov incident.

"Do you know who he is, the senior physician?" he asked suddenly.

"No?"

He mentioned a name with Professor and Academy and Doctor in front of it, and added:

"He's one of the great names in Russian medicine, one of the greatest surgeons they have, and that's saying quite a bit. But he has his hours of duty here at the clinic like everybody else. That's the way it is here."

We lay talking softly, while it gradually got light outside. It still was no later than four o'clock, all was perfectly still. There was only the night around us.

Everywhere, far out over the city and the land, the same white night lay around us. What we talked about I no longer recall, it was something about Russia and something about books. He was with the cultural attaché in this city. The nurse came in with a tray bearing glasses and needles, and we each got our dose again. Then things were quiet, and it was a relief to see how his pain eased. He laughed feebly a couple of times, and I was glad that the night was long and that the conversation continued, and we drank another bottle. . . . I had never seen him before, have never seen him since, but I felt that he was closer than people I've known for decades, and nothing in the world made me happier than that his pain abated. I saw that the dose must have been very strong, and with the wine it made him forget everything, likewise the thought of whether he'd ever be wholly well again, or be able to walk normally. . . . At times it was like sleeping with one's eyes open—the room, the light and the shadows were near and unreal at the same time, and I felt that I was a human being, and the night was long, and we heard the breathing of the two others in the room. Slowly, without knowing it, I dozed off for a bit, then I was awake again and saw that he was still lying with open eyes, and we exchanged a few words again. . . slept a little, or dreamed. . . .

By morning I'd really gone to sleep, but only after he did. So it was. This was my first night in Russia.

When I woke up a young, blond Russian was sitting beside my bed. Since there was no vacant stool he sat on the floor, supporting his back against the bed. When he noticed that I was awake he took my hand and smiled. He held it for a long time, and went on sitting beside me into the afternoon, perfectly still, without trying to make himself understood by word or gesture. He just sat there, silent and friendly, as if he were supposed to take care of me or protect me.

Now and then he held my hand.

In our room there were only foreigners, all dark-haired; the two others, besides the Frenchman and me, were a Cuban and a North Korean boy. During the bath and the morning ritual they were both as bashful and embarrassed as young girls; they held the sheet and blankets around them as if to defend their virtue against the nurses who were supposed to be helping them. One of them—the Korean—even drew a towel over his head out of shame. The Frenchman lay smiling, his lips pinched together.

This room with the foreigners seemed to be very popular among the Russian patients, and when after the morning bath the door to the hall was opened wide, it swarmed with friendly guests. My friend on the floor remained sitting faithfully by my bed—it was obvious that I was his foreigner.

Later that afternoon, when I'd got my clothes and was leaving the hospital, the Frenchman was once again in great pain. No sound came from him, and since he was forced to lie only on his stomach, I couldn't see much more of him than the back of his head; but he was unable to speak when I said goodbye and wished him a good recovery. He just looked up and smiled with his lips pressed tightly together, and waved to me with the fingers of one hand.

My Russian walked down the hall with me, clapped me on the shoulder and waved through the bars of the staircase railing.

The city was big and strange.

All this was very near to me as I sat there telling it to Lefèvre. And I saw that it cheered him up to hear it, and that he'd soon be in a condition to sleep.

I was still thinking about this endless night with a stranger long ago as I walked down over the gravel in the park on the way to my own house, my own room.

THE BUTCHERS

Stars for you and stripes for me
Prairial 9, the year 176

Lord God and Jesus Maria, where will this end!

That damned stinking tear-soaked tomcat, the excrement-general from Coca-Cola-land, has been here bothering me, he disturbed me in my work with the roses in the park and emptied his whole rotten garbage pail of an American conscience all over me! As if one murder isn't just as good as another! As if a yellow corpse doesn't smell just as sweet as a black or a brown one! And why kill people at all, if you're going to go around whimpering and whining about it afterwards?

My task on this syphilitic and cancer-ridden bomb crater of a planet is to simply and quietly remove the condoms from the park and clean up the madhouse—and then this eight-star idiot from Sing Sing comes along, yammering and wailing like a professional mourner over a corpse which in the first place he produced himself, and which in the second place is utterly and totally dead. I don't give a single sou, not a used rubber, for that kind of murderer.

According to his own laws—which he respects and esteems and admires—he should have been fried like all the others in his electric, American national shrine of a chair instead of strolling around in one of France's most beautiful landscapes fishing trout and eating crayfish tails at the taxpayers' expense. Besides, as a general he favors capital punishment—

at any rate for others, if they've done the same thing he did. On top of the whole dung heap he's also started being a Christian. He thinks that rabbi Joshua died on the cross for Americans too.

That is obviously an open question.

But it all began while I was up in the park clipping stragglers off the roses. Since I'm not a regular gardener—and for that matter don't have a thorough knowledge of anything else either—I can't do any garden work except simple things like that. I was standing there in peace and equilibrium, I could still feel the resonance of Whitsunday's journey to the sun, and my senses were sharper than usual, the colors kept getting purer and clearer and stronger, and all sounds were newborn and tinkling—it wasn't easy to recognize them. Besides, the morning was fresh and dewy and very lovely; life was full of meaning and beauty.

When I came out into my vineyard, the old newspaper was still lying on the table, the one which the hospital cat had made water on, and it was still lying with the same picture of Strauss turned upward; His Holiness Franz-Josef the Beshat was staring contentedly up at the shining Gallic morning sky, as if he'd bought the whole of France already. The paper was dry as tinder now, but yellow and wrinkled from the cat-piss. It immediately put me in a radiant humor to see the Finance Minister's urine-disfigured face.

So I was tranquil of heart and content with my lot when I was disturbed by the Pentagon person.

He was just as usual, quiet and meek and sad—and he trod so carefully on the gravel in the road that you could hardly hear him. He apologized for his existence with every single movement—light and supple and lean as he is.

He looks so civilized with his walking stick that you'd think he was British and not from Amerikanienland.

We exchanged a few words about roses and sun and wind, but I could clearly see that he wanted to talk about something else as well. His glance was flat and wandering, and as he stared up at the sky and the treetops he suddenly asked if I'd like to come along to the village and have lunch with him. He even named the place where he was thinking of eating: *Le Soleil Rouge*, which in fact has one of the best cuisines in this part of the world. All in all it's an utterly splendid little village, and I've always been pathologically fond of really good food, and in this case the Pentagon would pay for the meal.

So I accepted, and we set out on foot for the village.

On the way down I hardly noticed what we talked about. It was scattered, unconnected things—the way people usually converse, in other words not a conversation which entailed anything irrevocable, anything which couldn't be undone, any truth which, said once and for all, could turn the relationship between two people into something insupportable and unendurable. No, we just talked chiffon, as they say here. Just words.

I myself was engrossed in the landscape around me, by the flat but still faintly undulating lines, by the colors, the flowers and the veil which lay in the air and turned all distant objects into something blue and hazy, covering them with a sort of mild silver sheen. And it struck me again that we inhabit an earth which is filled with a beauty beyond all understanding—and that we've turned this paradise into a slaughterhouse and a criminal asylum—into an all-embracing La Morgue, stinking of benzol and chloroform—instead of making water on the finance ministers (as the hospital cat does) and singing, drinking wine, praising the solar system, frolicking, mating with each other, writing plays, and praying to the stars.

When we'd sat down at the table in the lovely old inn, *Le Soleil Rouge*, I noticed that he seemed tormented and wrought up. His glance was wandering, and he ordered one dry Martini after another. All at once I *saw* him, I *saw him* as he was, and not the way he looked. I saw the narrow mouth, the slightly protruding ears, the shaved nape and the idiotically short-cropped back of his head—but I saw something more; I saw the thin hands, and I saw that the lean, sinewy wrist under the gold watch and the gold band was as hairy as a beast's. I saw straight through the quiet, meek, polite creature and knew that he was nothing but a common executioner and a ruffian of a mercenary soldier.

Then he began to cry—that is: at first his watery blue eyes just became moist, and then he started talking about his miserable, ridiculous little murder.

He told about the brown girl who had worked as a maid for him and his family after he came home from the war in Southeast Asia, and about the night they'd been alone together in the house, while his healthy, normal American wife and his equally healthy, normal American children were away visiting relatives in Dakota, or wherever the hell it was, and how the mahogany girl didn't want to do it with him, and he had used force on her—after all, he was accustomed to doing what he wanted in Southeast Asia—and at length had torn off her panties and made her lie still by twisting her wrists, and so had eventually managed to force his way into her; and how she had gotten all crazy and hysterical afterwards and tried to shout for the neighbors and the police and suddenly she was dead, and had emptied her bowels while he was only trying to stop her screaming, and then what in hell should he do with the body—after he had tried to dismember it but stopped midway—and how he didn't know anymore what he was doing when he hid the remains under some sacks in the basement. And then all this about how he had no initiative in the days following, but just let her lie instead of getting her out of there, and he walked around in the yard and couldn't do a thing, until it began to smell and there was a police investigation and the body was found, and he couldn't manage to talk anymore at all. And what would people think of him and the general staff after this.

And he sat there talking and talking and crying on the tablecloth, and spoiled the whole meal for me, the frogs' legs and the Alsace wine and the cheese.

For awhile—during the hors d'oeuvres—I felt sorry for him, and tried to console him.

I said that when you came right down to it the death was nothing at all, and considering how many people were killed every single hour of every single day, it really wasn't worth talking about, just a bagatelle when seen against the background of world history. And besides, I said; after all, he himself as a military man in Southeast Asia had been involved for several years in burning hecatombs of both women and children with the aid of highly developed technological weapons. But he didn't want to listen to that, he yammered and cried, and said that that wasn't the same thing as he was talking about. I said further that the world had always been like that, and that judging by all the solar signs it would continue to be like that for several thousand years more, if we didn't succeed in exterminating all life within the near future, so that the earth eventually became a silent and marvelously dead moon continuing its journey in space for all eternity. One sex murder more or less. . . .

Between sobbing fits he stammered out that it was something entirely different he was talking about, and that I didn't understand him at all. And when I asked him to explain himself, he stared at me with dripping eyes through his gold-rimmed glasses and said:

"You must understand what it will mean if it comes out that I, with my position in the Air Force, have had intimate relations with a Negress!"

But then this hasn't come out, and the honor of the Force is still undefiled. And during the meal he changed completely several times, even if the tears flowed all the while, and even if he was homesick for Texas and the golf course and his cozy bridge club.

He went on sobbing and dripping on the tablecloth and drank ice water with his food and spoiled the whole meal, until I sat there wishing that the cat would do the same thing on him as it had done on the picture of Franz-Josef the Mighty.

And this shitty yakkity-yak about his nice wife back home in Detroit and about his brother officers and his garden and the retirement age and his country place, this I had to sit and listen to, while the sun was of fire and gold and went its wonderful golden way across the sky.

No, the little Belgian is really another breed of sex murderer; he neither cries nor regrets, he laughs and laughs at the
whole thing, and is entirely of the opinion that one sex murder more or less, that's—well now, there's nothing particularly
extraordinary about it. . . .
    Of course one can understand the general too.
There's practically nothing in the world one can't understand. But I don't like to have my meals ruined.
    When we got back to La Poudrière I told al Assadun that
le général must have a little extra ataraxic for his conscience.

    "What the hell does the old gynaecocide want with tran-
quilizers?" said the assistant doctor. "Isn't it better for him to
have a little pain in his soul for awhile?"
    "Hush!" I replied with a warning finger toward heaven:
"Allah hears all. We are all Allah's sons, not only our highly
cultured French brethren, but even the overfucked and
overfed Amerikanians are His children. And He will not forgive you if you speak contemptuously of the White Man."
    "*Tant pis*," said al Assadun. "He can have the pills."
    "Why are you so nice to us whites?" I asked. "Have you
no racial pride, after everything those sodomitic Frenchmen
have managed to do down there?"
    "We've forgiven you," he replied, heading toward the
medicine cabinet. "We've quite simply forgiven everything."
    "Is it only the Jews you hate?"
    "No," he said seriously, "we hate the blacks too. But you
Frenchmen and Eskimos we've forgiven. We've forgotten
you."
    He was bent over the medicaments:
    "What do people actually do up there?"
    "The same as always," I replied; "they drink cod-liver oil
and eat blubber, and inside the igloos they beget their common progeny on the snow floor. Nobody knows who's
descended from whom."
    al Assadun was now ready with the ataraxic for *le général*,
and sent a male nurse over with the pills.

"Shall we smoke tonight?" he said to me.

"No thanks," I replied, "I've got to work on the lecture. It has to be finished in a couple of days."

He nodded. I went on:

"Neither the Moslems nor the Hindus nor the Buddhists have had anything resembling the Christian heresy and witch trials, at least not so far as I know. Do you know of anything like that?"

"No," he said, considering it: "I know of nothing to compare with the Christians' burning of heretics or their witch trials. That hasn't occurred among us."

I went around thinking about that all afternoon: that if one wants to characterize the distinction between Christianity and all other religions in one single phrase, then that phrase is "the stake."

It's the center of our culture, and only if we understand this can we understand the culture. Christianity holds nearly all the rest of its ideas and concepts in common with other religions, as borrowings or from a deeper source. Only heretic- and witch-burning is our own invention; the Inquisition is Christianity's *sole* original product, its greatest contribution so far.

In my privy chamber I have read all four gospels anew, but I haven't found a trace of the sickness in them. The falsification began with Paul—the first Leninist.

When Paul brought democratic centralism into religion, he simultaneously proclaimed the doctrine of the magical elite, the "elitist theory," which ascribes to the party and the church elite a divine and magical power to express the people's true and deepest will, even if the people themselves have not the slightest inkling of this will, or even might want the direct opposite—just as heretics and witches were burned over a slow fire to save their souls—against their earthly will, and because others understood better than they what was best for them.

Here we're at the heart of the matter.

We've roasted each other for thousands of years without achieving any noteworthy results from our kitchen labors.

There's also some importance in our own geographical situation in Alsace, south of Trier, where much of the roasting took place—with the Eifel Mountains to the north and with some of the loveliest varieties of roses ever to be forced by man. A landscape created by God, with some of Europe's most beautiful architecture—created by human beings.

Once again I've walked in the cool of the evening beside the brook, I've seen the ice-cold, brownish water and the shadows of the trout gliding through it. Under the leafy treetops the whole garden lies in a shadow, clear and strong and blue. Some few poppies shine with the maddest red in creation. But the flowers are closing now. The flowers are closing. In the midst of all that blue, the flowers are closing up.

I know that something is going to happen tonight.

That the little pederastic sex killer from Belgium would come down to see me after dinner is something I should almost have known beforehand. But inevitability is just what one never perceives. There's nothing one is less able to foresee than precisely that which is the result of a strict and logical conformity to law. He *had* to come this evening. It was the only thing that was missing.

He writes and writes almost around the clock, and for all I know he may end up as an internationally recognized writer. But amid all this writing there are always things which don't get said, words which he doesn't dare confide to paper. Then he sneaks down and uses me for a garbage can, just as all the others do.

He began with bits of news from the Institute: that the Russian ambassador's wife had stopped howling her wolf-howls and was almost perfectly normal and calm—and that Lacroix had acquired a veritable ruff*of a bandage around his neck and showed no signs of dying after his operation, but on the contrary went on living against all reason. They all go on living and living, as if nothing had

*prestekrave: clerical collar, which in Norway is a ruff.–Tr.

happened in the whole history of the world.

Afterwards he told me about the first time he had been with a boy—after he himself was a grown man.

Of course I told him that it was nothing, a pure bagatelle which had been going on around the clock, year in and year out, in every city and every land, so long as the world had existed—men sleeping with boys; but he wouldn't stop talking about it, he went on and on while I sat at the garden table drinking wine and listening to him in the dark, and he kept going further and further back, all the way to his own childhood. What may seem surprising is that he has practically no inhibitions when it comes to telling about his two murders, he writes it down so that the ink spurts, with every possible detail, all that he thought and felt; but as soon as he gets onto the innocent and utterly harmless affairs with the boys, it's as if everything stops for him. And the reason, so far as I can see, is that the butcheries don't really tell anything about him, but the small intimate experiences say more than he knows himself, and he senses that; he senses that he may be telling more than what he himself can control. The obscenities entail a far greater nakedness than what they actually describe. A person who is capable of telling about his own true obscenities is capable of anything, perhaps even of speaking the truth about other things as well.

And he doesn't dare do it in writing. He dares to kill people and cut up their bodies afterwards, but he doesn't dare to tell the truth, not about his own insides, not about the innermost darkness.

When the darkness draws near, he laughs—he laughs and laughs. He laughs at the boys he's amused himself with, he laughs at the trial and the judge, at everything. But he doesn't dare reveal himself. He—like everyone else—is deathly afraid of standing there without his shorts.

It's very clear that one has freedom only to the degree that one isn't ashamed. He who no longer wants to hide anything, he is approaching freedom.

We boast of having fooled people, we boast of our dishonesty and our brutality, but we're ashamed of having unbuttoned a boy's fly.

Actually it wasn't much our little Belgian had to tell; something about too little time, abut hotel rooms and pissoirs, things not the least bit ugly or mean in themselves, but characterized by dirty, dishonest surroundings. Things that had to be kept secret, done hurriedly and without peace or patience, without joy.

The only really beautiful things this man has experienced were the two murders—both times of boys around the age of puberty. In contrast to our Amerikanian rapist of black girls, this young Belgian managed to dismember the bodies. He had better nerves than the general.

Still they aren't good enough.

The best nerves, basically, belong to old Lacroix, but not even they could stretch far enough—not in the long run. As is evident from the wolf-howls, the ambassadress's nerves aren't on a level with the solar system either. Strictly speaking, the one with the worst nerves of us all is probably the chief physician himself, good old Lefèvre, and in his way he actually gets along the best in this world.

A couple of the male nurses have it really bad.

On the other hand al Assadun seems to get on for the time being, even if only Allah and Mary know how he'll end up.

Meanwhile, as long as we're talking about things eternal, I must be allowed to mention something I myself experienced with a boy I once met on the street in Lyons—a city memorable, among other things, for its pioneering criminological institute. It was in Lyons that police investigations became a science.

This boy I'm going to tell about I met on one of the streets near the river, and I noticed him at once because he was beautiful. He was around fifteen, not especially tall, and had remarkably light, almost white hair. He was beautiful in a way that was both masculine and at the same time enchantingly feminine—and as soon as he sensed that I'd noticed him he swung into the nearest lighted shop window. It was a bookstore, and nothing was more natural than that I too should stop to look at the books. I remember very clearly a French edition of *Faust*. He looked up at me and smiled faintly, and gradually we started talking about books. What we both wanted lay in the air, you could have touched it.

Afterward we went to a bar and drank coffee and a couple of glasses of cognac. His clear, blue-gray eyes sparkled with cheer and good humor; the boy was full of gladness.

Already in the elevator up to my hotel room he threw his arms around me and kissed me with a spontaneity and abandon, with a strength which no woman could have equaled. I could feel that his whole body was rigid, it was just one single taut muscle.

Going down the hall he held my hand with the same hard pressure, breathless and impatient.

The minute we were inside the room he looked at me and smiled as he opened his trousers and drew out his cock, which was hard and stiff. Then there was an explosion: he literally tore off his clothes and threw them on the floor. What followed was like being in bed with a panther; he was in complete, almost senseless ecstasy, squeezed me in his arms and writhed his hips and belly against me, back and forth, back and forth. He couldn't speak, but kissed me with open mouth all over my face, rubbed his moist lips and tongue against my eyes, mouth, neck, and ears.

I raised my head slightly and looked down toward his belly and his bristling cock. Almost instantly I saw a gleam of something wet and lightning-swift. At the same instant I received the warm jet up along my torso and across my face. He pressed his mouth to my neck and bit me rather hard a few times, but otherwise it had no effect on him; his penis was just as stiff as before, and the violence just the same. Never in any other person have I seen such passion.

The blow-by-blow details are irrelevant here; the point is that it repeated itself three times in a few minutes, without his erection subsiding. Only later did he have to rest a bit, and lay there holding my hand.

Today the story reminds me of just one thing: what an enormous strength Eros can have at this boy's age—and *what kind of forces* we're tampering with when we try to suppress Him—when we try to lead Him into other channels which we don't know and can't comprehend.

We have a culture which idiotically digs and roots around in people, which wants to "form" them, "improve" them, without a spark of insight into what is being done. And behind it all stands the same evil need to dominate, to wield power, the same old sins.

Twice in my former office I investigated sex murderers' backgrounds as carefully and thoroughly as possible, and both times I arrived at the same results.

They had both murdered girls, but were of different ages and nationalities. The one had killed only once, by strangling. The other had killed twice over a period of several years—the second time after the doctors had discharged him from the criminal asylum as "cured," or at least greatly improved. He had committed both murders with a pocket knife and a large hatpin. In both cases he had driven along the highway and picked up the girls as hitchhikers.

Of the first, the strangler, one can only say briefly that he came from a monstrously puritanical and fastidious Christian sexual milieu. From the time he was a little boy he had learned to hate and fear the lusts of the flesh as the most evil thing in the world. He was a deeply religious, excellent, and solid man. This is no theory, just a fact.

The other, the double murderer with the hatpin, had a far more imposing background, marked by an insane and fanatical hatred of life. His father died when he himself was a small child, and he was brought up by the immensely pious woman who was his mother. This mother had set herself just one goal in life: to keep her son pure, to keep him away from all the women in the world. He was likewise hindered from committing the sin of self-contamination. Right up until the boy was eighteen or nineteen years old, he had to go to the john with the door open and the mother standing outside to see that he didn't indulge in carnal lust with himself.

Both boys became murderers in their twenties, and when I've progressed further with my work I shall inquire into all sex murderers' backgrounds and put everything into a defensible statistical form.

But where does this murderous urge come from?

Later we shall look at the witch trials.

Of this boy in Lyons, my wildest and most passionate love, I know nothing more. A few days later I left the city. He was going to school. But I know that we spent some splendid hours together.

Meanwhile, I've hardly been as happy anywhere else in the world as at La Poudrière; the strange brown color in the clear, ice-cold trout stream, the air here, the park with the huge, age-old trees, and the glittering flower beds—it's all a retreat from the world, a fine seclusion, a last great chance to understand anything at all of what we have taken part in.

Of course: courtrooms, prisons, madhouses—that is and will remain my world.

I have a very special relationship to medical folk. I've met doctors everywhere, and most are half-mad and delightful. With jurists too I have an intimate relation, possibly because they're almost the only people, aside from the convicts, who fully share my view of the courtroom. They know the lie.

Why I have such a patently tranquilizing effect on the mentally ill, I don't quite know. But perhaps they feel that I share much of their conception of the world, and yet manage to scramble through the garbage heap without being taken into custody. Our little Belgian is one of the sweetest sex murderers I've met; he has a peculiar charm. And he has killed two boys in a fashion which—by bourgeois standards—is so inventive that one must go to the American freedom fight in Southeast Asia to find a match for his artistry in butchering children.

The Belgian—M. Fontaine—had dispatched the two boys with a knife, and in a manner which shows that the world gets along splendidly without the advanced technological machinery of our time. A large, sharp-edged knife answers amazingly well if it's in the hands of a man with imagination and initiative. He had, among other things, cut off almost all there was to cut, by no means contenting himself merely with balls and penis. Quite the contrary.

This is quite funny to think about when I sit so quietly and intimately in conversation with him. The murders entered M. Fontaine's life as an utter surprise, when he was twenty-four years old and was studying for his doctorate in law. Fontaine is short, actually rather quiet, and of a very slender build. It's not easy to imagine him at work with one of those butcher knives. But I tell myself that just such things happen unceasingly every time God's images on earth hold their wars, and indeed we've hardly had time for much else. No matter which war you take, you find the kind of amputations and surgical operations which Fontaine performed, and which are by no means necessarily a part of the general staff's tactics or strategy. They are almost always done as voluntary extra labor, often on overtime or off duty; so the conclusion is obvious that the tendency is latent in a great many of God's images.

Fontaine grew up in a highly protected rich man's milieu, surrounded by servants, cars, and every imaginable luxury. To be sure he had previously caused his family concern because of his sexual peculiarity, but no one had expected anything like this of him. He had an excellent head and managed his studies with playful ease and with very good results—in return he was allowed to do as he liked in almost every sphere. The only thing the family totally denied him was permission to be a homosexual.

The first scenes took place when he was twelve or thirteen, after his mother had caught him with a schoolmate, both with their pants unbuttoned, enthusiastically engaged in mutual masturbation.

After the family scenes which ensued, he had been dragged to a series of doctors, to psychiatrists and psychologists, they had tried pills and diets, and they ordered the servants not to serve him eggs and to keep an eye on him. All his friends were regarded with suspicion, and were investigated as thoroughly as possible. But all this loving care came to naught, and it wasn't much longer before he was discovered anew—this time with the gardener's son, who was sixteen. As an emergency exit he began to seek out younger boys, but was caught again doing the same thing with them.

He eventually began to do disappearing acts, in which he tried to make contact with grown men—which didn't suit him very well, and which he stopped altogether after one of them reported him to the police for prostitution. But his parents continued to watch him for many years afterwards, and it wasn't until he was twenty that he was able to assert himself enough so that they couldn't check up on him. By then, however, he had become wholly fixated on adolescent boys, which put him in danger of being hit by the criminal law.

Furthermore, he had acquired very special needs. He was emphatically anal-erotic, and wanted to be the passive partner—in other words a real *enculé*, as Lefèvre is always saying.

It's clear that for Fontaine it's his adolescent years which are hardest to talk about. He gets tense and anxious when he tries. The murders which followed much later, and only five days apart, are much easier for him to discuss.

This evening he mentioned them again, and sat looking at me for awhile. Then he said:

"These two murders were my real birth."

"What do you mean by that?" I asked.

"It's hard to express it exactly," he replied; "but it was my own life which began then. Since then I've been totally different. I've come into being; I've received an existence."

"You could very easily have brought your own life to an end on the same occasion," I said, "if it hadn't been for certain first-rate lawyers and psychiatrists. And in the real good old days you could have managed to be burned just for pederasty. Remember Calvin."

"Yes, yes," said he; "that's just it. That's just it!"

He sat in silence for awhile, then started laughing loudly before he spoke again:

"Do you know that my family, my family which used to regard me as a kind of spiritual monstrosity, as a blot on their escutcheon, the same family now regards me with respect, you might say with *deference?*"

I understood what he meant.

"You've risen in the ranks," I replied. "A little pederast who runs around trying to get fourteen-year-old boys to satisfy him from behind is regarded only with contempt, but a murderer, he *is* something?"

"Exactly. A murderer is a *man.* A murderer is regarded with deference, not with contempt."

I said nothing, and after a moment he went on:

"Of course I was more or less insane when I did it, but who is really the craziest?"

I saw him partway up to the clinic and wished him good night.

It is certainly not very dangerous to let Fontaine walk around the park as freely as he does. Lefèvre's methods of treatment are effective; Fontaine has it better here than he's ever had it before, and he doesn't have to miss being with boys. Lefèvre has made an arrangement with the police doctor in one of the nearest big cities, everything works splendidly, and Fontaine regularly gets his wishes fulfilled to such a degree that he sometimes can't sit down the next day.

We all have it very good here at our beloved La Poudrière, among our two-legged brothers in the criminal asylum. Lord knows we have our quirks, but what about those on the outside—I don't mean the publicans and sinners, not the pimps, slave traders and necrophiliacs, pederasts, murderers, and pickpockets who are still at large—I mean those who really are of this world, those who lead it and look after it?

I walked down into the park and made my way across one of the lawns where there's a dense clump of trees, a kind of grove. And as I looked into it, I thought I saw something inside which was even darker than the darkness. I stopped and stared at it; there was something like a kind of giant sack floating above the ground. For a moment all stood still for me, before I dared go in among the tree trunks. It was a stout, heavy man.

Only when I came right up to him did I see that it was Dr. Báthory, the Hungarian engineer.

I sounded the alarm at once, and we got him up to the first-aid room. But it didn't turn out this time as with M. Lacroix; Báthory had had better luck.

"Twice in the space of only a few days," said Dr. Lefèvre; "that's just like in the prisons. Once one has begun, the others follow. Sometimes there are epidemics."

"Well!" said al Assadun, looking over at the splendid muscular corpse: "If it had to be somebody. . . ."

It was he who called the police, and a great part of the night was taken up with investigations and hearing witnesses, and the poor policemen were given red wine and wrote and wrote until it was past three o'clock. Then they left. The hanged cadaver they took with them.

Afterwards, down in my garden, I had a couple of slices of dark bread along with a couple of glasses of wine.

I thought how astonishingly much I've been able to recall of my own life, and at the same time what compactness and inevitability lies in it all. From the point where it begins there's an unbroken, logical line of necessity leading forward to the present. All being the way it was, it had to go the way it did. In a sense everything is good and right.

The two murders which M. Fontaine committed took place in a room he had rented in the city. The first of the boys had come to him as agreed, but unexpectedly demanded about twice as much as usual for his services. Fontaine became irritated, not because of the money, but because in some way he was hurt. And in the quarrel which followed, the demand escalated to blackmail: the boy threatened to tell all he knew about Fontaine's intimate pleasures. There was a brief fight, in which Fontaine completely lost control of himself, and the moment the blood started to flow he began the butchering. A few days later—still before the police investigation had gotten started in earnest—the second boy came up to him at the agreed time. But he didn't come just to perform his friendly offices toward Fontaine; he also asked about his comrade, who he knew had been at the same place before he disappeared.

This time the murder took place deliberately and consciously, and just as ritually as the previous one; among other things he performed the same, extremely conscientious castration.

As we know, the chief problem with every murder is to get rid of the remains; it's practically impossible. But M. Fontaine did it intelligently and thoroughly, and since the room was rented under a false name—he only used it as a love nest, and nobody in the district knew him—it took quite a long time before the case was solved.

Fontaine confessed at once, and was immediately brought to the clinic.

It's much on my mind that no one has the right to say the truth about others if he doesn't dare say it about himself. At the same time: is it possible to avoid doing it? Can one possibly record a protocol with real care without writing down the text in such a way that they can use every word against one?

I would probably even set up this basic doctrine for record-keepers: Write so that every word can be used against you!

THE WITCHES' REVOLUTION

Prairial 18, the year 176

So in God's name, I've given this cursed lecture from hell on the witches' world empire and the battle of the forces of good against them! I was prepared for just about anything afterwards, but I hadn't expected the kind of reactions that followed.

But first let me say that incidents with M. Lacroix and Dr. Báthory by no means brought others in their train. No, there was no epidemic. On the contrary, stillness and quiet have reigned in the asylum, truly the deepest idyllic peace.

Even M. Lacroix and the Russian ambassador's wife are over their momentary crises. Old Lacroix stumps around with his cane greeting everybody, a trifle weakened and with huge bandages around his neck, but he seems at peace with himself and the world—as if the bloodletting had done him good.

The ambassador's wife isn't howling for the nonce; pale and smiling faintly she walks about the park with the greatest diplomatic dignity, yet human and democratic enough to nod to everyone—exactly as befits a representative of two hundred million happy Soviets.

However, not a word of criticism shall be said about her here. In the first place she has her problems with herself and her nature, and in the second place she has a deplorable family background. Her father had fought on the barricades during the Revolution and was in the front lines all through the civil war; but alas, in 1936 he turned out to be one of the countless hyenas and bloodsuckers who right from 1917 had been paid by the capitalist powers to poison, sabotage, murder, and deceive the Soviet people, to mix ground glass in the flour, to undermine the Revolution, plotting armed acts of violence against Soviet man's heroic leaders, being all the while in league with the imperialist Trotsky and later on—after the takeover in Teutonia—collaborating with Adolf Hitler and the Gestapo.

Since the bloody dog confessed everything during the trials, there can be no doubt of the fact: he was so manifestly guilty of seditious crimes against the state that in calmer times there could be no question of redemption for him.

Despite her descent, however, his daughter—who in 1936 was barely born, and not demonstrably guilty of complicity—had later been redeemed to the point where she could now function as an ambassador's wife. The business about her father wasn't the only thing: acquaintances, friends of the family, relatives and others had in turn been exposed as imperialist bloodsuckers, deviationist hyenas, and revisionist murderers, not least after the war. So she certainly has lots to think about in the lonely hours between wolf howls and rape attempts, not least because the friends, relatives, etc., etc. who were convicted of hyenaism in the 1950's and also from the mid-'60's on—they too had all confessed their hatred of the people and their love of capitalism.

It isn't easy to come from such surroundings when you're a true and overflowingly grateful Soviet citizen yourself.

I've talked with her now and then, and she gives an impression of quiet despondency—as if she had once been crushed, and had never knit properly together again. But before her breakdown she was the perfect, self-controlled ambassador's wife who wholly and fully complemented her correct, regime-defending spouse, a true representative of Soviet Man's revolutionary virtue and heroic strength. Of course there's really nothing left of that now, even if she says she's often homesick for Russia and the villages there. I may have been both tactless and thoughtless when I've sometimes talked with her about her country's courts and prisons, where conditions have been improving steadily, not least after Stalin's death—until today they're actually so excellent that it's almost only writers who are in jail. She smiles at that, but doesn't look happy—though I know that it doesn't bother her to talk about it; on the contrary it seems to be a need. People can show so many strange sides, especially when talking about youth and childhood. I know that several times she's considered seeking political asylum in France, but is waiting to get well enough to make a decision. And when the attacks come, she thinks about something entirely different.

Once or twice she's had a couple of glasses of wine with me on the terrace, and that has been a great pleasure, at least for me. But we've never talked about the Bible. Like so many post-revolutionary Russians, she's never read it. She doesn't know other revolutionary writings either, only Lenin's creed and his little catechism—only the apostolic commentaries.

Fontaine too has had a nice peaceful time. He's had at least one visit, and seems content and relieved. He stands while you talk with him.

So we're still no scintillating assembly here at La Poudrière, and there are other madhouses with more eminent clients, but we get along pretty well, and we keep together for the most part.

The lecture was held in the banquet hall, which is furnished as irreproachably as any in a first-class hotel—with taste and refinement, as Lefèvre's level of culture demands.

After we had eaten—an unusually bad meal—I got out the manuscript and betook myself up to the lectern which we use at these gatherings. To avoid misunderstanding I reproduce here the manuscript as it was used—*in extenso*, for its interpretation of the great signs and deeds which later were made manifest.

But before we come to the heart of the matter I must, as the nearest representative of the Trinity—not as Son or as

Father, but purely and simply as Paraclete, Comforter and Holy Spirit—declare my antipathy to the monstrously shitty and syphilitic form of communication known as "the spoken word" (or among the profane, "lectures")—a form which has arisen for the sole purpose of swathing all exactitude and precision in a veil of fog beyond all power of discernment and all criteria. This form has much in common with the fashions which sporadically break out in record-keeping, but it has nothing to do with the analytic, microscopic naturalism which is all record-keeping's main artery; which dissolves reality into a shimmer of metals and minerals and precious stones; and which by force of its precision, its truth and its scientific method is the only record-keeping which has anything to do with the final apocalypse. I speak of that practiced by such caretakers as Schulz, Bulatovic, Genêt, Malaparte, and above all our beloved Céline—whose contemporaries don't reach to his ankles—along with many, many others who don't run with the fashions, and who therefore don't always receive their reward in this life, but are more or less burned at the stake or silenced, so that like a corn of wheat they must first die in order to gain eternal life.

I write this to explain the *imprecise tone*, which is and ever shall be the style of the *lecture*, "the Spoken Word"; and which I hereby dissociate myself from:

THE WITCHES' REVOLUTION
Satan's takeover of power, the witches' world empire, and the Great Dread

LADIES AND GENTLEMEN:

The absolute precondition—the *sine qua non*—for understanding the historic, heroic struggle against the Spell of Darkness is as follows: Witchcraft, i.e. witches' and wizards' crimes against the worldwide empire of the Trinity $(3 = 1)$, has always existed. But in the period around 1500, God's bloodhounds, the *Domini canes* brethren—aided by the day's greatest scientists and above all by the acumen of the *jurists*, by the trenchant thoughts and mighty labors of those versed in the law (see: Paul, Augustine, Thomas the sharp-witted of Aquinas, Luther, Lenin et al.)—undertook the following worldwide exposé:

Satan's plan for the Great Revolution: Satan's hegemony over all of Europe, to be accomplished with the aid of his mercenary soldiers, the witches and warlocks—with tens of thousands of hired troops, an army larger than Alexander's and Caesar's legions put together. Through this host of conspirators the dire event would come to pass: God's kingdom in Europe—"the Land of Christianity," as Novalis says—would be caught unawares and conquered, taken over by witches and warlocks, and forever incorporated into Satan's Realm of Darkness, there to mock God and break down HIS ORDER AND JUSTICE.

The decisive proof, for Christians versed in divine and secular law, was the vast increase in the number of witches on earth. For every witch who confessed and was justly punished (Moses: "Thou shalt not suffer a witch to live") there appeared ten, twenty, or even forty—up to a hundred—new ones, named by the condemned before God in the days ere the witch was to die the great death—at that moment when no one could lie, and with instruments blessed by the Lord Jesus Christ guaranteeing the truth of the testimony.

Among the community of the faithful these thousands and hundreds of thousands of witches created *the Great Dread*—the great November.

The faithful understood that in each person you met, Satan might have taken up residence. In every brother, sister, friend the evil duality might have conquered heart and reason, leading him or her to serve Satan's carnal lust—the portal to Satan's worldwide empire after the revolution.

In every person, lay or learned, you might meet a spy, an agent of the Powers of Opposition, a doomed sold soul, a servant of the Rebel Forces in their struggle to rule the world, in their fight to cast out the temporal princes and executioners and hatchet men—who, in the words of Paul, are installed by

God the Lord, and who are to be slavishly obeyed and served by every single Christian—without doubt, without rebellion, without disobedience; the Powers of this world, who at first opposed the Son's Kingdom of Love, but who since the fourth century have served God's Kingdom with the sword and the stake, and whom the Christian is to obey—according to Paul, Augustine, Calvin, and Luther—unto death, just as the Gospel of Love tells us. So long as these temporal powers are baptized and Christian.

In these hundreds of thousands of spies and servants of Satan's Kingdom the church and the secular jurists had a great and prodigious task—inasmuch as the truth, the sexual congress with incubi and succubae which forms the basis of the pact with Satan, could be exposed almost solely by the Church's most drastic means of coercion.

It cannot be repeated often enough that we're talking here about *Deus Caritatis*, the God of Love, and that only with sorrow did His servants turn the obstinate over to the temporal courts, to the jurists—who served the Trinity's fight against the black ones with at least as much zeal as did the clerics. The war that followed was endlessly and indescribably heroic on the part of God's servants.

For fully two hundred years they carried on the battle according to the dictates of Love: tens of millions of false Christians, spies and agents of the black Majesty, with spouses and (often very small) children, were put to the rack and the fire (plus all the scientific instruments which Father, Son, and Spirit have bestowed on us), and were then turned over, without bloodshed, to the punitive justice of this world. After this great and cosmic World War, which lasted for more than two hundred years, theology and jurisprudence emerged victorious over the many who had placed themselves in the service of Satan's Kingdom. The victory was the Church's and the Law's.

Ladies and gentlemen, honored listeners:

This is a short and introductory orientation to the topic we shall approach this evening.

We shall only note the theme which runs through the struggle: in these crucial centuries it was a question of world domination, of the Opposition Powers' insurrection and revolutionary acts against existing institutions, against God's eternal, loving establishment of the world order as it is, and as it ever shall be—or to repeat Martin Luther's explanation of that order's claim to continued existence for all eternity:

Art. XVI (De Rebus Civilibus.)
"Of police and the temporal rulers it is written that all authority in the world and all ordained rulers and all laws are created and installed by God, . . . that the Christian shall pass death sentences and punish evil deeds with death, wage righteous wars, fight, buy and sell, . . . own property, consummate marriage, etc. . . ."

Further:

Art. XVII (De Christi Reditu ad Iuditium.)
". . . give to the believing and the elect eternal life and eternal bliss, but condemn the demons and the godless to eternal torment. . . ."
"Therefore we reject the Baptists, who teach that the devils and the damned shall not suffer eternal torment and agony. . . ."
Today it sounds idiotic when an unenlightened and foolish pagan says—and here I choose the first words taken at random from among other just as idiotic pagan utterances, there are thousands to choose from:
"When you have been lost in the wilderness and return to the dwellings of humanity, you no longer make a distinction between Hellenes and barbarians—but feel how kindred one human being is to another."
This was uttered three and a half centuries before our Christian era, by Aristotle; and what a leap from darkness to clarity has not been made in less than two thousand years, from Aristotle to Luther:

Catechism, Haustafel, Appendix No. II: "Everyone shall be obedient, for above us all is the authority which has been installed by God. He who disobeys *authority* is disobedient to *God's own order.* . . . Therefore it is needful to *obey.* . . ."

Once again we go back to paganism and darkness, this time to the rabbi Joshua, who said (and he too ended as a criminal on the cross, after scoffing at the power of the State): *"Woe unto you, when all shall speak well of you!"*

How different, and how infinitely much deeper, is not the sound of Paul's own words:

"For I would that all were even as I myself."

Luther:

"Remind them to submit to princes and authorities. . . .

"Wives should submit to their husbands, as Sarah was obedient to Abraham and called him master. . . .

"Ye children, obey your parents in the Lord. . . .Ye servants, obey your masters after the flesh. . . . Ye youths, obey the old, and clothe yourselves in humility. . . . To the humble He gives grace."

After this came the outbreak of the witches' revolution! But before we describe in earnest the thoughts and lewdness which the witcheries entailed, we shall dwell yet a moment on the fact that Dr. Martin Luther owed his wisdom and clarity of thought not merely to himself. His spiritual fathers were the Ancient World's brightest intellects: Paul and Augustine.

For the kind of people who come into conflict with the state and who are punished by it, Paul, Augustine, Thomas, Luther, and Lenin have no words harsh enough:

"Strike them down like mad dogs!"

The deep wisdom which resides in this we'll return to later. Before we take the first break I'll just briefly cite the thoughtless and superficial words spoken by a certain Socrates, just before his death—approximately as follows:

"If I haven't protested against the laws before, then it's too late to do so now. *That I myself am to be executed* is no argument, when I've previously seen others die by the same ungodly laws."

And from there to only six or seven centuries later, from
dark Antiquity to the shining world of God, with all the
wealth of perspicacity, wisdom, and love which marks the
Athanasian Creed! (What is the laughable Greek mathematics
to this?!) I shall only mention Socrates's doubling of the
square—the slave boy and Socrates, which purported to show
that the foreign, barbarian slave had more thoughts in his
head than the class which, according to Paul, Augustine,
Thomas, Luther, and Lenin, was endowed with the wisdom
we know it possessed. From there to the shining, soul-enlight-
ening Athanasian Creed:

". . . . Except every one do keep the faith whole and undefiled [from Socrates, who is Darkness, to Paul, who is Light]:
without doubt he shall perish everlastingly. For there is one
person of the Father, another of the Son, and another of the
Holy Ghost. But the Godhead of the Father, of the Son, and
of the Holy Ghost is all one, the Glory equal, the Majesty co-
eternal, and the Father uncreate, the Son uncreate, and the
Holy Ghost uncreate, and the Father incomprehensible, the
Son incomprehensible, and the Holy Ghost incomprehensi-
ble, *and yet they are not three eternals but one eternal, and also there
are not three incomprehensibles nor three uncreated but one uncreated
and one incomprehensible,* and the Holy Ghost is of the Father
and of the Son neither made nor created nor begotten but
proceeding, and none is afore or after another, and none is
greater or less than another. . . ."

What a growth in purity of spirit!

Let us dwell for a moment on the great correlation.
Originally the Church was without laws or means of combat-
ing witchcraft; since the old canon law declared that there
were no witches, the Church was even forced to regard belief
in witchcraft as heretical. But when it turned out that the great
heretic regions were the home of monstrous witcheries, and
that nearly all heretics not only killed small children and
lived in debauchery, but also used the debauchery and the
children's blood to cause other persons and their cattle great

injuries in ways which could only be due to sorcery, there could be no further doubt of the connection: it was obvious that sorcery came from heretics, and ergo also that heresy came from witches.

This opened up the judicial possibilities of the Holy Inquisition for the first time; no longer must the Church stand powerless against the darkness. By justly condemning witches and wizards according to the laws against heretics she was thus eventually able—after battling for a full two hundred years—to check these servants of Satan, and by then it had turned out that Europe had housed millions and millions of them.

Which of the Churches put forth the greatest and most Godfearing effort in the holy battle is impossible to say. Not only within the Mother Church did the great witch-*doctores* arise; Calvin and Luther too were devout witch-burners and contributed greatly to purging our continent of devils and sorcerers and witches. With the aid of the many pious men of God among the judges and lawyers the work was accomplished, and many of these produced a life work comprising the burning of several hundred witches—even thousands.

It goes without saying that witches hate truth, and their pact with the devil obliges them not to tell the truth to the high court. Witches or wizards will never confess their black arts of their own accord, and thus it was always incumbent on the men of the Church or the Law to procure proofs and confessions by another route.

From the very beginning, of course, the Holy Inquisition had at its disposal the Church's most drastic means of coercion, such as Spanish boots, racks, thumbscrews, red-hot irons, and warming-basins—but these alone weren't enough, and now legal science developed rapidly, it steadily conquered new technological ground, finding ways to keep the accused alive until all deeds were confessed and all accomplices in the witches' sabbaths named by name. If a witch or a wizard could be kept alive long enough, you could induce one subject to name from sixty to more than a hundred new witches, who each in turn—if kept alive long enough—could then yield as many new names. Thus it sometimes transpired that whole villages were caught in Satan's toils, and the entire population could be led to the stake. Not a few villages, especially in Gallia and Germania, were depopulated for this reason—villages where not just old and ugly witches, but even the priest and the mayor—yes, and often very small children, too—confessed relations with incubi and succubi when interrogated with instruments.

Today we have trouble comprehending the prodigious number of witches, and thus the vast extent of the trials. And this number was steadily mounting. For each witch or wizard who was caught, twenty, maybe sixty or eighty new ones were exposed. And this happened all over Europe; there were districts where the stakes stood thick as trees in the forest.

And it's hard too for us to comprehend the awful dread and terror which these throngs, these hundreds of thousands and millions of Satan's servants, awakened in right-thinking Christians.

As a Christian you knew that you were surrounded by witches who wished not just to ruin good folk's property, health, and lives, but whose ultimate goal was to seduce you into becoming a witch yourself and spending all eternity in unending torment in hell.

Thus an understanding of eternal hellfire is an absolute precondition for grasping witchcraft's essence, as well as the evil allure of the heterodox—including that of the Moors in Spain and the infidel, heretical Jews throughout most of Europe. These too were treated by priests, bishops, and jurists in the same needful manner as ordinary witches and heretics.

So in many ways it becomes hard to differentiate between heretics, witches, Arabs, and Jews—and today it would be impossible to give exact figures in connection with all these trials and persecutions. One can only say that millions and millions had to be burned.

Still, the main point is evident: how appallingly far Satan and his black host had advanced on their way to revolt and

revolution against God and the forces of Heaven. It's no exaggeration to say that the outcome of the battle against the witches was long in doubt; for at least a hundred and fifty years it looked as if these hordes and legions, these countless multitudes, would get the upper hand and make their ruler master of heaven and earth, with the Christians writhing in everlasting fire and Satan himself debauching for all eternity with heretics, sorcerers, Jews, witches, and Arabs.

Where steel doesn't help, there's fire. And fire helped.

In the long run it turned out that the old rack, or "ladder," formerly so supreme, had a disadvantage: especially obdurate witches could withstand it, because their joints got used to being stretched. Persons who had been interrogated never became quite firm in the joints again; hence during later stretchings they no longer felt the right degree of pain upon extension of the rack. Their joints slid apart all too easily.

Something could be achieved by turning the ladder so that the person was suspended under it, adding body weight to the pull of the rack as it was screwed outwards.

But very often they had to resort to the warming basin, setting it either under the rack—for roasting—or on the accused's lap or stomach or chest. But this could result in the death of the accused before the accomplices were found.

Gradually, however, Christian science invented a long series of instruments of different types—instruments for piercing, crushing, burning (needles, etc.), pinching (tongs to draw out nails with and the like), plus many, many others which were of great benefit to the Church and the true Christian faith.

Sometimes the accused might be of an especially stubborn and malicious character. This happened especially in cases where, for example, the witch's daughter too was accused of the same horrible sin, and where the mother, the older witch, was unwilling to give information about the daughter's magic arts.

It might also happen that witches and wizards as well as heretics neither confessed nor denounced their accomplices,

but withstood every torture the human mind could devise—
even the Spanish boot, which produces one of the greatest
pains we know: as the screw is turned it slowly crushes the
shinbone, the fibula, and the foot. Still, those were rare cases.

But before employing the most drastic means of force, the
court gathered ordinary external evidence against the witch.
It could be warts or toes grown together which proved that
Satan had set his mark on his servant—or insensitive places
on the body, or places which didn't bleed when stuck with a
pin. It could also be that the witch looked like a witch, so that
everyone could clearly see it.

A great many witches were forbiddingly ugly, old, and
extremely poor—so that ugliness, age, and poverty often had
the status of legal proof.

Others perhaps were wont to curse and call names and
blaspheme against God's servants, or express evil wishes that
came true. In the latter event the case was perfectly clear, and
it was just a question of finding the witch's accomplices.

I can mention a case of that type of witchery in a northern
region, a case which led to a series of bonfires.

There was an old woman who had met the executioner on
the street, and he had struck her hard across the arm with his
crop. The woman had then threatened the executioner, saying that it would ache longer in his arm than in hers. A short
while later the executioner broke his arm and reported the
witch to the tribunal.

It turned out that just through this one witch they managed to expose a mighty conspiracy of witches, who among
them gradually produced a long series of names—there was
even a priest involved in the sorceries. But this priest must
have been a great wizard and devil, for he confessed nothing
and yielded no names of other wizards, but withstood every
degree of interrogation, even being burned over a slow fire—
right up until he died on the rack.

And of course execution by fire could itself be varied in
the most diverse ways. You could be burned in rainy weather
and without wind, and thereby suffocate from the smoke; or

you could be burned in a fresh wind, in which case you wouldn't be troubled by smoke, but would die directly from the flames. It also made a great difference whether you were thrown onto a huge flaming pyre and thereby died a swift death—or whether you were bound to a ladder, say, and laid on a very small pyre, or on a pyre which was first lit after you had mounted it.

In cases of special clemency the condemned might sometimes be hanged first, and only the earthly remains consigned to the fire.

Of extreme importance too was the realization that those burned alive would not be able to rise after death and thus could not serve Satan's power in the hereafter.

Since all witches and wizards had habitually debauched with the Evil One, often thousands of times, it was wholly natural that theologians and jurists—priests and lawyers—should show a particular interest in the sex organs of the accused, in whether they were especially large or especially small, and whether there were visible traces of intercourse with one or more devils.

It's also of great importance that Satan has never been a pederast or a homosexual, but always appeared to female witches in a male form, as an incubus—and to warlocks as a female, a succubus. The Church has a deep understanding of this, adducing Satan's noble descent (from a fallen archangel) as proof that despite everything his character is too noble for pederasty.

Beyond that it was frightening what the judges and priests found out concerning forms of sexual congress between witches, wizards, and devils. For instance, all had kissed Satan under the tail, on the opening itself, and most had also eagerly licked and kissed Satan's balls and his long but ice-cold penis. This penis penetrated way up into the breast or even the throat of certain witches, and gave them—despite the cold—a tremendous feeling of pleasure. Naturally judges and priests were very much taken up with such celebrated sex organs, and examined all witches—not least the young ones—

very thoroughly, in order (among other things) to purify the infected female organs by a burning-out process which involved the insertion of a red-hot iron rod into the suspect's vagina. On wizards they performed a more routine crushing of the testicles.

Priests and judges were just as concerned with sex organs back then as they are today.

Regarding the Devil's power of reproduction, in other words whether the Devil can beget hominoid creatures on witches, great disagreement has reigned; many scholars are of the opinion that congress of a witch with Satan can produce only lizard- or snakelike progeny, while others believe that it can engender small, black, hairy children, more like devils than like humans.

However, the best argument comes from Catholic circles and weighs strongly in favor of Satan's procreative power: ". . . . for how else can you explain Martin Luther's existence?"

Of course it may also explain a great deal about Luther's frequent association with the Majesty.

One more thing should be noted in this brief sketch of the witch trials' apocalypse: namely, that the Greek Orthodox Church never saw the necessity of these prosecutions; hence the Slavic—Orthodox—countries never had their heretic- and witch-burnings. The one exception is Poland, which was Catholic; there they burned away with a will, thousands upon thousands.

In England witches were not burned but hanged—but in Scotland they burned them, to the delight and satisfaction of all.

At the end of the seventeenth century the trials ebbed out all over Europe, which had once again been wrested from the Devil. And in the eighteenth century the very last stakes burned down.

The church and the courtroom had finished their work.

The Great Dread wasn't over, but it retired to other regions.

We shall glance at the system of temporal courts, led in part by the same lawyers, scientists, and judges who so faithfully stood by the Church's side through two hundred years of holy bloodbaths. And we shall simultaneously note that these two hundred years of witch trials lay not in the Middle Ages but in the Renaissance. The witch trials were the glorious introduction to our time, attended by a complete revolution in cosmography, by empirical science and by scientific heresy. And they blossomed right here in our beloved, beautiful Alsace. People painted the loveliest pictures and built the most splendid cathedrals while at the same time they incessantly roasted old women and small children alive.

Child-burning was not so widespread as the burning of adults; often the Church allowed even heretical children and those versed in sorcery to get off with being whipped before their parents' pyres. Strictly speaking it was only under the most intense pressure of the Great Dread, in the mid-1600's— that is, when the danger of Satan's victory was overwhelming—that they also burned children at the stake. It didn't come to so many thousands.

Compared to the child-burnings of our own time, by napalm, phosphorus, sulfur, and ordinary firebombs, the child-burnings in the days of the great witch trials would look modest.

Still, they had their points.

It goes without saying that at our beloved nerve clinic, where we're all nervous wrecks to some degree—here at La Poudrière I haven't wanted to go into detail about the use of instruments and fire; it seems far more important to spare both my own and the audience's nerves. After all, it is *we* who are nervous wrecks.

But I wanted to draw your attention to three things:

A) The Great Dread which walked the earth.

B) The witch trials' *enormous* extent.

C) Satan's plan for revolution and world dominion.

The Great Dread—or if you will: the Greatest Dread—we shall find again in other parts of history. We find it wherever one can really talk about history; it's the history-creating force. Without the Great Dread nothing would happen. It's the driving force behind everything. There are things which indicate that the Great Dread is the flight from meeting the ritual murderer in ourselves.

I mean *meeting* him.

The ritual sex murder must therefore lay claim to our very greatest interest. I don't mean the private ritual murder so much as the sex murders we know of on the part of the Church, the courtroom, and the State. In short: *history.*

After good and God fearing men—priests and judges—had waded in blood for two hundred years, this one episode was past. They had discovered evil—i.e. outer space—in themselves, and crazed by terror they set about eradicating the evil in others.

We are now at the heart of the Law—for even the witch trials were only a limited part of the general legal system. You must first have courts before you can set up witch tribunals. The witch trials were not an isolated or a unique phenomenon, but a characteristic detail. You must first have the tongs to tear out nails with before you can use them to pull out the nails of witches.

But now we'll have a piece of cake and drink a cup of coffee.

LADIES AND GENTLEMEN, DEAR FRIENDS:

When we approach the Root of Evil, as we're doing now, we'll discover that the real Evil lies far deeper than the witch trials, and that it involves every attempt yet made by human beings to create a society on this earth. The Great Dread, the Great Paranoia, comes from the earth's interior.

I mean that literally.

Today every child knows that our globe's interior is one gigantic mass of fiery porridge, a seething stew of glowing molten rock and metal. It's on a frighteningly thin crust around this cosmos of liquid minerals that we roast, boil, and mutilate each other; it's here that life has arisen, green, cool, luxuriant, and moist. Just above this crust lies outer space where the cold reigns—an eternal, limitless cold.

Both of them—the fire under us and the lifeless cosmos

above us—are just as totally meaningless, just as dependent on their "laws," just as absurdly idiotic as all other galaxies and all other stars and masses of fiery porridge which exist.

And in this lunatic world between the deadly cold and the foaming sea of fire there lives—logically enough—a lunatic humanity.

This is the Root of Evil.

On this madhouse of a planet, a madhouse from the beginning by sheer force of its meaningless existence, we wish to keep *order!* But as long as the totality is insane and meaningless, it's also meaningless to keep order here. But we fuss around arranging things, and we keep the Great Dread out of our lives—at least for the most part; only occasionally does the Dread awake and get the upper hand, it breaks out of the earth's seething interior and takes possession of us. We may flee into outer space, out into the endless cold, into the clear, logical, mind-forsaken universe; but we won't succeed in escaping from the earth's interior, from the seething, bubbling magma under our feet.

The age of the witch trials was also an age when we were conquering outer space; for the first time we observed the planets through a lens, calculated their orbits, and mapped the watchmaker's workshop.

Now we're doing it again. But now we're setting foot on strange planets; five hundred years ago we exposed the planetary spheres with telescopes, now we're landing on the stars.

But we have the fiery porridge with us.

Every time we meet the cosmos, the unending void, the Great Dread breaks out.

For two hundred years it looked bad for the witch trials; early in the eighteenth century the bonfires burned down, and only at the beginning of the twentieth did the trials come to life again.

I'm thinking, of course, of Lenin. He laid the foundation for them in the same way that Paul, Augustine, Thomas Aquinas, Calvin, and Luther had laid it centuries earlier. Lenin was the titanic rediscoverer of the witches' revolution, of the plan for

Satan's takeover. The great demonologist reinstated the devil and his hierarchies, and Lenin understood the conspiracy.

He instituted a flood of prosecutions, which through his heirs was eventually to engulf more than thirty million witches. It first reached full strength in the proceedings against the great warlock Leon Trotsky, of whom it is clearly shown in the court records that he had simultaneously, on the same day and at the same hour, been in three different cities: Berlin, Copenhagen, and Oslo. In Copenhagen he had even shown himself to the physical eye at a hotel which doesn't exist in Copenhagen. What more proof of sorcery do you need?

It must also be noted that the new witch trials were produced by the same old schools, by the jurist Lenin and the theologian Stalin. The two sciences are inseparable.

I know very well who Satan is: He is freedom.

He is the uncontrolled, the incalculable, the antithesis of order and discipline, the antithesis of the legalism of outer space. Satan is the rebel against God's Kingdom, which is order. Which is ellipses and pendulums and mathematics and planetary orbits and necessity. We know where a planet will be in twelve years, four months, and nine days. But we don't know where a butterfly will have flown one minute hence.

Therefore the butterfly is of Satan.

A little later than in Russia the Great Dread broke out in Teutonia. Metaphysical paranoia took possession of country after country in Europe. And Jew-burning too likewise became popular again—it came back into style.

In land after land it reached new and unheard-of heights; in land after land the worldwide conspiracy was exposed; but the Jewish revolution and takeover was prevented. This time too the Church and the jurists abetted the powers of righteousness; the Church supported the defenders of society, and the jurists served them meekly: law after law was written and passed and interpreted, nothing happened which was not blessed by the diligent, honest, and righteous lawyers whom the world has never lacked, and who have fabricated laws on an assembly line every time the rulers wished it. Thus nothing happened which wasn't fully legal.

In Poland the burning of Jews was more festive than in other lands; when the Teutons slaughtered the whole ghetto in Warsaw, the Poles living nearby sold places in their windows to the grateful populace, who could then witness the massacres from orchestra seats in the neighboring houses.

The Rumanians worked out methods of slaughter and education of such quality that even trained Germanic Jew-burners blanched at the sight. They lent an extra sheen to the festivities by hanging the Jews on meathooks in the windows of butcher shops.

But it all happened justly and legally, with the aid of thousands and thousands of solicitors, barristers, and Supreme Court attorneys.

I'll ask you to note that point, for it illustrates the fact that the witch trials of the Renaissance were in no way exceptions or especially remarkable as high points, but merely followed the rule. There was nothing special about them.

Nor should we think that particular types of theologians and jurists were used by the courts of that time; they were just the same as in any age.

They were fine people, obedient citizens, and good husbands and fathers. They were and are the bedrock of the state.

To illustrate what I want to stress, I'll mention a trial from Amerikanienland where our brothers dwell—and I'm picking one at random, I'm just reaching blindly into the pile of similar cases. The one we shall look at here is known as the "Haymarket trials," and it took place in the year of Our Lord 1886, the month of October.

In those days a great dread walked over the earth.

The anarchists' revolution was imminent; their takeover of world power was at the door, and there went out a decree from the Supreme Court that all the anarchists should be numbered, so that the police and the judges and the executioners and all the powers of Light might be victorious in the battle against the darkness.

For many years the Christian countries waged a heroic Christian battle against the demonic revolution, and it took nearly forty years before the victory was fully won—through a collaboration between Cardinal Lenin in Russia and the Justice Department in Washington. Trotsky, Lenin, and the American government so decisively defeated the pacifists and the anarcho-liberals that these were physically annihilated. On one particular occasion Saint Lenin slaughtered over 17,000 anarchists in a few weeks.

But in the Haymarket affair only seven were convicted. The really interesting thing about the case is that nobody has ever *believed* that the five who were sentenced to death were guilty; even the judges, the police, the district attorney, the executioners, and the journalists were quite aware that the guilty party was never haled into court. Who threw the bomb at the Haymarket in Chicago has never been determined. It could have been one of your many average lunatics, or it could have been a police spy or a provocateur.

The point of the executions was clear and unambiguous: to maintain peace and order.

And they succeeded.

After all the anarchist trials and illustrious executions of these forty years, both the U.S. and Russia had gotten rid of their labor movements—which have never since made a comeback in either country.

A bomb was thrown at the Haymarket in Chicago during the revolts in the month of May 1886. At the mass meeting five were killed and two wounded, making a total of seven, and the authorities and the police arrested seven live anarchists. After an amazingly honest trial, in which no one claimed to know who had thrown the bomb, two were condemned to life imprisonment, five to death. But the interesting characters in this connection were the jurors: of the twelve honest, incorruptible citizens, husbands and fathers who had pronounced the death sentence, *five* ended their days in a real, genuine lunatic asylum—just as raving mad as we are ourselves. And it speaks in their favor that they cracked up. The story is interesting too because of its cogent numerology: five killed, five condemned to death, five gone crazy. And all of the condemned were flatly innocent; but the country clamored for the hangings, and the judges had no choice.

Judges in every age have done this, again and again they've deliberately condemned the innocent. They're doing it today, and they'll do it tomorrow. But few are so tender-minded that they die in the madhouse.

The events of October 1886 were repeated as late as 1927 with the anarchists Sacco and Vanzetti—and this time too there wasn't a soul who believed that the pair was guilty as they were executed amid the cheers of the populace.

It wouldn't be difficult to write a history of the world—or rather, a history of Christian culture—taking as its point of departure cold-blooded, deliberate, conscious judicial murders carried out by honorable men. And now once again we're on the trail, we're approaching the center anew: we have a culture which was ushered in by a judicial murder. Common law has been involved from the very beginning. It *must* be so.

And still we can broaden this: all culture we know, which today includes the culture of science, is a continual, mounting Culture of Dread—a chronic, growing paranoia.

The more insight, the more dread.

The Great Dread is greater today than ever before, because our insight into the idiocy has grown: the fire under us and the deathly cold over us, this literally godforsaken world of numerical relations.

And then our former religion in the midst of all this! Is there any other religion with a similar picture of hell? They all have their worlds of shadows, their Hades, their realms of death—but we're the only ones who have pictured the kingdom of death as a cosmic torture chamber where we'll be spitted, flayed, boiled, and roasted over and over again *for all eternity.*

We've painted this tableau of eternal torments as an image of our own souls, we've filled it with hate and dread of an exceptional strength. This is a matter of significance for the understanding of our culture, and of why things went as they did.

About Heaven and paradise we know almost nothing, and we've never managed to imitate these wonderful places on earth—probably because we knew too little about them.

On the other hand we know disconcertingly much about hell. We know almost everything about hell, and therefore it's been easy to establish it on "earth," on the small, thin habitable crust between the fiery porridge and the minus 459.7 degrees above us. We've recreated excellent models of hell on earth.

And why, dear friends, why have we done it?

Here we're at the center of the problem.

The unique feature of the witch trials is that they build on a precise, unbelievably tidy science of devils. Only by dint of their exact, enormously comprehensive demonology do the witch trials distinguish themselves from our other activities.

However, I must express reservations about the very expression "recreating hell on 'earth'"; even putting the word "earth" in quotation marks, as above, isn't enough of a precaution. There just isn't any *earth* to talk about. This brittle green crust, this indescribably thin shell between the aforementioned fiery porridge beneath us and the aforementioned minus 459.7 degrees above us—in God's name you can't call this an *earth*! So I want to protest loudly against this word, and to propose that the designation "the earth" shall be stricken from all vocabularies in all countries and in all languages.

Instead we shall introduce the term *the Crust.*

We live on the Crust.

And we're waiting for it to crack.

During my many years of wandering, while I was studying the landscape painting of many countries in its highest and most spiritualized forms, I naturally made a significant study of devil imagery as well. The iconography of devils, which encompasses and embodies the most profound thoughts of our greatest demonologists, has flourished for centuries. And it has always interested me much more than the written demonologies. Of course I've studied such books as the Most Christian King James's *Demonology* or *Malleus the Witch-Hammer* from cover to cover, but I don't want to burden you with details. Anyone can go to the source.

But the pictorial art, devil painting, has engrossed me more; partly because of its beauty in form and color, partly because of its power and expressiveness—because of the *concrete* things in the pictures. Here I shall only draw your attention to a few scattered facts.

In their concreteness the devil pictures far surpass the angel pictures, which of course also exist in great quantities. The iconography of angels is always marked by a certain theoretical abstraction, and lacks the devil paintings' concrete resemblance to life, their spontaneous reality.

The explanation is not far to seek: people knew a lot more about devils, and also understood them much better in a purely human and devilish way—while the angels were, and remained, strangers. The only one who has really described angels at close range is Swedenborg, who also gives upsetting descriptions of their eminent lewdness. The heavens are full of mating and passion. But no painter has painted lewd angels in the process of satisfying their sexual needs. They all stuck to the gold background and six or eight pairs of wings.

One of the devil pictures which I would like to call to your attention is the great devil-painter Stephan Lochner's portrayal of doomsday—of the last gigantic trial which will be held against devils, witches, heretics, warlocks, Jews, Arabs, Negroes, anarchists, and hyenas. The picture, which is one of the high points of eschatology, hangs not far from here—in the magnificent city of Cologne. It is characteristic of our cosmography that everything, world history and the solar system, ends with this enormous prosecution; it's a lawyer's dream.

The Day of Judgment describes how on Christ's return the world will be divided in two: the resurrected humanity from the Crust streams toward the God of Love, who forthwith divides them into good and bad. The good are very fair, and blond almost without exception. Many are also tonsured. Rejoicing they stream in a dense throng into the castle of heaven, where they are received by angels and embraced. They're all stark naked, and the embraces seem hearty. One of them is even kissing an angel on the mouth, which evokes the memory of Swedenborg. None of the good are too fat or too thin; they are slender, graceful and delicate. All the angels have very light skin and yellow hair, along with wings in several colors.

On the right-hand side the bad ones are streaming in, and are being received by the devils—no less enthusiastically. The evil, are much darker and almost without exception have black hair. Many have Arab or Turkish turbans. Many are fat or very thin. One fat man is dragging a sack of gold with him. Others are obviously sensual.

The devils are having a jolly time.

Here people are being stuck and impaled and bitten and crushed—but above all: burned and burned and burned.

So Hell is presented exactly like the Church's own operations, precisely like one of the Inquisition's pious workshops.

But there's a fundamental difference. Under the church's rule the sticking and impaling and crushing and burning were done by good and pious servants of God; here it's carried on by devils, under the leadership of the chained-up Satan himself—who sits amid the fire, an element he thrives in, as he bites and burns people. Of the devils it can be said that there are several distinct kinds of them.

There are hairy ones, black and brown. Then there are dark hairy ones without horns, and dark hairy ones with horns.

Then come the flying devils, who are green and seem to be made of a rather smooth and shiny material. In the air there are also many flying angels, who are blue. The blue and the green ones stab and impale each other energetically in flight.

Then you have the large green ground-devils. They have
to walk. They also come in two main versions: with and without horns. Several have imposing exteriors.

In the middle of the picture stands a huge green devil,
without horns. But he does have a lot of other things: above
all he's liberally provided with devil faces—a large one on his
belly, one on each knee, and one on each shoulder. His main
face combines a horse's head with a tiger's mouth, while the
ears are like those of a bat, and are green on the outside and
red on the inside.

All the devils are busy gathering people together and
dragging them up to the Majesty, to Satan, who is mighty to
behold.

He is red and green and much larger and stouter than any
of the lower devils.

Some of the devils and angels are fighting over people,
but the angels are winning because they have long thin for-
bidding things to stab with, which seem to cause great pain to
the green ones and the hairy ones.

We shall dwell for a moment on the Majesty himself.

HE is clearly the emperor of the realm, the true gathering point for all, and He has a few clergymen around him.
He has the same green, slightly metallic skin color as several of the others, and he too has a huge devil face with an
open, blood-red mouth on his abdomen. It's clear that these
devil faces on his belly signify sex organs, but that they're
both incubus and succubus in one: the nose and eyes corre-
spond to penis and testicles, while the gaping red mouth
forms a vagina. The Majesty has the largest vagina of all,
but still the most impressive thing is the face he has on his
face. It's huge and blood-red, with horns. His teeth are very
big and sharp, and there are red flames issuing from many
places on his body, so that he burns those whom he
embraces and bites. There's a chain going straight across his
abdominal face.

This picture is eternity; this is how our culture imagines
eternal life.

And we walk around with this picture inside us, whether we know it or not.

Now let's take a look at the development of our legal system—at the history of crime and punishment, this fascinating expression of human nature, which also confirms the kinship between heavenly and earthly justice.

We may begin with a picture of common life from humane and democratic England.

The always popular child executions were especially beloved in England. One of the pleasures of hanging children, especially young ones between seven and thirteen or fourteen years of age, was that because of their low body weight they could live much longer than grownups when dangling from the rope. Adults seldom live for more than fifteen minutes, even if they don't break their necks on the drop and die immediately.

In the year of our Lord 1801 a thirteen-year-old boy broke into a house and stole a silver spoon, but luckily he was discovered and punished. The punishment was carried out the same year by hanging.

The previous year a boy of ten had been hanged, likewise as a deterrent for other children engrossed in criminal thoughts.

In 1808 they hanged two sisters, the one eleven years old, the other eight; it is supposed to have been a particularly lovely and entertaining spectacle, because both girls wriggled so long on the rope. And law, justice, and morality continued to exist in the realm.

In 1816 a ten-year-old boy was hanged for shoplifting, again a great success with the public.

In 1831 they found a nine-year-old boy who had set fire to a house, and they hanged him the same year.

In 1833 a boy of nine was walking down a street in London; as he passed a window of a paint store, he discovered that the window was broken. So he put a stick through the broken pane and in this criminal manner appropriated paint to the value of two pence.

But the police apprehended him, the court convicted him, and the hangman hanged him—in the venerable prison Old Bailey.

It's only the very youngest criminals who are briefly mentioned here; children of fourteen, fifteen, and sixteen were hanged in droves.

Nevertheless the child executions declined, and the serious and righteous men in parliaments and courtrooms had other things to do. The loss was first righted in our own century, after Russia had been freed from the barbarity of Czardom. In the 1930's child executions were reintroduced in the Soviet Union, although they were limited to children twelve years old and up. There were a great many.

Meanwhile, it goes without saying that crimes against the Crown and the security of the state had to be treated with considerably greater firmness, even with harshness.

Counterfeiters, for example, were long punished by being boiled alive—in some countries in water, in others in oil. This took place publicly for the most part, and there are a number of records from the popular festivals. The criminal was hoisted up over a great big cauldron provided especially for the purpose, and was then lowered into the boiling liquid.

Direct crimes against the majesty's person, such as rebellion or blasphemy, were punished by drawing out the criminal's tongue and intestines before breaking him on the wheel or hanging him up on an iron hook. At the same time we must point out, in connection with the witch trials, how much less serious are these crimes against the security of kings and emperors and states than the crime of wanting to rise up against God and threaten His supremacy—even if the penalty for crimes of this sort was on a level with that for political crimes and transgressions against goods and property.

For example, Queen Mary was a zealous burner; for a while she had about a hundred persons burned yearly. The method was also evolved of making a bonfire under the gallows; the condemned was suspended alive and merely roasted slowly in the air above the fire. In England they also

invented a large apparatus for crushing the whole body at
once, with such force that blood spurted out of nostrils, ears,
and fingertips. The cook who poisoned the Bishop of
Rochester was publicly boiled alive; on the same day a right
fresh and healthy servant girl was boiled in another part of
England, in the middle of the marketplace before a huge
crowd of onlookers.

Persons who trespass in print against the temporal powers
have likewise in every age been punished just as harshly as
those who blaspheme God through heresy or witchcraft—by
having their tongues and sex organs torn out, for instance. (As
I said, sex organs have always been of great interest to jurists.)

As an example of a punishment for criticizing the king we
have the famous Collingbourne, who had written disparagingly of King Richard III: first he was hanged symbolically
and then cut down alive; next his belly was opened and his
intestines taken out; after that his chest was opened so that
the executioner could take out the traitorous heart—while the
author himself cried, "Jesus, Jesus!" This was a very common
way of proceeding against the enemies of the State, and executions of this sort acquired a steadily more ritual character—
a ritual murder with strong sexual connotations, performed in
the name of justice. The ceremonies and the ritual often
ended up as the most important thing about the punishment.
Cocks were slaughtered at the same time, and there was an
official whose sole function was to carry a can of vinegar and
ice water to be poured over the condemned man's head if he
fainted during the treatment. Bread and wine were also par-
taken of while the executions took place; in some countries
this was prescribed by law.

There was often a considerable apparatus employed during the gorier executions—towels, tubs, medicines, all of medical expertise was brought to bear in order to stop the bleeding and to prevent a premature death.

Part of the reason for all this was the deterrent effect the
sight was supposed to have on the public, who often streamed
to it by the tens of thousands. But like the witches, transgres-

sors against the security of the state and against goods and property just became more and more numerous. Under Henry the Eighth those executed by fire and iron and hemp numbered considerably more than 70,000 persons.

Public quartering, in England as well as in France and other cultured countries, was especially popular with the people, although nobody learned anything from it. And this in spite of the fact that quartering was the most ritual execution of all.

Boiling was extremely popular for a while. Often salt was used in the water; the bodies would keep longer afterwards and could thus be exhibited even on warm summer days.

One funny thing is that women weren't quartered, but burned; quartering entailed undressing in a public place, and an undressed woman would be contrary to morals and religion.

Many things have been misunderstood, not least the use of the pillory—which in reality was very often a death sentence, because the public amused themselves so thoroughly with the person on display. And often its use was an introduction to further and more solid punishments; it could also be combined with several simultaneous operations.

Still, people most commonly used the delinquent as a target for throwing stones; and to keep him from bowing his head to avoid the stones, his ears were nailed to the planks. Sometimes the criminal was suspended so high up that only his toes touched the platform, and he was strangled by the pillory.

The always eager people often threw things at the delinquent until his face swelled up to an enormous size; they also amused themselves by hanging on his back, so that strangulation occurred. Homosexuals were often treated this way, and many of them died in the pillory or afterwards in prison.

The Bishop of London once prescribed the following treatment for a doctor of theology who had written disparagingly of kings, noblemen, and prelates: first whipping, then the pillory. In the pillory: cutting off one ear, slitting the opposite nostril, and finally, branding on one cheek.

Then, after a week's imprisonment, the pillory again, with

a repetition of the same treatment—this time with ear number two, nostril number two, and cheek number two. The sentence speaks well for the bishop's imagination and morality.

Naturally after a week the man hadn't entirely recovered from the wounds on his back and face, but the treatment was repeated to the great delight of the public.

He is supposed to have survived.

That physical attacks on the crown and the monarchy had to be dealt with severely goes without saying. After the attempt on Louis XV, who ruled France up until twenty years before the Great Revolution, the rebel was first punished by having his hand burned off; after which they poured melted lead and boiling oil over the stump. Then they laid him down in the marketplace and hitched him firmly to four horses, one for each arm and one for each leg. Then they whipped up the horses, each in its own direction. But the operation proceeded slowly; time after time the horses took off and threw themselves with all their strength into the work. Again and again the sweating, snorting animals strained at their harnesses. It took so long, and was so exhausting for the horses, that finally the executioner had to take a knife and cut across the tendons in the criminal's hip and shoulder joints so that the horses could finish their task. Still it was heavy work, and only gradually—to the unbounded delight of the masses—was the rebel against the monarchy torn limb from limb.

The Great Marquis, de Sade, was himself an eyewitness to the execution and has left us a delightful description of it, not least of the French nobility observing the spectacle from the palace windows, while ladies and gentlemen fingered each other's sex organs.

This brings us to the revolution and its methods of execution—which were used on, among others, this same king's successor, Louis XVI.

In the context of the time the guillotine seems like a mushy and sentimental method of execution, typifying a legal system in a state of debilitation and decay. It's often mentioned as a special French invention—fast, effective, and painless.

However, it doesn't come from our beloved Gallia. It probably originated in Italy, where the apparatus had already been developed in the 13th century; a few years later Germania and the British Isles had it too. But it never attained the popularity of boiling, roasting, breaking on the wheel, disembowelment, etc., etc. The machine made its first real breakthrough in France, and then in the century of Reason.

The great record keeper Lord Byron describes a meeting with the guillotine in Rome, where it was being demonstrated in connection with the execution of three robbers. There is no doubt that the performance made a powerful impression on the lord's artistic and sensitive temper, and he enthusiastically writes of the incident that:

> The ceremony—including the *masqued* priests; the half-naked executioners; the bandaged criminals; the black Christ and his banner; the scaffold; the soldiery; the slow procession, and the quick rattle and heavy fall of the axe; the splash of the blood, and the ghastliness of the exposed heads—is altogether more impressive than the vulgar and ungentlemanly dirty 'new drop,' and dog-like agony of infliction upon the sufferers of the English sentence.

One can understand his enthusiasm, and one can see why France was the country where such an artistic procedure made its breakthrough with the people as well. Of course its adoption on a wide scale was due to the thousands and thousands of traitors and assassins, immoralists and seditionaries who threatened the revolution. The men of the revolution were no weaker or more vacillating than the men of the Church. Furthermore, although the witches' takeover had been averted, Europe was now the object of a Conspiracy of Criminals—and in every land, quite aside from the Church and the revolution, public executions of a purely secular kind became widespread. In one year in a region like Auvergne, two hundred seventy-six criminals were hanged, forty-four beheaded, thirty broken on the wheel, and three burned. But this doesn't quite measure up to the achievements of the clergy in the days when witchcraft flourished at its worst, and when it was possible in a brief period to record figures like this: one single bishop in Geneva burned fully four hundred witches in three months, but was surpassed by a colleague in Bamberg, who managed six hundred—although both were beaten by that man of God, the Bishop of Würzberg, who had nine hundred people burned alive.

In those days all this happened publicly for pedagogical reasons, and in our beautiful France public executions were a matter of law until the year 1939—by guillotine, of course.

In Western Europe public executions were revived only a relatively short time after Teutonia's collapse, not least in Poland, Holland, France, and Italy; while in England and the U.S. they now took place only behind closed doors. During the war, of course, there were public executions by the millions all over Eastern Europe, and a number of eastern countries continued this practice long after the peace had been concluded.

For several centuries the public hanging of Jews was a widespread popular entertainment; the Jews were hanged in the most ignominious and painful manner possible, most often head down and along with a couple of dogs, who in their rage bit and lacerated the Jew beside them.

We may ask ourselves why public executions were so popular with the people—with the steady, credulous, hard-working people, who must surely have had many other uses for their time. But that's the way it is: at the World's Fair in Paris in 1889, for example, the Eiffel Tower was the big sensation; but the public streamed to a double execution in far, far greater numbers than to the Tower. The great tourist leader and travel agent Thomas Cook could fill all his spare buses with visitors to the execution—which brought him a welcome bonus. At the last execution in Versailles, in the year 1939, all the rooms in the city with a view on the guillotine were rented out in advance at very high prices.

The last public performance in the U.S. had taken place three years earlier, in 1936—by hanging, in front of more thousands and thousands of people. The question is whether public hangings and guillotinings don't meet a need in the common folk which it's easy for us to overlook today, and which can be dangerous if it's never satisfied.

Today it might be therapeutic to revive them—especially in the prosperous welfare states of the West, where the population is increasingly a prey to psychological and psychosomatic ailments along with a deep-seated, unsatisfied aggression which can lead to political catastrophes.

In Asia and Africa punishments are still carried out publicly; this has proved to have a tranquilizing effect on the masses. There the pursuit of spies, traitors, enemies of the fatherland, devils, revolutionaries, hyenas, and witches brings *visible* results.

In the West the process of humanizing the penal system and making it invisible—combined with our insight into the absolute cold and deadness of outer space and our knowledge of the eternal liquid fire under the green and living crust we inhabit—has certainly helped to increase our dread of the great meaninglessness in the universe's mechanical-mathematical chamber of horrors.

As I've said already: the more insight, the more dread.

Now we'll look at the Great Dread's outbreak in just the past few decades. Again it will support the basic thesis of this talk: that the Church's witch trials of the sixteenth and seventeenth centuries were by no means separate witch-hunts, but only an ecclesiastical variant of the Permanent Witch-hunt, of the eternal witch trials which are the most salient characteristic of the race which inhabits this planet.

The simple basic fact is that here on our thin, thin crust, with the fire under us and the unimaginable cold above us, we've never ceased to hunt, stab, flay, crush, hang, and burn each other—and moreover there's no sign that we ever will.

The acceleration in the spread of the witch trials, in their effect and in the number of those condemned, burned, and maimed has been colossal just in the last fifty or sixty years. Today we can work with figures which are without parallel.

The big devil scare broke out in earnest in the 1920's. Now we shall look not at details, but at figures. The acceleration corresponds to the acceleration in the world's total production of horsepower—of physical and technical energy.

And this acceleration in the production of horsepower is again only an expression of the accelerating growth of our insight into the so-called laws of nature. This insight = dread.

Two of the clearest and most intelligent minds of the time functioned as seismographs: comrade Lenin and comrade Trotsky. More acutely than others they felt the dread which proceeds from the swinging pendulum in that renowned Russian church, the pendulum which proved irrefutably that the globe is round and that it moves all alone through an outer space where no god dwells.

Their dread was carried further and converted into action by the theologian, the great comrade Stalinissimus the Bloodthirsty. The fruits of his enormous cleanup can be reckoned today at ca. thirty million dead.

With the same volcanic violence the Great Dread broke out in Germania, in the homeland of theoretical physics. Now the populist defenders of society rescued Germania from the Great Dread, and they exterminated six million Jews alone.

Simultaneously all countries rushed at each others' throats. Today we calculate that the purges which the great wolf-howl brought with it may have involved at least eighty million lives.

A new type of human being was in the making. Humanity met the wolves in itself, and the insight was thereby achieved: *Homo lupus* was born. And the dread grew; the wolf-man's loneliness and insight into meaninglessness was complete.

Since the first decades of our century *Homo lupus* has ruled the earth.

In the 1940's the Dread reached the U.S. and China.

With that a new epoch had begun.

Once again the wolves were obsessed with the discovery of

the witches' revolution; the evil ones strove in earnest for mastery of the world, and in all countries the wolf-folk saw through each other's plans for taking over power on the planet.

In China within a few years they caught and executed around twenty-five million witches, all spies of Satan and His host, all agents of Satan's empire.

All the specimens of *Homo lupus* in every land hated each other with a hate born of mortal dread. They made bombs which could smash the crust, so that we wouldn't have to live there anymore. They made more and more of them. The Russian wolves hated the wolves of other lands and continued to hunt them and to condemn their spies along with their own.

In the U.S. the Great Dread climbed more sharply than in any other land.

No longer could it be satisfied with roasting Negroes, for *Homo lupus americanus* knew that if he didn't gain mastery of the world, then other wolves would.

All the wolves hunt all the other wolves.

But this is nothing to the hunt which is to come, nothing to the wolf-howl which is coming, but which has not yet been howled.

It must be stressed that the two most important ideas about freedom which the human race has had—Christianity and socialism—have the remarkable similarity that they've both been twisted around into their absolute opposites, to the antithesis of what they are. Equality and propertylessness have been totally abolished in both ideas; in both, enmity toward the state—which was one of the most important points of all—has been changed into devoted worship of power and of the state; the original emphasis on peace, pacifism, has in both cases been transformed into a wild cult of weapons and military power. The fundamental idea of love, which can be summed up as a belief in equality, liberty, and fraternity, has been transformed into hatred of everyone who desires or believes in equality, liberty, and fraternity; love is transformed into violence and brotherhood into oppression.

And both times this has happened through certain individuals who laid the groundwork for the theologies by which many diligent theologians were to rebuild these ideas into their exact opposite. It's also typical that these same great falsifiers of the truth have since come to be regarded as holy men; I mention out of many the apostle Paul and the jurist Lenin. In both the Church and the Party the source has been destroyed: in the Church there is no Christianity, in the Party no socialism.

We know from days of old that the Devil is God's ape, the one who turns all the Creator's work into its opposite—who twists, distorts, and perverts; so it isn't hard to figure out that our Great Brother with the Tail has been around again. Our beloved prince is to be found in Paul and his theology, in Lenin and the dogma which builds on him. In them we see the great perverters, the great falsifiers—those who explained away the whole thing and proved that it was the opposite of itself, just as judges and lawyers through the ages have proved that injustice is really justice.

The great devil-hunts have an apparent external similarity in the fact that the courts have always arranged for the accused to be interrogated in two separate stages. The first task was to obtain his confession that he himself was guilty of the accusations. This could often take a long time and be enormously demanding for the interrogators, but sooner or later almost everyone confessed.

When the confession was complete, invariably with endless masses of detail, they proceeded with the second stage of the interrogation. Now the aim was to persuade the accused to name his accomplices in the conspiracy. This stage often took longer and demanded correspondingly greater tenacity and strength from the interrogator. Many times the accused showed great reluctance to give away his fellow conspirators—so that only the most extreme inventiveness and perseverance on the part of the interrogator brought results.

It was the element of genius in the procedure—never to let anyone die before the accomplices were revealed—which exposed the incredible extent of the conspiracies. No witchhunt has been able to get along without the method. All the great hunters, from Calvin to Adolfus Germanicus and Stalinissimus the Great, have been dependent on it.

With the achievements of these great men the Great Task is accomplished: the human being is unmasked, the mask is torn away, and the wolf's fangs are visible. *Homo lupus* stands forth in all his glory. This phenomenon, the outbreak of the Permanent Witchhunt in a whirlwind of persecutions, happens every time the *faith* is threatened. No particular faith, just the belief that everything has a sure and certain meaning. When the faith that the cosmos—the fire under us and the empty, dead, and endless space above us—when the faith that the cosmos has a meaning is threatened, then *faith* rises up and crushes *unbelief.* This is the great Dread, and it appears in times of skepticism, reason, and enlightenment—in times of criticism.

When we conquer outer space in the future, the Great Dread will rise to new heights; and there's been nothing like the hunt which is to come.

My dear friends!

I myself have seen all this in a dream, and you know that such a man as I can read the future. Wolf shall hunt wolf, and the universe shall resound with the wolf-howls from this planet, and the Dread shall mount and mount, and the hunt shall go on and on. And *Homo lupus* is still new on the earth, but *Homo lupus* shall reign over it.

Over the beautiful rich earth, over all its splendor, over the sunrise and the sunset and over the flowers which close and over the blue shadows in the tops of the trees, *Homo lupus* shall reign. Over the mountains and the sea, over everything on our beloved, beauteous earth the wolves shall reign, and their howl shall last until the crust no longer divides the sea of flame under us from the dead stars above us. And the beauty of the stars and the wind and the desert and the forests, of the ocean and the plains and the mountains and the rivers and the strand, all shall be drowned out by the wolf-howl which is the last voice of humankind.

And the Dread shall tear at the wolf's heart.

In this sense and in this connection I ask you all to regard the Christian witch trials as a small colored stone in a large mosaic. And now I thank you for the patience you've shown me this evening—not in the hope of having answered the question, but in the hope of having posed it rightly. For only a correct statement of the problem can lead to a correct answer."

I was totally exhausted after the lecture.

Then a howl cut through the room, a familiar voice, but not a real wolf-howl. The ambassador's wife had risen, white-faced: "You have spit on Lenin!" she shrieked. "You have sneered at my people!"

Things got terribly restless in the hall, and I headed for the exit. At the door stood our little general, and all at once I knew how his face looked when he was murdering black girls.

I don't remember exactly what he said, but it too was something about having spit on and sneered at and dishonored a great and mighty, golden and godlike fatherland.

Beside him stood Lefèvre, with his cigarette in his mouth and his drooping mustache. Without taking the cigarette out he said:

"Too bad we don't have a Chinese here too!"

al Assadun was standing on the other side:

"We'll have to order one from the embassy. They have their psychiatric problems there too."

But the general went on, he shook his fists at me and yelled. The little gynaecocide suddenly struck me as danger-ous. He yelled that he loved his country and was loyal to his government—unlike certain other people present, who obvi-ously didn't have any fatherland in the first place. And didn't I understand that the U.S. invested both money and young men's lives in saving types like me from communism? At the other end of the hall the ambassador's wife was still howling.

Then a hoarse but powerful voice sounded from the lectern where I had just been standing. It drowned out the others, and the hall became quiet.

It was old Lacroix who spoke, and he was a strange sight with his round head and the bandage atop his old but still vigorous body.

He was perfectly calm, but pale and very serious.

"Ladies and gentlemen," he said, "may I have your attention for a moment?"

Now it was quiet, except for a sort of mixture of howls and sobs coming from the ambassador's wife. Dr. Lefèvre was on his way over to her.

"I would like to remind you that here at our dear La Poudrière we have a tradition that whoever has something to get off his chest may volunteer to give a lecture. And I would like to avail myself of this excellent tradition, because I have things to tell—from a different viewpoint than our honored last speaker, whom I also take this opportunity to thank for his contribution to the understanding of our intrinsically so excellent planet—and I would request to be allowed to speak in this hall as soon as is in keeping with the practical possibilities."

He looked questioningly at the assistant doctor, who had listened to him with the greatest attentiveness. al Assadun gave a decisive and friendly nod, and the matter was settled.

Lacroix thanked those present for their attention and came down from the lectern.

Lefèvre had reached the ambassador's wife and was holding her arm while he talked to her. At the same time al Assadun was talking in a soothing and friendly manner to *le général.*

As for me, I left the hall and walked down through the darkness in the garden toward my own place. It was very dark and still, and the evening air was cool and fresh.

When I came to my grape and tomato arbor, I heard the sound of the brook. Running water and the smell of earth and plants. There were stars in the sky, but no moon.

I walked over to the edge of the brook and looked down into it. I could only just barely see the water moving, but I could hear the brook very well as I stood there.

I no longer thought about the fire under us and the endless cold above us, nor about how thin this crust is which divides the fiery porridge from outer space. I only felt that the night was dark and full of life, of snails and moths, of growing plants, and I knew that there were trout and frogs in the brook. Sometimes the frogs here croak all night long, in a great chorus.

There are bats and owls, and deer roam the neighboring forests.

The flowers have closed. From the hospital there was not a sound. All was silence.

Then a great golden tone rose through the night, and it was followed by new tones. The nightingale had begun, and now filled the world with its abnormal voice.

There's something I'm thinking about.

Several years ago in Africa, below the equator. In a small capital city, abandoned by the colonial administration and with buildings more or less in a state of decay as remnants of the colonial rule. I walked around the town alone, and the heat was really tropical. You could recognize the smell of the marketplace long before you got there, and as you reached the market it began to stink like a carnivore's cage. The heat was terrible, and half the people in the square were asleep among the wares, which lay on tables or were stacked behind them. There were people lying and sleeping on their stomachs, straight across a table—with their legs hanging down on one side and their arms on the other.

I've always—ever since I was a child—been very fond of saying hello to people, and here I found others who liked the same thing. We greeted each other with deep bows and with deference as we exchanged friendly words.

At the harbor I took a ferry across the mouth of the river. It was a simple, roomy, open motorboat, but with an awning over it, so that you could sit partly in the shade.

When I'd sat down, a young woman with a little boy five or six years old came on board. Everybody smiled, everybody said hello.

The boy was naked and dark brown.

She was tall, very black, and wore an orange cotton cape which reached from her shoulders to her feet. She was one of the most beautiful women I've ever seen, with a long neck and a firm, round face. Otherwise I could see only her long, thin fingers, her slender wrists, and a little of her feet.

The boy placed himself beside the bench which ran along the deck; it was as if he were waiting for something.

Then she put down her basket, and with a single movement of her hand took off her robe and stood there just as naked as the boy.

The slenderness and suppleness of the tall body went through me like lightning.

Then she folded up her robe into a kind of pillow, put it on the bench and lay down with her head on it. At once the boy bent over her and fastened his mouth to her breast. He was thirsty, and she seemed to go to sleep the minute she stretched out. She lay halfway on her side.

The boy, the five-year-old, stood for the whole crossing with his back bent to drink, and he drank for ten or fifteen minutes, only moving once: to change breasts.

I often walked through the streets in this town, and I always greeted everybody.

We said:

"Bonjour, mon cher monsieur!" and *"Bonsoir, mon cher monsieur!"*

And there was always the same smile, the same quiet bow, the same friendly dignity.

Since that time great misfortunes have befallen the country, as happens in Africa. And I think about how things were with the mother and the thirsty boy then. First come the ministers, then come the massacres. Finally come the rats.

✧

Then there was another time when I saw someone drink in the same way. A very little girl in a south Italian village, one hot noon on the piazza. She was drinking from the pump, and she was standing in the same position as this boy—with her knees slightly flexed, her back curved, her elbows bent, and her hands hanging down like empty mittens. She stood like that and drank and drank with her whole body.

And you could see the water ripple through her. For to slake one's thirst is the greatest of all delights.

This night is eternal. I'm still sitting at the table in my garden, with my shirt open and my pants unbuttoned down to the crotch, so as to enjoy the coolness of the night after a long hot day. It is dark, and a heavy golden-brown moon is slowly rising over the treetops. The night teems with life: growing plants, mating animals. The bats flutter among the trees. The wine decanter stands on the stone table.

Across the terrace in front of me moves a soundless black lump, barely visible in the dark. Slow, sniffing. The hedgehog which always goes alone at night, searching for water. I've put out milk for it, and it knows where the milk is.

What did God intend by the hedgehog? What is nature trying to say by having produced the hedgehog? What does it mean when midway between a dead and sterile lump of matter, a moon which follows its idiotic path in the cosmos, midway between this moon—which we shall also soon poison and syphilize and pollute—midway between it and the flaming hell of seething liquid minerals under us, on a green and living crust of the only life which exists in the cosmos—what does it mean that in the middle of all this a lonely hedgehog goes around in the night sniffing for water?

But this evening the hedgehog is different from usual, and quite rightly: for after it comes another hedgehog, a mate. It's not just a question of water or my saucer of milk tonight; they've come out for the purpose of mating. And how in Jesus Christ's and Allah's name *do hedgehogs copulate?*

I've seen the frogs in the spring, in the clear ice water in the brooks, where they lie clinging to each other for hours, the female on her belly, the male behind her with his forefeet around her. For hours they lie like that in the icy water, utterly motionless. But the *hedgehogs?*

The heat has been intense, and it's a relief to sit like this with my shirt open and my pants unbuttoned all the way to my groin, with only the night and the animals—mice, beetles, snails, and hedgehogs—living and mating around me. There's nothing but stillness, nothing exists but a hushed, indefinable murmur which says that something is alive.

And there's also a smell in the night, a smell of something decaying and something alive, of bacteria and mould, of humus which is not yet sterile and destroyed, mould which the earthworms can still live in, snails leave sticky wet tracks on. Something we haven't ruined yet.

And the moon has risen higher now and has changed color: it's reddish and golden, and you can see the mountains on it.

About this moon we know everything. About the whole machinery, the whole insane, mechanical apparatus, the solar system, Andromeda's nebula, ellipses and periods, motions, metals. We sit here on our feeble-minded, explosive planet and sail around in an utterly meaningless, monomaniacal bedlam of a watchmaker's shop. About other solar systems we know everything; but go up to the ambassador's wife who howls her wolf-howls and clings to the barred window, go up to the little black-slayer of an American general—and you'll see that we don't know anything about them.

We know everything about the cosmos, about outer space, but we don't know anything at all about Fontaine, our little Belgian sex murderer.

After this conquest, this assault on the dead, frozen space—after this there must follow a conquest of something else.

We've conquered outer space, but not our neighbor.

And we must conquer him *now.*

For either all is totally insane and meaningless—and ought to go under—or it has a *meaning* and ought to survive.

Conquering Lefèvre will be just as dangerous as conquering outer space, only scarier—but *there* lies the solution to the riddle. For this spiritual torture chamber in the absurd dead space is insane if it has produced us all by itself—us and our scared little consciousness on the little green crust of grass and flowers and life, a tiny little Paradise of moist greenery and oxygen where we, so long as history has existed—between the earth's boiling interior under us and the minus 459.7 degrees above us—have hardly done anything but boil, burn, maim, and slaughter each other. It fills me with horror and dread. Our situation between the masses of lava under us and the deadly cold above us is frightening. But we must turn inward, toward Fontaine. If we conquer the cosmos, we must also conquer the general's interior, for there lies the secret. It will be just as dangerous, just as frightening—but there lies the meaning, if there is one.

Meeting *homo lupus* will produce a greater dread than the Great Dread we have felt of outer space.

I would like to beg everyone for forgiveness.

Not many years ago I could still think: Maria, we are all thy sons, we are all thy children. Today I can't say that any longer; I can only say: *they* are all *my* children.

Ye are all my children, with prisons, madhouses, churches, gallows, schools, with La Morgue and Verdun and Dachau, with witch-burnings and torture chambers and headsmen. . . . Ye are all my sons, ye are all my children. I think this is God's loneliness. *Mea culpa.*

And I would like to beg everyone for forgiveness.

And in the night two hedgehogs go around sniffing for water before they can mate. And a little black boy still drinks from his mother's breast, and an old man sits on a bench under a tree.

The hedgehogs have found the saucer of milk and are drinking from it, quiet and motionless; for the greatest desire on earth is to slake one's thirst, when one is thirsty—for plants, children, and hedgehogs.

All at once I hear something from out in the darkness. It isn't the sound of an animal or a bird. It's human footsteps. Cautious, furtive, careful. And they come not from the park, but from my own grape and tomato arbor. A couple of steps at a time, then silence, before I hear yet another couple of stealthy footsteps. I become afraid, because a human being is approaching.

Then there is silence again. For a moment. Then the watchful, almost soundless, careful steps come closer. All at once they become firm and decided, and I see something white between the tomato stalks and the grape vines.

It's the little nurse Christine.

"I didn't want to wake you," she said, "if you were asleep. But then I saw your lamp burning on the table, and figured you were still up."

She came all the way over to me and sat down at the table.

I haven't told about Christine. She's very young, only a little over twenty, and she belongs to the type of girls who grow up here in Alsace: slender, with firm, slender limbs, a small waist, and square shoulders. In Northern Italy you have girls of the same Gallic type—a kind of gazelle race. Christine is a nurse, specializing in mental hospitals.

She sat down, and she was wearing her white working uniform. I gave her some wine, and she drank. Angelo Bevitore.

She, like the hedgehogs, was also out after a warm day to enjoy the cool of the night. It was strange to see the slim brown neck and the long supple brown legs against the chalk-white nurse's uniform.

The night around us was replete with life and growth and abundance, the frogs sang in the brook. *"Buon rifrescamento!"* she said. Her mother is Italian.

The two silent hedgehogs crossed my little terrace, two nearly invisible lumps in the dark. They had drunk now. Then they disappeared among the plants to their marital duties.

"It's becoming—that severe, nunlike nurse's uniform of yours," I said; "it functions as a proof that nurses are sexless."

"But I'm not sexless," she said, and took another sip of wine.

We were sitting so close that I had only to stretch out my hand to stick it in under the cloth and feel her breast. She had nothing on underneath, and her nipple was taut and hard. After a moment I withdrew my hand and drank some more wine.

"What happened up there after I left?" I said.

"There was a real fracas; the whole assembly was scandalized by the ambassador's wife and the little American general. The atmosphere in the hall became totally anti-American and anti-Russian. Finally they both left."

We laughed for a minute, then we sat still and took in the smell of dew and earth and of the brook. The moon was higher now. It seemed like a big dead lump out there in space.

"Why did you come to me?" I asked.

She smiled and tilted her head, her thin face with its concave cheeks:

"Because I like you," she said. "It's something about your eyes—something utterly hopeless and utterly despairing. You seem more desperate than any of the patients."

"And so you came here to see if I was asleep?"

"I thought we could make an evening of it," she said.

I took her hand and held it awhile. The moonlight was strong and the shadows very black. I blew out the lamp, it was light enough without it now. The frogs were protecting us. The night was a fortress around us.

When we stood inside my whitewashed room, I lit the lamp by the little desk and put down the manuscript I had used. "I locked your garden gate from the inside," she said. Then she looked at the desk: "Do you really always have that picture hanging there?"

"Yes," I replied; "its been hanging there for months, maybe a year."

"It's a dreadful picture," she went on; "a terrible picture."

We both looked at it.

It's a very grainy black-and-white photograph of a young man who is about to be hanged—a Yugoslav partisan. He's standing on a wooden plank which will be kicked out from under him in a moment; above him is the rude, heavy cross-beam of the gallows. The rope around his neck is very thin, so thin that it must be of wire to bear the weight of his body when the plank is kicked away. But the young man, still with the classic partisan cap on his head, isn't bound, either hand or foot; the only thing is the loathsome thin wire around his neck, fastened to a solid iron hook on the gallows. Behind and around him stand a number of men in uniform, grinning spitefully at him. But all this isn't the main point; the point is that the young condemned man shows not the slightest sign of dread or despair. He stands erect with his feet slightly apart—his arms stretched straight over his head, his fists clenched. He stands there showing not even a sign of anger—only peace, and unending confidence in victory; in the straight arms and the clenched fists there's nothing but an incomprehensible, calm triumph. In a moment his bladder and bowels will empty automatically.

Christine looked at the picture for a long time, then she said:

"It's a marvelous picture, but it's terrible."

"It's the most beautiful picture I know," I said.

"Why do you have it over the desk?"

Christine looked at me with the strange, somewhat melancholy look which she almost always has.

"I have it there to be sure that everything I enter into the protocol will bear being read by him," I replied.

"You let him read it first?"

"Yes. I want what I write down to be true. Therefore he reads it first."

"How long have you had it hanging like that?"

"At least a year here. But I also had it up where I lived before. And it hangs on the other wall too—over there." She turned and beheld the same picture on the opposite wall.

"Doesn't it drive you crazy?" she said.

"Yes," I said.

We ate a piece of bread and cheese, then I undressed and lay down.

She took off the white uniform and was brown and strong with her thin, square shoulders. Then she sat on the edge of the bed and bent over me, offered one breast to my mouth. I lay perfectly still and did as she wished.

"Turn over," she said, and I rolled over on my stomach.

As I lay thus, she kissed me all over my back—but shiftingly, so that I never knew where the next kiss would come. It created a strange and almost childlike tension, and I lay there without moving.

"Turn over again," she commanded, and I lay on my back.

As she bestrode me I saw that she was glistening wet all the way down to her knees, and when I was inside her she slowly drew her own legs together and lay forward, on top of me. We lay like that without moving, I only felt her head on my shoulder and some of her fine, sandy hair in my face. She had both hands around my head, and I put mine around her shoulders.

We lay like that for a long time, almost without stirring. And around us was the night, the Alsatian night full of insects, frogs, hedgehogs and snails, and growing plants, full of scents and of grapevines and high treetops.

My walls no longer bleed in here.

I have no dread of the empty space over us or of the fire under us. For I know that all, all has a meaning—not just the hedgehog who sniffs after water, and not just the flowers which have closed. I know that there's a meaning in lying thus and being among those who live in this night. And when I noticed that she was fully satisfied and her body relaxed and soft, I let her slide down beside me with her head in my armpit. She was utterly still, she just lay there beside me, but she stroked my head a couple times. The thin body was moist with sweat.

I caressed her too, over her neck and shoulder. Her eyelashes were wet.

"Do you want to sleep here tonight?" I said.

She opened her moist eyes and smiled.

"No," she said, "I have to go on duty early tomorrow."

When I saw her up to La Poudrière we didn't go by the gravel path, but walked barefoot across the dewy lawns. Hand in hand.

"Will you come back to me again?" I said.

"Yes," she said. "As often as you like."

All at once we both stopped and stood still in the grass. We had heard people. And they were coming closer. Out of the big clump of trees—"the wood," as we call it—came two people. They walked quickly over to the garden path and up toward the light in front of the main door. There was no mistaking who they were.

The ambassador's wife and *le général* had been out sniffing for water.

When little Christine had gone in the back way to the clinic I walked down again, and again I met a person—a large heavy man with a drooping mustache and a cigarette in his mouth.

"Bonsoir, mon vieil enculé," he said. And he looked at me as plaintively as a child.

"What's the matter?"

"The police," he replied. "It's about that damned syphilitic foreign legionnaire and parachute-idiot you cut down in the garden a couple days ago. The coroner has concluded that hanging wasn't the cause of death. The man had a broken neck before he was strung up. It was an outstanding professional job."

Lefèvre accompanied me all the way down to my house, and we drank some cognac before he went home.

He sat heavy and distressed in the garden, with his massive head bent forward—so that the cigarette smoke rose up into his mustache, followed his nose and forehead before it parted company with his face.

"Well, well," he said. "If they don't hang themselves, they hang somebody else. That shouldn't surprise us."

"So now there'll be police investigations and interrogations and hell—and right here at La Poudrière, which was supposed to be a refuge of peace and rest for people with extravagant habits!" I said.

He looked up and poured himself another large glass of cognac:

"Extravagant? On the contrary it's quite ordinary; people don't *do* anything but take each other's lives, even if the methods vary."

"Can't you bribe the police?"

He shrugged:

"Of course that's the first thing I'll try. It's just a question of how much those damned gonorrhea-infested cretins want for burying the case. I'll have to talk with the police chief."

"Of course it'll be an uncommonly disgusting business to have them snooping around out here."

He groaned and passed his huge right hand over his head.

"It's just Harun-al-Rashid and I who know the result of the autopsy, so keep your mouth shut about it for the time being. If the patients get any inkling of it, it'll be a madhouse here in earnest."

"I'll try to control myself," I said.

Lefèvre poured himself another glass and turned his face to me, sad and pleading:

"Tell something," he said. "Tell me a story!"

I thought about it, then I replied:

"It would have to be about Tu Fang. That's a story I remember from Paris.

"Yes, yes!" said Lefèvre. "Tell me about Tu Fang, please do!"

Tu Fang was the man with the golden throat. I met him in Paris in the old days when I was still wandering around.

He had a tenor which was a totally abnormal phenomenon. Now if there are really angels, and if angels really can sing—as the collected European angel paintings testify—if angels really can sing, then they sing like Tu Fang.

Tu Fang was a Korean, and he was studying voice in Paris.

Everyone at the conservatory knew for sure that he would be one of the very great names among the angel choirs' soloists.

We often strolled together along the Left Bank; I'd gotten to know him in one of the innumerable small bars. Tu Fang had many friends from both Gallia and Amerikania and from many other countries. And you couldn't help befriending him—nobody could meet Tu Fang without becoming fond of him. He was very small and slight, with a beautiful, thin Asiatic face and a smile which was always there, but which wasn't superficial.

Tu Fang drank.

He drank desperately and to excess, like Modigliani and Utrillo. And when he drank, he neglected his studies and the conservatory. To get free drinks he often made the rounds of bars and nightspots all night long—and for that matter in the daytime too. He sang with his golden voice so that people stood paralyzed around him.

Tu Fang also had a lot to do with women, and like all alcoholics he awoke both the matrimonial and motherly forces in them. He lived with woman after woman, and they all tried to get him to stop drinking. Tu Fang tried everything, from drinking mineral water to taking Aversan; and it happened with one woman after another that he'd stay on the wagon for awhile, often for several weeks, during which he went regularly to the conservatory and worked hard. But then—after a time—he was standing once again at a bar in the Quartier Latin and singing to get more glasses of Beaujolais. He went so far as to go around with a beret in his hand collecting coins for the next glass. And his voice was just as golden, just as angelic. His smile was the same, only deeper and gentler. Tu Fang sang and drank and remained his old self. But he also made progress in developing his voice, in spite of his perambulations through Paris. When you met Tu Fang on a sour gray rainy day, it was as if the sun burst forth.

Then came the change.

Tu Fang met a new woman, and she achieved what no one any longer thought possible; he stopped drinking. I don't mean that he stopped for a week or two, or that he stopped for a few months. No, Tu Fang *stopped*. Nobody knows what happened, or how it came about—what she had done to him. But he didn't drink anymore. At the same time a gradual change took place in him; I don't think he had the desire to drink any longer. It was as if he no longer expected any consolation from the wine, as if he had abandoned all hope once and for all. He was doomed to sobriety.

He smiled as before, but in a totally different manner—a kind of still and anxious child's smile. And he became reserved, he talked less and less, and he was almost never to be seen anymore in bars or bistros. We saw him only occasionally, and now he no longer smiled.

I wasn't along to help cut him down.

But all his friends went in to see him on the sofa afterwards, with the horrible blue-black mark around his neck.

She—the widow (if one can use such an expression)—maintained total silence, but we all took her by the hand and said a few words to her, and we were also present at the foreigners' cemetery.

I told all this to Lefèvre, but with many more details and at much greater length.

Lefèvre sat listening in silence as he emptied my cognac bottle, glass by glass.

The cigarette hung from the corner of his mouth the whole time, and occasionally he nodded at certain points in the narrative.

At the end he looked up.

"That was a good tale," he said, "a very fine story. There's nothing in the world so sad as an abdicated alcoholic."

"What do you think about Tu Fang—as a doctor?" I asked.

He thought for a bit, then he said:

"We need our consolation in life, if we've understood the terrible madness in the world and in the solar system. And probably Tu Fang stopped drinking without really wanting to. He didn't want anything anymore, his mainspring was broken. He died of shock. Call it a trauma. Call it *frustration*—he was bereft of his expectations."

Over the terrace walked a black, soundless lump. The hedgehog was out again. This time it was alone. It went right past our feet and disappeared among the tomato plants, into the darkness.

I saw Lefèvre up to the gate in the palisade around my garden. He looked tired and at peace.

"Sleep well, old pederast!" he said.

And for a while I could hear his steps on the gravel in the path.

LACROIX

Prairial 24, the year 176

In the morning, while I was busy tying up the tomato stalks in the garden, I heard faint, almost soundless footsteps behind me. I turned to find the little nurse Christine standing there barefoot, with slender brown feet, and wearing a short, thin blue dress.

She was smiling because I hadn't realized that she'd been standing there watching me for quite awhile. In her hand she had a shopping bag.

I walked forward between the plants and kissed her. She stroked me over my thick black hair.

Then she put the shopping bag down on the stone table, which stood cool and airy in the shade. Out of it she took two bottles of Alsace wine, carefully chilled and wrapped in wet newspaper—and then two hunks of cheese, a couple of smoked fillets of trout, and a loaf of fresh white bread—the long, thin kind.

"This is for you," she said, "but I have time to help eat it up. It's a thank-you for yesterday—and now I have my lunch hour at the clinic."

Then she took my hand, and with her naked big toe she drew two letters on the ground. They were my initials.

The wine was of a considerably more expensive sort than I usually have here myself. She must have gone down to the village to buy it.

I went down to the brook and rinsed my face and hands and feet in the fresh water. Then we sat down.

"You said yourself that I could come again," she said. "But I'll only come if you want me to."

We had both gotten up early, and were hungry and thirsty. It was very still now, just before the noon hour, and the sun was of gold and fire and the sky was golden. I don't remember what we talked about. Maybe we hardly talked at all, but I was terribly unshaven, and my beard is almost completely white now—even if my hair is just as black as before. Christine is nearly thirty years younger than I am. "It looks as if you're on a visit to your grandfather," I said, *"chez ton grand-père."*

She laughed. Then she broke off a piece of bread and laid one of the trout fillets on it. She put it into my hand, and we went on eating.

"We must drink the wine before it warms up," she said. "Drink, it's supposed to be cold."

When we'd eaten, and had only half a bottle left, she looked at her watch. "I have to be up at the clinic at twelve thirty," she said, "but there was something I wanted to ask you."

"Yes?"

"May I look at your picture first?"

"What picture?"

"The one of the man—the man who isn't afraid to die."

"Ah!" I said. "The Yugoslav partisan!"

We went into the house, and she bent over my desk and stood for a long time studying the picture of the young man with the wire around his neck and his hands clenched above his head. She stood utterly motionless, staring at it.

Then she straightened up, turned around, and held her hands over her eyes for a few seconds.

I saw her to the gate, and when she'd gone some distance across the lawn she turned around and waved.

Then she disappeared into the park.

I had yet another visit later in the day.

It was from a man I haven't mentioned yet—Ilya. He's our other Russian, besides the ambassador's wife. He doesn't howl.

Ilya is one of our male nurses, and he's important to the place not only because he can beat al Assadun at chess, and al Assadun has won honors playing for Algeria in international tournaments—but just as much because of his good temper, his patient disposition, and his thoroughly Christian nature.

It was Ilya who came down to see me in the afternoon, and I could hear from a long way off that it must be he: he moves neither soundlessly nor invisibly in the landscape.

When we met, he did what he usually does:

"Ivan!" he said; and grabbing me with one hand under each armpit he lifted me up, the way I myself can lift a child—and held me like that, with my feet dangling in the air and my face on a level with his, while he kissed me first on one cheek and then on the other. Then he carefully set me down again, as if I were a little girl who mustn't be injured by careless handling.

He sat down, took a bottle of vodka out of his jacket pocket and set it on the stone table.

I got some glasses.

"You're a good man, Ivan," said Ilya, looking at me out of small blue eyes in a huge round face. "I've come to remind you that Lacroix is holding his lecture this evening."

I nodded.

"Good," I said. "Anything else new?"

"Nothing except that that damned Hungarian parachute-idiot from the Foreign Legion unfortunately didn't die a so-called natural death, namely by hanging—which would have been natural for him. The homicide commission has concluded that somebody broke his neck first, and strung him up afterwards."

"That's at least as natural," I said; "there isn't a single person in all La Poudrière who didn't detest him."

"Oh yes," said Ilya. "There are two people here who thought a great deal of him—the nymphomaniacal Leninist-fascist of an ambassador's wife, who's always howling her Siberian howls at night, the wolf-maid from the Kremlin—and the little butcher of blacks from the Pentagon. They both set great store by him, as a man and as a murderer. After all, he'd worn that marvelous green-spotted uniform which has spread France's culture all over the underdeveloped world."

Ilya downed a beer glass of vodka in one gulp.

"But *you* knew about this, I see?" he said.

"Yes," I replied, "I just didn't think that anyone but al Assadun and Lefèvre and I had been informed that someone had taken justice into his own hands."

"I was the first one Lefèvre told about it," replied Ilya. "He was in utter despair and said he'd kill the first policeman who showed his face at La Poudrière, and with his own hands. I had to console him and sing Russian songs for him almost the whole night afterwards. Finally I even sang 'Stenka Razin' for him."

We both sat in silence for awhile, thinking.

"I have an idea," I said. "A solution to the whole problem. I've been sitting here mulling it over all day, and I think it can be solved in such a way that Lefèvre won't be hurt. A friend is a friend."

"Yes, Ivan," Ilya nodded, "a friend is a friend."

(It's a very funny thing here at La Poudrière: Ilya calls me "Ivan"; the French-born ones, like little Christine, call me "Jean"—so does Fontaine, the killer of boys. The Italian gardener calls me "Giovanni," and the little sodomitic Semite al Assadun calls me "Jochanaan." In other words, everybody after his own lingo.)

"When you come right down to it, Ilya, we live in Transalpine Gaul, and in spite of everything these damned blood-stained degenerate frog-eaters have *culture*. They're *civilized* people. That means that neither the homicide commission, the coroner, the district attorney, nor the police chief has great scruples about taking bribes. We're in civilized territory."

Ilya blinked at me, then he shook his head.

"Ivan, you're really a child. Lefèvre sounded them out about how much they wanted only a couple of hours after he got the report, and it involves sums which Lefèvre can't raise. Just the DA and the coroner and the police chief amount to a fortune—and on top of that there's a homicide commission of six members.

"La Poudrière is already so heavily mortgaged that our poor friend Lefèvre can't up the mortgage by so much as a franc."

"I didn't think for a minute that Lefèvre should pay them. And I know he can't. Besides, that would be immoral. To get the case dropped and to get a false death certificate made out I figure would take in the neighborhood of half a million new francs."

"That's not a bad estimate."

"My idea is totally different," I said. Then I told him my plan.

He approved of it.

There are a number of things to tell about Ilya, not just that he's a sovereign chess player. Ilya is a wrestler by trade, or more accurately: he was for many years. Outwardly he's marked by it: both his ears are so-called "cauliflower ears." They were twisted off in the heat of many wrestling matches, so that today he bears only some small, crumpled traces of what he once had. But that isn't his real profession. Originally he was a clown, acrobat, and trapeze artist, but he eventually got too heavy for that. For awhile he was a weightlifter and strong man in a circus. Later he became a wrestler.

He's a couple of years older than the century—in other words, a little over seventy today.

When I met him for the first time, in Paris, he was working at a theater—which was easy because his old clown talent has qualified him once and for all as a splendid comic—in mute roles, of course. He was doing various other jobs around the theater as well.

We met in the theater cafeteria, where he was sitting and drinking at a table beside some of my friends. I talked with them both for a bit and then went out to the pissoir.

Right afterwards Ilya also came out to empty his bladder, and stopped beside me. I perceived him only as a tall, very stout man. As we stood there pissing, the following conversation unfolded:

"You must really excuse me for not introducing myself in there at the table; my name is Ilya Aleksandrovich Coldoni."

"*Goldoni!*" I exclaimed. "Are you descended from the great Goldoni?"

He smiled and shook the urine off his mighty penis:

"Not Goldoni, *Coldoni.* If it had been Goldoni, I wouldn't be standing here."

"Are you an actor at this theater?" I asked.

He shook his head.

"No, no. I'm an *artiste.*"

"How's that?" I asked. "What kinds of things do you do?"

He leaned his head back and looked up at the ceiling:

"I work in the air."

"In the *air?*"

"Yes, yes. . . . originally on the trapeze, that is, or if someone is supposed to fall six, eight yards, or something like that—they may need somebody to be a strong man, or . . . suppose they want someone to instruct the actors in karate or acrobatics and that kind of thing. Once in awhile I have mute roles—this awful Petersburg accent of mine!"

This conversation in the pissoir led to a lasting friendship. But of course all this stuff about wrestling, karate, acrobatics and weightlifting, and pantomime is only Ilya's outer being—his outer man, so to speak. He was born in Petersburg in 1898, and was thus nineteen years old in the year of our Lord 1917.

He took part in both the revolution and the civil war, and belonged to the anarchist faction whose aim was to unite communism with freedom and equality. After comrades Lenin and

Trotsky had begun the slaughter of the anarchists and had realized the apostle Paul's vision of Power and the State—and while the blood ran in the prison cellars, along stairs and floors and walls—Ilya managed to escape a few hours before his own execution: he broke a couple of MPs' necks, kicked a few doors to pieces and disappeared into the masses whence he—in contrast to Lenin and Trotsky—had come.

I hardly think that there's anyone in Western Europe today who knows much more than Ilya about the concrete reality in that fraternal pair Trotsky / Lenin's paradise. People don't *know* anything!

It was several years before Ilya managed to get out of Holy Russia, and during his illegal existence in Petersburg he accumulated many experiences.

He *thinks* in revolutionary dates, and it's typical of Ilya that when I once told him my birth date, in *krasny oktyabr* 1920, he went into a gale of laughter, he wheezed with laughter, he screamed.

"What are you laughing at, little father?" I said.

"Ivan, Ivan!" answered Ilya. "How can I stop laughing when I think that *you—you* of all gentle people—were born in the same month Lenin published his treatise on *Terrorism and Revolution*—a treatise which is the very apotheosis of terrorism and the definitive ruination of Marxism! Aside from the Pauline-Lutheran apotheosis of state power."

He's also the only person who has given me a concrete explanation of the Red Army's effectiveness. Ilya's explanation is as follows:

"The secret of the Red Army is that it doesn't exist, and never *has* existed. That is to say: the army exists, but it isn't *red*! Everybody knows that eighty per cent of the officers were old czarist officers, and that only positions which didn't require professional expertise were filled with Bolshevik police spies and commissars. There's never been any *red* army.

"Trotsky understood what a soldier *is*; he knew that a soldier has four desires: food, liquor, money—and *fine uni-*

forms. While the Russian population was starving and in rags, the Red Army walked around *well-fed and content in beautiful, well-fitting uniforms with red stars;* and for this pay they would shoot their fathers, their mothers, their sisters, or their brothers, if it were required of them. The same goes for the police. The judges. The prosecuting attorneys. History knows no exceptions."

But this belongs to Ilya's inner man—along with the fact that he's a believing Christian, in the same way that al Assadun actually believes in Allah. That same evening after Ilya and I had met in the men's room of the theater and had spiritually more or less mingled blood—that evening turned into a very jolly one, because along with the other guests from the cafeteria we ended up at—I don't remember exactly where, but it was either at the Soviet embassy or at a hotel in Paris which the legation had rented in its entirety. Some of the hosts even wore uniforms with red stars. It was a long night, and we slept with our clothes on.

But the night was jolly, we sang, we smashed furniture and windows, we played leapfrog, we threw knives and we shot pistols at empty vodka bottles. It was cozy and delightful, just like home.

And this happened at a time when everything looked brighter for the future of Soviet Man: *Homo sovieticus* was breathing more freely than before.

In other words, this was awhile after Satan had taken Stalin's soul and was, let us hope, giving it the prescribed treatment—with stabbing, impaling, pinching, and especially burning, roasting, and eternal boiling.

The next morning Ilya and I sat on the Left Bank with a quiet bottle of calvados. Neither of us was so sick after the night before that we couldn't both enjoy the invigorating, silver-gray morning air and the gray-green water in the river—in this river which has seen everything there is to see on this earth, from the guillotine to Paul Cézanne.

Let me add that we were sitting right by the bridge which goes over to the Place Dauphine.

Beside us sat two young people who were kissing without pause. They kissed each other in the ears, on the nose, on the eyes, and on the mouth.

"Ilya," I said, "one really has to admit that your intellectually gonorrhea-ridden countrymen at this politically most syphilitic of all embassies (leaving the Americans out of account)—that your spiritually hunchbacked countrymen are in fact utterly enchanting to drink with."

He sat still, scratching one of the ears he didn't have; it was only a hole with a fringe around it.

"Ivan," he said, "little father! I won't start telling about the Neva or about the tulips by the Volga—but there is some good in everybody—*even* in Russians.

"Did you notice that the chauffeur was at the party?"

"Of course," I said. "That was a nice democratic ingredient."

"The embassy chauffeurs are always in on everything, Ivan. That's because they're invariably police spies. Their job is to keep the whole embassy staff under surveillance in order to report them to the secret police—at piecework rates."

"Ilya, police spies are people too!"

"No," said Ilya, "police spies are not people. They are *insects*. The only thing they understand is insect powder, and it's the only thing which works on them. If you don't grab them by the scruff of the neck in a free moment."

He said "scruff of the neck" in such a way that I could *hear* the vertebrae snapping. "Crack!" it said, sharply and clearly.

"But the others, then? All the others were very pleasant yesterday."

He sat there, quiet and serious, then he said:

"Yes. And they're good people. They're *nice* people, and I often get together with them—but only when the chauffeurs aren't around. They're good and loving people. I mean really *good* people, Ivan. And this is the strange thing: I've often been at their homes, these people from the embassy. . . but. There's a *but*. It's something I don't understand. . . something I can't comprehend."

He turned his head and looked at me with his penetrating

little blue chess-player's eyes in the round face atop the enormous bull neck. Then he went on slowly:

"I've often been at their homes in private, and they're *good* people—but they don't have any icons in the corners. They're *good* people, *but they don't pray. They don't pray!*"

This is Ilya, the chess master above all chess masters—revolutionary theorist, practitioner, and historian. Except for al Assadun—here the Semite is superior—I don't know anyone who knows so much about European literature as Ilya, anarcho-communist and male nurse at our madhouse.

After I'd told him my plan about the homicide commission and the district attorney, the coroner, and the police chief—and after he'd expressed his approval of it—we sat there for a while longer. We agreed that I should go to Lefèvre and tell him before Lacroix began his lecture.

The afternoon sent steadily longer shadows in across my grape and tomato arbor while we emptied the vodka bottle.

"Listen," I said, "have you ever gotten a licking, Ilya?"

He thought about it for a long time. Then he said:

"Yes, once. That was in Paris too, I'd gotten into a quarrel with an Englishman. A thin little guy with a red mustache. I remember him very well; his mustache was small and trimmed short, and he was little and thin. I must not have been much over sixty at the time, and he was around your age, he must have been about forty then. We fought for almost two hours, and the police didn't dare intervene. The thing was that the man was trained as a commando during the last war—a specialist in silent killing. And after a few minutes we both realized that it was a professional meeting—between brothers, so to speak. He almost killed me, and it turned into a sport while we were at it. But he was a decent sort; he came to visit me in the hospital afterwards. I was there for almost six weeks. He was very nice, he brought me books and wine, and he said that his nerves had been ruined during the war, which is why he sometimes drank too much—otherwise he wouldn't have manhandled me so. But then I wasn't exactly sober either, so we were both very sorry about the incident. But that's the only time I can remember."

"It's funny," I said. "Now they're landing on the moon, and they're going to leave a box there with a letter from President Nixon. But that isn't all. . . . The thing is that it's almost impossible to go to the john in outer space. So beside Nixon's thought-laden autograph they're also going to leave a plastic bag of excrement."

"You sound like Fontaine," said Ilya. "One would think you were a Belgian."

"Have you talked with him lately?"

"Oh yes, he's progressing—he has talent."

"For writing, you mean?"

"That too. Now he's writing down his *vita sexualis*, but I was thinking more about his lessons."

"Lessons?"

"I'm teaching him karate. He has indisputable talent."

"Ilya!" I said. "You're teaching that little sex murderer karate? Only Russians can be so immoral! Do you know what you're doing?"

"Dr. Lefèvre fully approves. It's healthy for him—it gives him more self-respect, and hence less hatred of humanity."

"This is really a madhouse!" I said. "Are you stark raving lunatics, all of you?"

"Yes, we are," said Ilya, "but do you think it's any better outside?"

I didn't reply. Ilya went on:

"You know our little vivisector of black girls from Texas or whatever the hell it's called, you know him well. Do you think he seems especially American?"

"Internally, yes. But externally, in style and manners, even in his language—after all, the man knows English!—he seems rather British."

"Quite right, Ivan, quite right. Do you know what that comes from?"

"No. I've thought about it some, but I don't understand it."

"The explanation is this: *le général* was educated at a British training station for commandoes—silent killing plus. It's left its mark on him. He even learned the language."

We sat in silence for a while, and since the vodka was all gone I got out a couple of bottles of red wine.

"This is better than Smirnov," I said.

We took a short walk around the garden, looked at the tomatoes and the grapes and stopped beside the brook, where an occasional shadow glided swiftly through the water. The tomatoes are doing fine now, and the trout look good too. Earlier the brook was overpopulated, with small trout whose heads were too large; but since my intervention this fall the population is now about right, and the fish have gotten much better—less head, more fillet.

Their flesh isn't really red, but it has a fine light pinkish-brown color, and the skin turns delightfully blue when it's boiled right, in vinegar water.

The frogs also look very good. Sometime in the next week Lefèvre and I are going to have a little meal here. The most fascinating thing about a frog is that you can eat the hind legs without killing the animal; like all cold-blooded animals it will grow new hind legs, which you can eat once again. The operation is very simple: you take the frog by both hind feet, one foot in each hand, and let it hang with its head down over the water; then you twirl it around, the way little girls do with a jumping rope, and in a minute the frog is gone and you're standing there with two delightful frog's legs in your hands. The new hind legs never grow as big as the first ones, but they taste just as good—better than any chicken. You go on like that, and the frog gets used to it. Next week we'll have a little dinner here, of frogs' legs and trout. I'll cook it myself. I'm the best cook at La Poudrière.

Ilya was deep in thought.

"Tell me frankly, Ilya," I said; "who do you think killed that damned parachute-cretin?"

He looked at me quietly, and his small eyes looked wiser than ever:

"I think I can tell you something about this Hungarian hero of the fight against barbarian socialism and communism. Do you know that the man was *famous?*"

"No."

"Well, he was famous in Algeria, Tunisia, and above all in Indochina—in Vietnam, as it's called."

"That idiot was *famous?*"

"Oh, yes! He was famous. He was a renowned chief of interrogation. Of course you know that it was our two-legged Gallic brothers who invented the telephone method? *N'est-ce pas,* Ivan, even you know that?"

"Yes."

"Do you know what the man was famous for?"

"No, of course not."

"As you can imagine, even among these perverse, sadistic frog-eaters, your two-legged French sodomites, it isn't always easy to find people with the nerve to make a phone call. You know: the field telephone has two electrodes, and one is usually fastened to the nostril, the other to the rectum or penis— or if it's a female partisan, to nipple and vagina. Lefèvre, who doesn't usually talk nonsense, has told me that he's seen people die of shock—not *during* the treatment, it isn't physically life-endangering—but afterwards. He also told me that he's experienced a French officer who died after having *administered* the treatment. So as you can imagine, it's—even among the frog-eaters (among Russians it would be easier), but *even among Frenchmen* it *can* be difficult to find people who want to telephone.

"That's how our little Hungarian patriot and guardian of the morals of Attila and the Gauls became famous. He was always willing to telephone. And he was famous for having developed the method further: he always fastened one electrode to the vagina or penis, and the other in the rectum. That's how he got *his* kicks.

"So actually I never took his crying jags very seriously. The man was an engineer by profession, and like almost all these good defenders of society he had an intense interest in sex organs. For France, his new fatherland, he was the ideal paratrooper and foreign legionnaire. It's been established that he directed a squadron of legionnaires in burying a whole Arab family alive. The adults had to dig the grave first, after which both children and adults were shoveled in by the legionnaires. He was a *man.*

"Do you understand now that our friend Báthory, Doctor of Engineering, was a *celebrity*—and *deserved* a pension for life, along with marriage to one of France's richest heiresses and a correspondingly high position?"

"Of course I perceive the man's patriotic services."

"Báthory had really contributed something in the fight for culture—not least for French culture, for Rodin and Paul Cézanne."

"Ilya," I said, "that wasn't what I asked about. I asked if you had any idea who broke his neck."

Ilya smiled his good Russian smile:

"You know that both Lefèvre and al Assadun fought on the Arab side during those little wars in Africa, and that they were very well informed concerning the Gallic interrogators' records. al Assadun was trained as a guerrilla soldier, and as a doctor he has—in common with Lefèvre—a thorough knowledge of anatomy besides."

"So you're implying that al Assadun. . . ?"

"Oh, no. I have no evidence. Besides, do you know that Lefèvre is almost as strong as I am?"

"Yes," I said. "I know him very well. But who the devil is left, then?"

"Well. . ." said Ilya, "the most highly qualified, the real specialist, of course, is old Lacroix."

I found Lefèvre up in the music room in his private quarters, the original La Poudrière, in the ancient stone building itself—the tower. He was sitting perfectly still and listening to his marvelous Swiss recording of the Ninth. To the last movement, as always—from the place where the theme is first stated in its entirety: before *"Oh, Freunde, nicht diese Töne!"*—

there where the whole melodic sentence is played all the way
through for the first time. It has often struck me that the
Ninth is more French than German, Beethoven's passionate
climax is the true French national anthem—and not only
musically: Schiller's poetry likewise has a deep bond with this
hard, austere nation of winegrowers and painters. I don't
know any Teutons who love the Ninth Symphony the way
the French do. It's a Gallic world, and Lefèvre was sitting
there consoling himself with it.

"*Bonsoir, mon bon vieil enculé*!" he said, looking up. He
knew that Lacroix's lecture was to begin in a few minutes.

"I've come to propose a solution to this whole damned
mess with the homicide commission," I said.

He gave a friendly and appreciative nod.

"It's too late," he said, "I can't raise the money."

"You won't have to," I said. "It will be done by far more
solid circles in this country."

He raised his eyebrows, and for the first time I can
remember he took the cigarette out of his mouth—between
his thumb and forefinger. He held it like that for a moment,
then flicked the ash onto the rug and put the cigarette down
on the table—directly on the surface, without an ashtray, the
way the Italians do. There it lay, searing a small brown point
into the tabletop. He looked at me.

"Listen," I said, "has that infernal parachute-cretin's family
heard about the homicide commission's findings?"

"No," he said, "of course not. It's only Harun-al Rashid,
you, I, and then of course little Ilya from Petersburg who
know about it."

"Well," I said, "for a family of that sort, who are not only
industrial magnates, but who also own several banks, half of
Brittany, and most of the original Indochina—the death certificate as it stands, namely hanging by his own hand, would
be the biggest scandal the family could imagine. One just
doesn't do things like that. Going crazy is bad enough, but on
top of that he goes and hangs himself.'

"Yes," said Lefèvre, "I know them—they'd rather see him

burned alive than accept the medical opinion that he died by his own hand."

"But so far that's all they've gotten—a declaration from al Assadun, from you and from the coroner, that one of your colleagues cut him down in the park after death had occurred?"

"Yes, that's all they know."

And he sat for a minute thinking about it:

"But in a few days they'll receive a new and more encouraging death certificate, namely from the homicide commission."

"You've talked with the police chief and the district attorney?"

"They want over four hundred thousand new francs to drop the case for lack of evidence."

He stared at me despairingly.

"Then the case is clear," I said. "Call the police chief and say that the money will be there in a few days, and ask them just to go a bit slow on the whole thing. Everybody will get his.

"Then you contact the widow and the in-laws, and tell them that you understand their desperate and disgraceful situation, but that the coroner was called immediately after the accident—as well as the commission from Lyons.

"That's why there's this painful certificate of death by his own hand."

He looked at me, and stuck the cigarette back in under his mustache.

"Okay, and then?"

"Then you tell them that for the sake of discretion you've tried to get the death certificate altered to spinal fracture after a fall from a tree in the garden, and that both al Assadun, your excellent assistant doctor, and the man who stumbled upon the all-too-prematurely exanimate corpse of this brave champion of all enduring values—a certain renovation worker at your madhouse, by the name of Jean—both are willing to confirm this, out of respect for the family's good name and reputation; but that the coroner and the commission are dead set against it—every Gallic businessman will understand what

that means. In short, you tell the billionaire father-in-law that
the coroner and the commission together demand half a million for signing a more tactful death certificate. That just
means that I swear on oath that I found him in the grass, and
that all you doctors write out an affidavit saying that our patriotic friend died of a fracture of the cervical vertebrae—which
is the medical truth, after all."

Lefèvre sat totally expressionless for a minute, staring
straight ahead; then he got up and brought a bottle of
Napoléon out of the cupboard. He poured out two large
glasses, then he said:

"You good old shitty *enculé*! This is worth a mass!"

We drank up.

Then he picked up the telephone on the desk and dialed a
number; in a moment he got an answer.

"Hello!" he said. "Yes, well, this is me. I just want to
report that the hygienic conditions out here will be put in
order in a few days. I've just gotten a very friendly and positive answer from the bank. It will hardly take me more than a
week to pay the bill. You just have to certify the hygienic conditions first."

There followed some words on the other end, from the
coroner, and though I couldn't understand the words, I could
hear that the voice sounded almost meek.

"You mustn't apologize," replied Lefèvre. "The Bible says
love your enemies, but it doesn't say anywhere that you have
to love your friends—Not even Mohammed had such a
thought! . . . I'll let you know when everything is arranged,
and you can come out here. . . . You know best yourself what
the procedure is for that kind of thing."

Again a couple of grunts from the other end.

"Tant pis!" said Lefèvre and hung up.

Then we walked together down to the banquet hall to
hear Lacroix's lecture.

The little nurse Christine was sitting in one of the front
rows, and smiled at us when we came in. The hall was full
of people.

Fontaine, al Assadun, Ilya, *le général* and the ambassador's wife were all sitting way down front—the last two next to each other.

Lefèvre and I went further back in the hall.

He took me by the arm and grinned:

"If your plan works, about Báthory and his illustrious French family, I'll blow you to three free shock treatments!" he whispered. He looked happier than he had in a long time; there was hope in his eyes again.

Then Lacroix stood up; and slowly, as if hesitating, yet steadily and with confidence, he walked forward to the lectern. It was literally so still in the room that you could hear one of his shoes creak. Clearly the whole thing took great self-discipline on his part.

When he mounted the lectern and turned toward the audience, you could see that he'd had the bandages changed on his neck. The new ones were smaller, and over them he was wearing a silk scarf which at least partly covered up the gauze.

Lacroix cleared his throat a couple of times, then began to speak. His voice was a bit hoarse, but powerful and distinct:

LADIES AND GENTLEMEN:

The trade which I have plied for more than a generation is hardly any secret to those present. There are things no one can hide, nor should they be hidden today. In my position of so many years' standing I was a servant of the state, I was paid out of public funds, and was thus publicly installed and remunerated by the taxpayers—that is, I've been a true servant of those present, I've carried out your will by implementing the decisions of society, because I meet the requirements of this office—"the possession of special qualifications." So no one should despise or fear me just because I've carried out the will of others through all these decades.

As a public executioner I have the same right to respect, friendliness, and even sympathy as any other human creature.

So I want to talk about these things from the public executioner's point of view—or to use a less ambiguous word: I want to talk about them from the headsman's point of view.

People think of the victims, they think of the guilty, the condemned, they even think of the invited witnesses who by law must be present at every execution—but who thinks of the *executioner*? He is a man "with unusual qualifications," they say; that's a prerequisite for the job, people think. But is it true? Is this really correct?

By "unusual qualifications" they mean in the first place so-called "positive qualities," such as sobriety, accuracy, integrity and, above all, having "nerves of steel." But they also mean other qualities, less engaging ones, which perhaps should not be publicly required of a servant of the state—such as "hardness, heartlessness, insensitivity."

Of course this applied especially in times when a public executioner's duties often entailed significant aggravations of the death penalty, such as whipping, branding, blinding, lopping off hands and feet, quartering or drawing out the entrails of the condemned—sometimes on top of execution at the stake.

Today torture is carried out by officers and policemen, no longer by executioners.

That a person in those days could have as his job the performance of such things led to the popular belief that only persons with sinister, unclean, and dreadful characteristics could accomplish this public but—like the sanitation worker's—necessary task. People didn't consider the fact that often the headsman had no other opportunities for employment than this one, and they despised him, they avoided his house, and his children were regarded as *unclean*—as persons whom no good citizen could take in marriage.

This led to an extensive intermarrying among Europe's executioner families, and in the course of the centuries there arose the so-called headsmen's dynasties, families which in a complicated way were all related to each other, and which often had the peculiarity that (for example) English executioners bore French names, French executioners bore German names, and the like.

Here I shall only mention a few of the great headsmen's dynasties by name—such as the Deiblers, the Sansons, and the Reicharts, servants of the state for centuries. Of course we have the names of other great executioners too, such as the Austrian Josef Lang and the Englishman Ellis, both known for their sensitive tenderness and for their love of all living things—not least our four-footed friends, the beasts. James Berry, the Englishman, should also be mentioned as a man of the very best qualities. Likewise Elliott, a thoroughly excellent person. We have such glorious names as André Obrecht, Desfourneaux, Henry Allen, the great Hungarian executioner Anatole Rozarek, and such worthy men as Schweitz or Paul Späthe. Just to name a few. One should also mention the Nuremburg executioner Hans Schmidt. A special place of honor goes to the English public executioner Albert Pierrepoint, morally as well as professionally an outstanding personality.

I won't conceal the fact that there have also existed executioners of an extremely low, even criminal character; several of them ended their own lives at the stake, on the gallows, or under the guillotine—such as, for example, Meister Friedrich, Meister Hans, Cratwell, Derrick, Brandon, Price, Rose, and Marwell. They were all executed for their leisure activities.

Many people are appalled to think that sovereign states have had criminals in their service.

But these executioners whom I just mentioned are by no means representative of their calling, and had none of the character traits which are prerequisite to the honorable and responsible practice of the profession. The ideal executioner is, to quote an English colleague, a person of an entirely different cast. If he has evil, cruel, or criminal tendencies, he must sublimate and transform them into higher forms. He should be a placid person, without too much imagination—and he's often markedly pious and religious. A competent executioner should be far more than an efficient technician and professional; a real executioner is an artist, a craftsman. Here I shall quote such an outstanding connoisseur as

Charles Duff, the Englishman, who uncompromisingly states the demand that the executioner be an artist, and a man with the true artist's ice-cold, self-controlled, and almost pedantic temperament. Mr. Duff says: "A man who can dispatch another person painlessly and without brutality, is he not an artist? There's a certain delicacy about the deed itself which requires a sure eye, a lightning brain, cool and calculating—and a proficiency which is encountered only within the realm of great art."

Unfortunately, however, my colleagues are often far from being artists of this dimension. Sentimentality and weak nerves are just as incompatible with the executioner's trade as with the performances of a great violinist or a great pianist. Not to mention the writer's or the poet's profession: Here everything is coolness, consciousness, and precision.

But in addition to this the executioner performs his solo number against stakes of a far more dreadful sort; a pianist who loses his nerve and self-control will hardly be trampled to death by the mob, as happened to many a headsman in the days of public executions.

It was in the later phase of the heyday of public executions that the headsman's profession acquired this new and dangerous character. This was due to a change in the public taste, which underwent a process of refinement in the 1700's.

The ordinary public—which usually assembled by the tens of thousands—had previously been most appreciative of long-drawn-out, extremely complicated executions, as protracted and painful for the delinquent as possible; but now they began to prefer the swift, elegant dispatch, performed with virtuosity—dazzling, ice-cold and *merciful* expertise.

I don't need to tell you what this meant in terms of the strain on the executioner's nerves, especially if he worked with sword or axe.

To undertake the dispatch of another person, alone with him on the scaffold, with a sword in your hand—surrounded by tens and tens of thousands of experienced and critical spectators demanding one single lightning-swift, brilliant stroke—this was a far greater strain on the brain and nerves than the earlier breaking on the wheel, flaying, boiling, etc., etc., which had been carried out before an always grateful populace, a crowd of spectators who cheered loudest when the action proceeded slowly.

I know of executioners who, when alone, during practice, could cleave a willow wand lengthwise with a sword or axe, and with such force that the block had to be split open in order to get the weapon loose—virtuosos of the very highest artistry. But on the *scaffold*, before the condemned—surrounded by the titled, clerical, and vulgar mob—they were seized with such uncertainty, such nervousness, that they were apt to hit the condemned on the back, for instance, or maybe just to scalp him—real artists who had to use five, six, or more strokes to sever the head from the body.

Add to this the frightful mess of blood, not to mention its smell, which can be very strong.

The circumstances were aggravated even more by the fact that the mob often attacked and killed the executioner after such unfortunate or unsuccessful executions.

Concerning a headsman in Denmark, a very small country in Northern Europe, there's a detailed description of how the executioner made repeated attempts to remove the head of a woman. He hit her three times on the shoulders, sheared off her scalp and struck twice across the delinquent's back. The mob stormed the scaffold, and the executioner had to take flight while the woman was still alive. He was pursued by the crowd, which overtook and killed him in the most gruesome manner.

The woman bled to death.

We have a great mass of material, of historically reliable quality, about such unsuccessful executions. I shall mention just a few of them, because they shed light on later developments in the art of dispatching.

They also involve technical details of a bewildering degree of fineness, and here I shall call to mind the crown prince of the Sanson dynasty, advising the Jacobins in connection with the planned mass executions. Charles-Henri Sanson explained: "After one execution the sword can't be used again." In other words, the edge had to be whetted like a razor blade after every neck on the block. So you get an idea of what is required of an artist, and a goodly proportion of unsuccessful executions are due to the executioner's not knowing his trade well enough to hone his instruments in a professional manner. But Maître Charles-Henri was one of the great ones in his field.

However, that wasn't true of a colleague like Jack Ketch in England, who had needed four strokes to take the life of Lord Russell. His next client was the Duke of Monmouth—and the historic scene is described by no one less than the great record-keeper Macaulay, who relates how the Duke calmly mounted the scaffold and gave the headsman a handful of gold coins.

"Here are six guineas," he said; "but don't hack me up the way you did my dear Lord Russell."

I don't need to tell you what effect this remark had on Jack Ketch's nerves. With the already suspicious mob around him, and the duke's dispiriting words in his ear, Ketch totally lost his self-control; and when he struck he hit not the duke's neck, but only his body. (According to the great Sanson the axe had now, after one stroke, already ceased to be usable.) The Duke of Monmouth got up from the block and looked reproachfully at the executioner, then laid down his head once more.

The trembling Jack Ketch heard the yells from the crowd and struck again and again, but didn't succeed in severing the head from the body, which continued to move. Howls of rage and loathing arose from the crowd, and in despair the headsman threw the axe down on the scaffold; the duke was still alive.

"I can't do it!" shrieked Ketch. "I don't have the heart!"

"Pick up the axe and continue!" ordered the commandant.

"Throw him over the railing!" roared the mob.

The headsman picked up the axe and struck twice more.

Then death occurred—but Ketch had to use a knife to cut the head loose from the shoulders before he could lift it up and display it.

Only strong military protection saved Jack Ketch's life after this execution.

But the great Macaulay tells nothing about how the executioner fared later in life, or about who suffered most on the scaffold—the Duke of Monmouth or the headsman Jack Ketch.

Just as unlucky as Ketch was the German executioner Valentin Deusser, who was to behead a very sick and feeble woman with a sword. She was so weak that she had to be carried to the scaffold, where she was set on a chair; the beheading was to be done with a sword using horizontal strokes—something which is extremely demanding technically.

Meister Valentin almost collapsed at the sight of her; he walked around the sick woman several times, trying the sword in different positions. When he finally struck out, he hit only the uppermost part of her head, taking off a piece about the size of a dollar. He also knocked her off the chair, but she got back up on it without help.

Now she began pleading to be allowed to leave the place of execution. But she was forced to stay on the chair, and Meister Valentin struck again. This time she didn't get up, and now the executioner had to *cut* off her head, which he laid on the scaffold. The furious mob thereupon began stoning Valentin Deusser, but with the help of the city's armed forces he was saved from death.

Such things happened often. The French public executioner, Monsieur Flurat, was pursued by the mob after an execution of this unsuccessful type, and sought refuge in his own house. The mob set fire to the house and burned it down over the heads of him and his family, all of whom died.

One of the most unsuccessful executions on record is the decapitation of the famous Comte de Chalais. I won't go into the historical and political background of the execution here—it ought to be well known in this beautiful country—but will

stick to the technical and psychological facts that the execution took place by sword, and that it took the headsman fully
twenty-nine—29—strokes before the head was chopped off.

The executioner's job was thus to keep his head cool and
his nerves calm while surrounded by a crazed, howling public
which demanded the utmost of him every time—and with the
headsman's life as the stake during the performance of the job
with which king, church, princes, state, citizenry, and the rabble in general had charged him.

On top of this he was regarded as unclean, diabolical, a
man to be hated and feared—this servant of the state, servant
of the people and—according to the churches and Paul and
Luther: *servant of God!*

Still, people through the ages have *loved* the executioner,
and as the proverb says: a beloved child has many names.
We call him *Meistermann, Meister Hans,* Official Executioner,
State Electrician (in the U.S.), *Henker,* Hangman, *Monsieur de
Paris* or *Monsieur de France, Schinder*—and we have countless
other names for the executioner.

Josef Lang, the Austrian, who was the undisputed world
champion in hanging, by a private, quick, and apparently
humane method—this same "Pepi" Lang, with his many pet
names, was popular and beloved among the Viennese, especially the women. Every young or mature lady of the world's
oldest profession rendered him gratis every service within the
possibilities of the trade. But not only this light brigade, but
also ladies and *fräuleins* of the middle class and of the very
highest social station offered Lang their services in love; Lang
exercised a fascination over women which no Don Juan or
Casanova possessed. His daily mail of love letters was a great
nuisance to the postman.

These are historical facts, ladies and gentlemen.

"Meistermann" was also the focal point in great popular
festivals, of which we have one eyewitness account by no less
than the great, titanic protocollist and bookkeeper, Charles
Dickens. I shall only repeat a few lines of his description of a
double execution, a married couple, taken from the excellent

London newspaper the *Times* the day after the festivities took place. Dickens says:

"The horrors of the gibbet and of the crime faded in my mind before the atrocious bearing, looks and language of the assembled spectators. . . . The *shrillness* of the cries and howls . . . made my blood run cold. . . . Screeching, and laughing, and yelling. . . thieves, low prostitutes, ruffians and vagabonds of every kind. . . . Fightings, faintings. . . tumultuous demonstrations of indecent delight. . . . Many places had the air of battlefields. . . . Crushed and trampled persons lay about, many of them insensible, some with broken bones. . . . London's hospitals were filled with the wounded. . . . *It was as if I were living in a city of devils. . . .*" Dickens says, word for word: "*I felt for some time afterwards as if I were living in a city of devils!*"

And I ask you, ladies and gentlemen: was it the *hangman* who was the devil?

Some become executioners of their own free will, others because they have no choice, because it is their fate.

I'll mention a single but central example from one of the great families—one of the classic dynasties, the Deiblers (but all these dynasties—the Obrechts, Sansons, Desfourneaux's, and Deiblers—carry each other's blood in their veins; they're *one* family, and almost all the great executioners come from it.

Anatole Deibler refused to take up the profession which his race had practiced for generations. He refused to become an executioner. He served his time in the army and was received with hatred, loathing, and repugnance, excluded from the other soldiers' *companionship*, which means so much to a *young* man (though not to mature men). After he left the army he experienced the same thing; everywhere his reputation preceded him.

So Anatole Deibler changed his name, and tried to disappear into the crowd. He tried new places of work, new names. But everywhere his origin and identity were discovered, and he was frozen out anew. He suffered from hemophobia, he couldn't stand the sight of blood. But again and again he was unmasked and identified.

At last, like the prodigal son of the Bible, he went back to his father and his guillotine—back to his *fate*.

But there are aspiring executioners of another type, without a fate. When Berry, the English executioner, was installed at the end of the last century, there were 1399 other applicants for the post. What kind of applicants were they? They didn't come from the dynasties.

Anatole Deibler, with his fear of blood, his nausea at the smell of it, and his hysterical screams after the beheadings, must have suffered beyond all human endurance all his life.

It's not too much, ladies and gentlemen, to say that the course of fate for the true executioners has been one long *via dolorosa*, it has been a *via dolorosa* of generations, leading through contempt, hatred, persecution—and through the performance of the job itself.

But among the applicants for vacant posts there have been medical men, journalists, lawyers, and even clerics.

A common sideline, in Austria and England for example, has been innkeeping—for the last hundred years.

In the foregoing I've described a few examples of unsuccessful beheadings. If I were to supplement them with unsuccessful hangings, it would take up too much space. Originally hanging was almost always "unsuccessful," in the sense that it led not to strangulation, to the closure of the large arteries in the neck, which produces rapid unconsciousness—but to a slow death by suffocation, to a painful and protracted death struggle—which may even have been part of the intention.

Anyway, it was usual for the friends and relatives of the condemned to gather at the execution and cling to the hanged man's body and legs to shorten the death struggle. Or the executioner often did it himself, out of compassion. But it might cause the rope to break, so that they'd have to start all over again.

We've had examples of hangings which were repeated several times. But these unsuccessful hangings or beheadings from earlier times are not what will occupy us today.

In 1793—during the Great Revolution—the guillotine was introduced as a symbol of the new era, to be sure an era of mass executions, but still the age of reason and humanity.

The ideal of our time is a fast, painless, and 100% effective execution.

It is the technical revolution on the scaffold.

Today we consider the following to be swift, painless and effective attempts at dispatching:

A) Shooting.
B) Hanging by the "long drop," in other words when the person falls from a height.
C) The guillotine, which swiftly severs the head from the body.
D) The electric chair.

Only a few relatively barbaric countries still hang people by stringing them up, or—as in Spain—suffocate them with the garotte, which means slowly screwing in an iron ring around the condemned person's neck. Otherwise we've gone over to shooting, the "long drop," the guillotine, and the electric chair.

Are these methods, so popular and respected today, and regarded as so humane—are these methods really fast, painless, and effective?

Are these methods sure?

After a long life in the service, after long personal practice, after studying the journals and visiting a number of countries and observing all these modern methods firsthand—with all this as background, ladies and gentlemen, I must disappoint you.

None of these methods of dispatch is sure.

I shall go through them point by point, the way they're practiced today in many countries—under extraordinary circumstances in *all* countries, almost without exception.

I shall describe them from the executioner's point of view.

But before we go on to this, we'll have some coffee and a couple of pieces of cake.

✧

In the intermission, just before the serving of coffee began, there were—as happens so often—a few seconds, perhaps a couple of minutes, of silence or soft conversation; then the cackling broke loose like a cloudburst, everybody cackled with everybody else. Still, there was one who drew the main interest, and that was al Assadun; he had received a happy communication, and it spread like fire in dry grass.

I've forgotten to tell that Harun-al-Rashid is married to a French girl, of the less Gallic, more Latin-rustic type; a round and luscious, black-haired Mediterranean thirty-year-old, intelligent and fat. During the first part of Lacroix's lecture she had given birth to a sound and healthy, well-formed French-Arab boy.

We were all delighted, and congratulated him—to which he responded in full seriousness by saying that it was Allah's will.

When the most noisy congratulations were over, and people had gathered around the cakes and coffee before the final part of Lacroix's remarks, Lefèvre clapped him on the shoulder, grinning at him with a friendly wink. As usual his cigarette hung almost vertically under his mustache.

"Harun-al-Rashid," said the physician-in-chief, "the fact that you've finally had a child must be regarded as a victory for your religion and as an enormous conquest of territory for gynecology: it's the definitive proof that anal coitus really *can* lead to conception. It's a rehabilitation for anal-eroticism in general, besides being a scientific novelty. It proves that you—as a *sal arabe*—are right: it is Islam and not Christianity which is the true religion."

al Assadun grinned his most lewd and frivolous boyish smile, then he said:

"I have always said that Allah is great. Even greater than you knew."

A moment afterwards Lefèvre was gone, and Harun and I stood there laughing.

Right beside us stood little Christine. Lacroix was on his way up to the lectern, and it became quiet in the hall once again.

I dreaded the rest of the lecture, because I knew it would be a strain—on *my* nerves, at any rate. Lacroix looked serious, but was calm.

"Come tonight!" I whispered to Christine.

She looked quickly around the hall, then she whispered back:

"I have to pass out a lot of ataraxic first—but I'll come afterwards. Just wait for me."

She sat down in her seat. I in mine. al Assadun remained standing by the door—with his grin.

MESSIEURS, MESDAMES, MESDEMOISELLES [began Lacroix]: I must ask your pardon for taking the liberty of starting the second part of this chat—I wouldn't call it anything else—with a digression. I entreat you from my heart to think about a couple of facts which I only touched on in the first part—namely, the many public executioners who have themselves been convicted of capital crimes, who have themselves committed deeds which qualified them for the total amputation which capital punishment, anatomically speaking, is. I would ask you to *think* about that.

The many executed executioners—I'll mention Friedrich and Meister Hans, the robber and murderer Gratwell, Derrick, Brandon, Price, Rose, Marwell, Thrift, Dennis, and Turlis—all were men who had seen and precisely observed the torments and agony of the death penalty at close quarters. *No one knew the horror of an execution better than these men.*

There's a common theory, ladies and gentlemen, about "the death penalty's deterrent effect." Almost all defenders of capital punishment build on this thought: the deterrent effect, the so-called "general-preventative consideration."

Who of all people should be more exposed to this general-preventative effect than these very colleagues of mine who have been the nearest witnesses of mutilations and the dread of death? Who should be more "deterred" by the example than precisely the executioner? Who should fear the scaffold and the gibbet more than the public executioner himself?

And what deterrent effect has it had to be the performer of maybe two to three thousand executions?

None, ladies and gentlemen, *none!*

The executed executioners' amputated corpses are the best historical and psychological *dis*proof of the punishment's general-preventative effect. When you've seen such things, or just *know* this—then your brain must have been ruined either by legal or theological studies if you're still enough of an imbecile to believe in the general-preventative effect.

The true effect is the opposite: the more brutal the punishment, the more brutal the crimes.

This was a digression, and I apologize for it. It isn't my task to propagandize for a different policy toward criminals; this evening my task is just to describe certain universal human customs and practices, seen from the standpoint of my own profession.

That was a digression.

But for me it was a necessary and justified one. And now to the matter at hand: the modern, humane, effective, lightning-fast, and painless executions which the Occident today is so proud of.

I intimated, before the break, that this humanization has been unsuccessful for various reasons.

These reasons are partly medical and technical—but also partly of a bureaucratic nature.

It may sound strange, but the purely formal and bureaucratic viewpoints play a major role here.

Nothing, ladies and gentlemen, *nothing* is easier for someone with skill and a knowledge of anatomy than to kill a man—even at my own advanced age—without instruments, with just one chop of the hand, painlessly and instantaneously. But that isn't permitted anywhere; everything must happen *ritually*. All executions are *ritual* executions. Everything must take place according to a formula established by the state—and it must be humane, effective, fast, and so forth—and the delinquent must be fully conscious, and in the best possible state of health besides—even with his teeth filled. Of course there's no such thing as a humane official execution—because, among other things, the delinquent must wait a considerable length of time for it to be carried out.

One could easily execute people humanely—simply by coming up from behind, wholly by surprise, and without the delinquent's having been informed of the sentence, and killing him on the spot with a reasonably powerful hammer. It's possible, ladies and gentlemen, to kill a horse with one single hammer stroke.

There's also the method, used during the earlier period of the great revolution in Russia, of shooting the condemned through the head from behind. They didn't let him—as they do in the Western countries—wait months or perhaps years for the moment of execution.

But this truly humane method is no punishment; it is simply the *liquidation* of a political opponent.

The forms which are used today are all intended as punishment, and even if we no longer quarter and burn our public enemies, we still see to it that the torture takes place mentally—through formalism, bureaucracy and long waiting periods.

To kill a person, from behind and by surprise, with a hammer—that is a method lacking all the sadistic elements which have been finely thought out and brought into civilized form by jurists, priests and statesmen.

Along with this we come up against the fact that almost none of the common civilized methods of execution is effective or fast. The rituals prevent it.

As a layman one would think, for example, that execution by firing squad was a fast and painless method of dispatch. A large number of men, all experienced marksmen, stand in formation in front of the condemned, who is now led forth by a priest and officers or prison officials to a post, where he is bound fast. Then a hood is drawn over his head. Usually a piece of white paper is fastened in front of the patient's heart. For those cases where the delinquent is unable to walk—the waiting time may have been very long, and a breakdown may have occurred—for such cases they have a long plank, a sort of stretcher, to which the person in question is tied—so that they can carry him or her to the post and there place both the plank and the condemned in a vertical position. Then preparations for firing are made. As everybody knows, four words of command are given—the last is *"fire!"* The condemned stands with the hood over his head, and he hears the guns being loaded and the words of command before the salvo comes.

They all aim at his heart—and the squad stands a significant number of yards from the subject.

But they are all experienced marksmen.

It turns out, however, and it has turned out again and again, that men may be able to shoot a dove in flight, but under these circumstances—when they're standing in front of a defenseless person and are supposed to fire—they absolutely *can't* shoot any longer. A marksman who with a pistol can hit an ace of hearts at fifty yards, will under these circumstances be capable of shooting completely wild, so that he doesn't even hit the target. Most commonly the result will be wounds in the stomach, chest, shoulders, neck—or even in the abdomen.

We have countless examples of this. It's part of the ritual that after the first salvo the doctor in attendance examines the executed person with a stethoscope. If he's still alive, they load and aim and fire again. Not seldom has it happened that even experienced marksmen, and soldiers psychologically trained for the front, have had to load and fire up to four or five salvos before death occurs—and then it's often due to bleeding from the many superficial gunshot wounds.

A person who is executed in this manner no longer looks like a person who has been shot, but like one butchered bloody lump hanging from the ropes which hold him fast to the post or to the planks he was carried in on.

His trousers and shoes are full of running blood, and the ground under him is likewise colored red.

As a classic in this connection we can look at the historic execution of the Tyrolean hero of freedom Andreas Hofer, in which Hofer himself finally called out to the squad, "Oh, how badly you shoot!" This is no rarity, but rather the rule with the firing squad; we have records of cases where it took more than fifty shots to remove life and consciousness from the subject. Thus "execution by firing squad" becomes—just like the old executions by sword—a slow butchering of the condemned.

According to the American Army instruction manual, the sequence "clear," "ready," "aim," "fire!"—followed by reloading of the guns and repetition of the ritual and the salvo— shall continue right up until the staff doctor has pronounced the person clinically dead.

The reasons for these difficulties in taking the life of the condemned are twofold:

A) The nervousness which grips the members of the squad, and the resulting uncertainty of aim which this produces.

B) The bureaucratic stipulation that the distance between the delinquent and the squad shall amount to at least twenty yards.

The autopsy after the famous American execution of the American private Edward D. Slovik—which took place not far from our own district, in Ste. Marie-Aux-Mines in Les Vosges—showed that all of the squad's eleven bullets had struck the body, but not one had hit the subject's heart; the bullets were lodged in his neck, upper arm, shoulders, and chest. He died from loss of blood.

Most of you here will certainly recognize this historically interesting landscape, of uncommon natural beauty.

However, we won't dwell any longer on the firing squad as a method of execution; it still gives an all too idyllic picture of what happens with the other modern executions.

It can be much more unpleasant to attend modern hangings—the scientific "long drop"; in practice the method is hardly better than the old-fashioned stringing up.

To the "long drop" belongs the trap door, which opens mechanically when the delinquent, with the hood over his head, hands tied behind him and feet bound together, is placed on it. It's astonishing how often the mechanism fails and the bolts get stuck, so that the attempt must be repeated several times. A certain Englishman by the name of—if I remember rightly—Lee, had to go out on the trap three times before it finally worked.

Another weakness of the "long drop" is that if the height of fall is too great, the delinquent can have his whole head torn off—which may not be so bad for the person himself, but which comes as a shock to all the invited witnesses, lawyers, clergymen, and so on, and is of course an extremely unaesthetic sight.

Hence for the executioner, hanging by the "long drop" is an unusually taxing and demanding process.

Here there are two schools, the English—which places the knot under the left mandible, in front of the ear—and the American, which places the knot behind the left ear.

Both have the aim of overstretching the cervical vertebrae so that the spinal cord will be crushed or torn off. They likewise produce a highly peculiar elongation of the neck.

This is the ideal hanging, which one always aims for; but medical postmortem examinations have shown that this ideal is in actual fact a rarity, and that most people die of strangulation or of ordinary slow suffocation—with the result that the delinquent remains hanging alive on the rope for at least a quarter of an hour.

When this happens, it's not uncommon for the public executioner and his assistants to betake themselves down to the chamber under the trap door, where they hang on the hanged man's back as in the old days, in an attempt to shorten the time of suffocation.

The hangman's technical problem is as follows: he isn't permitted to let the subject fall so far that the head is torn off as a result, since this means a mutilation of the corpse. He mustn't let the condemned fall too short a distance either, since this leads to slow suffocation.

For this reason tables have been worked out for weight and the length of the rope; but in the last analysis they can't be followed automatically because of the condemned's individual neck musculature. So the executioner must have an opportunity in advance to observe and assess his client individually, so that afterwards, with his experience and skill, he can give the rope exactly the right number of inches in length of drop.

This sizing up of the delinquent takes place through an invisible hole in the wall or door, giving the hangman an opportunity for accurate study and evaluation of the relationship between the prisoner's weight and neck musculature.

Yet other problems can further complicate the proceedings—such as when the condemned can't manage to stand up, or faints, and may have to be placed sitting in a chair on the trap door itself. Very often the feeling of the rope being suddenly placed around one's neck will produce such a strong shock that the bowels empty automatically and the urinary sphincter relaxes as well. This happens in any case with the jerk of the rope after the drop, and the smell of excrement can then become so offensive that it puts a further burden on the executioner's nerves and precision and calm.

When it comes to hanging ladies, the use of waterproof underpants of rubber or plastic has been introduced long since.

A further nuisance for the hangman is that even in the happy cases where vertebral fracture does occur, the deceased's heart will usually continue to beat for considerably more than half an hour.

In all cases they let the body hang—for technical reasons— for at least an hour.

However, the arrival of the moment of death can take highly individual forms. A funny and instructive example may be drawn from the record concerning the hanged murderer Takacs, who in Germany was taken down after only ten minutes on the rope. When Takacs was brought in for autopsy, he came to himself again about half an hour later, at first only halfway to consciousness, but fully alive. The interesting thing about Takacs was that he lived for three whole days after the hanging. He then eventually died from accumulations of blood and fluid in his lungs.

We have a disconcerting example from England in the hanging, well known to everybody in the field, of Mrs. Anne

Green. Mrs. Green was taken down after half an hour's hanging, and then came to her senses after the execution. In the
course of the half hour she hung on the rope they did their
utmost to shorten the death struggle—they hung on her legs,
struck her with full force on the breast and even lifted her up
several times, so as then to pull her down with their combined strength. When they laid her in the coffin, however, it
was obvious that she was still breathing; and one of those present, a strong and burly man, sprang on top of her and trampled and jumped with all his might on Anne Green's stomach
and chest, to end her sufferings.

Mrs. Green survived nonetheless, was treated by doctors,
and in later life is supposed to have had four children.

From prominent and highly reliable medical experts the
archives have acquired written observations of an often disconcerting sort—such as when the hanged person begins
coughing during the funeral and thus dies a second time of
suffocation under the earth.

A case from the city of Boston in our beloved USA offers
us a highly impressive, accurate record. The subject had been
hanged at ten o'clock in the morning, with a drop of almost
eight feet. Seven minutes after the hanging the doctors
recorded one hundred heartbeats a minute, two minutes later
ninety-eight beats, and three minutes after that, sixty beats.
After another two minutes the heart was still.

After a total of forty minutes they took the hanged man
down from the gallows. One hour and thirty minutes after
the execution the heart began to beat again; this time they
measured twenty-four beats a minute. Out of pure scientific
interest the doctors now opened the pectoral cavity of the
formerly deceased and observed regular heartbeats, and
even two hours after the hanging they still measured forty
beats a minute in the open chest cavity. After three hours
the rate had sunk to five beats, and only at two o'clock, i.e.
four hours after the moment of death, was the dead man
dead. He died, that is, of loss of blood occasioned by the fact
that they performed the autopsy while he was still alive—so

that this time the doctors finished the hangman's work.

The hangings after the War Crimes Trials in Nuremberg are notorious: there was one accident after another. Part of the explanation for this may have been—purely psychologically—the executioner's own highly peculiar fate. Working on the executions in Nuremberg was the *same* man who with such great efficiency and loyalty had performed public executions (chiefly by the guillotine, but also by hanging) all through Germania's happy Teutonic period, so beloved of the people—during all the blessed years between 1933 and 1945: my eminently effective, but also deeply humane and highly sensitive colleague, Jean-Baptiste Reichart, who today of all his professional colleagues (I don't mean mass murderers of the vulgar sort) most likely has the longest execution list in the world—a total of 3,010 personally performed. Jean-Baptiste (or in his own lingo *Johann der Täufer*, in Italian *Giovanni Battista*—in other words, "John the Baptist") was a symbolic name; if one regards death as a transition from one state to another, and thus as a kind of *baptism*, then this John the Baptist may have baptized more people with his guillotine than any priest with his baptismal font. Ladies and gentlemen, note the following:

Jean-Baptiste Reichart, the last scion of a dynasty of executioners more than two hundred years old: it was Jean-Baptiste Reichart's fate, after having executed thousands and thousands of fascism's opponents on commission from the Third Reich's great and beloved leaders—finally, *in his last action as executioner, to execute his old taskmasters!* He has since retired to the peace of private life and is now happily and contentedly pursuing the activity which always lay closest to his heart: a kennel, a dog farm, the raising of purebred animals.

It also sheds a peculiar psychopathological gleam of light on the victors of the last war that they unhesitatingly took over Hitler's, Streicher's, Goebbels', and Göring's loyal executioner—not only to perform executions himself, but also to serve as teacher and instructor to the American executioner Sergeant Wood.

How many were dispatched during this Teutonic golden age is something for which there naturally are no figures; but if you leave out the millions of Jews and such dispatched with Zyklongas from I. G. Farben Industries, you have at any rate around 50,000 *legal* death sentences, pronounced by honest and proper, legally qualified judges—local politicians—some of whom are performing their duties to this very day, just as Jean-Baptiste performed his duties in the service of the Allied victors.

Of course, Reichart himself executed only a fraction—in other words 3010 personal executions in all—and so can't compare with the jurists. Besides, Reichart was really a man of much more sensitivity and delicacy than judges by and large are.

From the foregoing you will have gotten the idea that even a form of hanging which uses the most modern techniques by no means fulfills our expectations of the "long drop." The method is anything but sure. A classic trait of all modern, humanized methods of dispatch—except for the guillotine—is that a large hood is always drawn over the delinquent's head and face, so that the latter is totally hidden. Many laymen have the impression that this part of the ritual is due to consideration for the subject, so that he or she will be spared seeing with his or her own eyes the very last preparations for what is going to be done to the person in question.

That, however, is not the case.

They hide the face out of consideration for the witnesses, for the guests who must always, even at "secret" executions, be present by law to testify that justice was done. Even the academics present—clergy, lawyers, and doctors—are made the objects of this consideration.

What the executioner sees when the hood is taken off a hanged man is a sight which human eyes ought to be spared—the color of the face, from violet to blue-black; the eyes pressed almost all the way out of their sockets; the tongue sticking black and swollen out of the mouth. On top of all this, if the relationship between body weight, neck musculature, and the number of inches of rope has been miscalculated, the skin and flesh will have been torn from the neck and face as well. Then if you take into account the smell, this strange, peculiar stink of blood, along with the odors of the urine and rectal contents filling the pants and shoes—and if on top of that you realize how often the executioner and his assistants must hang on the hanged man's back, or pull on his arms and legs with all their might in order to put an end to the strangulation, then you get a picture of the "unusual qualities" an executioner must possess. Add to this the fact that many of the great executioners themselves haven't chosen this profession of their own free will, but are forced into it by the family's fate, and that choice is nonexistent.

Before we leave the subject of modern hanging, I'd like to mention briefly a variant which was invented and practiced by the great Josef Lang in Vienna—who in his time was regarded as the world's best hangman. He used a method which completely lacked a "long drop," but which quickly produced unconsciousness in the client. He bound him with a rope around his neck to an erect post, positioned the rope very carefully and fastened it to a bolt on the back of the post.

At a prearranged signal the assistants would grab hold of the delinquent, hang on to him and pull him downwards with a force of several hundred pounds. This produced a mixture of the suffocation and strangulation methods: the main arteries were closed fairly quickly, and at the same time the supply of oxygen was cut off—so that the consciousness which had been extinguished by the strangling couldn't return, because of the lack of oxygen. Josef Lang performed these executions without putting a hood over the condemned man's head; from the color of the face he could thus observe the exact moment, first of unconsciousness and then of death.

An older variant of this is the far less pleasant garotte, an instrument which in our time is or has been used only in Spain and in certain Latin American countries—among others in Cuba, where it is now supposed to have been abolished—

and in the Philippines. In Spain it is still in use. The garotte is a chair with a high back, and through this back, at neck height, is bored a hole. Through the hole and around the delinquent's neck is passed a cord or metal wire, which is then tightened by a simple mechanism so that the larynx is crushed and the windpipe blocked. Today there are technical improvements which comprise almost a quadruple execution: two iron rings around the delinquent's neck are moved in opposite directions, so that the cervical vertebrae are broken, the veins blocked, and the oxygen supply cut off; at the same time a sharp knife is introduced between the cervical vertebrae, severing the main nerve between head and body. It goes without saying that out of consideration for the attendant theologians and jurists the operation is undertaken with a hood over the head of the condemned.

Through the ages an astonishing amount of acumen and industry has been invested in developing the different execution machines and methods.

It was thought that a new era in the history of the art of execution was being ushered in with Dr. Guillotine's invention, as designed by Dr. Louis in the year 1792 on a commission from the French National Assembly, and executed by the eminent (Teutonic) piano maker and performing musician Tobias Schmidt—a notable interpreter of Bach.

I won't discuss the construction of this unusual machine here, since it's all too familiar. But the main idea is that the heavy blade, sharp as a razor and with a weight of around a hundred pounds, swiftly and painlessly severs the head from the body without the slightest chance of accident.

According to all the theories, the separation of head from body was supposed to result in an immediate lowering of the blood pressure in the brain, thereby producing instant unconsciousness.

It has turned out that none of this is correct.

It once happened to my honored colleague, Jean-Baptiste Reichart, that the blade got stuck a few inches above the delinquent's head and stayed there while the latter shouted that he was innocent, that the accident was God's will. However, God's will expressed itself only once; the operation was repeated, this time successfully. But Meister Reichart suffered from nervous disturbances for a long time.

Still, technical accidents are so rare with this machine that in practice they don't play any role.

The following is far more serious (and here I shall quote a prominent Russian researcher, Dr. Vladimir Aleksandrovich Negovsky of the Resuscitation Laboratory in Moscow):

He assumes that the brain, when cut off from its oxygen supply, resorts to an emergency system for breaking down sugar for energy production by anaerobic glycolysis, and that *"this works for five or six minutes. We must hope that the brain in a severed head, like the brain of a hanged person, isn't fully conscious."* I don't know whether Negovsky has also concerned himself with hanging.

The medical concern with consciousness in the newly beheaded has existed for a long time, however—i.e. ever since the introduction of the guillotine. Doctors, at least, have been performing experiments for over 150 years—beginning, naturally enough, in our beautiful and beloved France.

These experiments were begun so early because of the violent grimaces made by the severed head in the basket, along with the almost unbelievably severe convulsions and movements which the body exhibited for an astonishingly long time after the execution. The surprising display of life on the part of the beheaded was difficult for the observers to reconcile with Dr. Guillotine's theory of instant and painless death.

The beheading of the renowned Charlotte Corday—after she had murdered Marat because of his responsibility for the Jacobin Club's illustrious "September massacres"—attracted particular notice. When Monsieur de Paris had completed the operation, his assistant lifted Mlle. Corday's head up out of the basket to show it to the howling mob gathered around the scaffold. To demonstrate his patriotic feelings the republican didn't content himself with swinging the head before the grateful populace, but struck the severed head forcefully on the cheek.

What happened next was observed without exception by everyone in the immediate vicinity of the guillotine:

Charlotte Corday's face reddened, not just on the one cheek which had been struck by the blow, but on both cheeks, and showed unmistakable signs of anger and contempt.

In this connection I shall allow myself to mention that for a man of my profession this isn't something one jokes about or speaks of lightly. I beg you—I *beg* you, ladies and gentlemen!—to listen to this as something which I am able to speak about openly and publicly only with the very greatest self-command—even if I won't go so far as my highly esteemed colleague Mr. Pierrepoint, who made the following declaration to none other than the British Royal Commission on Capital Punishment: "I refuse to talk about it. It's something I feel ought to be my own secret. *It is truly holy for me.*" I myself am *willing* to talk about it, but I don't do so frivolously, and not without deep inner agitation.

After Mlle. Corday's severed head, held by the hair, had shown these signs of indignation and distinct consciousness, one of those present, an experienced official, made the following note: "Long after Mlle. Charlotte Corday's head was separated from her body, it betrayed an expression of unmistakable indignation. *Both* cheeks were red. . . . One can't deal with this by claiming that the slap produced the reddening, for one can't produce this effect by slapping a dead person on the cheeks; the dead never blush. Besides, the slap only hit one cheek, and still the other cheek reddened as well. . . . "

From the guillotine's halcyon days in Gaul, in the days of public mass executions, reports abound of how the heads of the executed, as they were ritually lifted up and shown forth to the mob, showed clear signs of *contempt for the people*; it is also often related that they even moved their mouths and eyes—usually in a not very democratic manner.

As noted, doctors have been continually occupied with the question, and one of the last investigations was carried out in Paris in 1956 by Drs. Piedlièvre and Fournier, both of them scientists and medical men above all suspicion, especially chosen and commissioned by the French Academy of Medicine to do this research on totally fresh corpses. Their investigation of the guillotined persons ends with the words: ". . . . A dreadful spectacle. The blood streams out of the vessels in the same rhythm as the severed arteries, after which it runs smoothly. The muscles contract, and the cramps are horrifying; the entrails are exposed to wavelike convulsions, and the heart contracts in irregular, astonishing movements. The mouth is distorted into horrible grimaces for several moments. It's true that when the head is severed from the body the eyes have dilated pupils, but they don't move; fortunately they are without a look, but even if they lack the sheen of death—in other words, are not glazed—still they don't move any longer. In their transparency they're alive, in their immobility they're dead. This can last for minutes, in really healthy persons *even for hours: death never occurs immediately*. Every single vital part survives decapitation. For a doctor what remains is purely and simply the impression of a gruesome experiment, a horrible vivisection, followed by a premature burial."

It wasn't the first time the two physicians, Dr. Piedlièvre and Dr. Fournier, had seen people die.

I know myself from my own experience and observation that the headless body usually moves for hours after being laid in the coffin. The state of the head has been experimentally investigated many times, and the results have often been more depressing than what Dr. Negovsky at the laboratory in Moscow expressly gives the form of a *hope*: namely that the head isn't *fully* conscious.

If one exposes the severed head to strong stimuli, sensory impressions or direct irritation of the spinal cord, the picture becomes very different. Here it must be stated, however, that there is one single, well-defined experiment which has never been carried out by modern medical men: that of stopping the bleeding from both head and neck, so as to measure how long the beheaded will then continue to show signs of life.

Only in the Renaissance was this done. At the same time it must be mentioned that in Germany all medical experiments with executed persons—because of the disquieting nature of the results—have been forbidden since the last century.

I shall mention, however—in the form of a quote—some of the results which were achieved. First there were the experiments performed by the physician Dr. Wendt and several professional colleagues, among them the surgeons Illing and Hanisch—along with a merchant named Otto, whose task was to time the different observations made of the beheaded, whose name was *Troer*. I quote an excerpt: ". . . . I observed the executed man's face sharply, and was unable to discover the least distortion; the face was utterly at peace, the eyes open and clear, the mouth closed; not a feature of the face could have disclosed the condition in which the unfortunate's head—through separation from the body—had been placed. . . . I moved my fingertips rapidly toward the open eyes, and this unfortunate head tried to protect itself against the danger which threatened its eyes by lowering the lids. . . . Herr Illing lifted up the head and turned the face toward the sun, which was shining directly on us, and in the same second the head closed its eyes. . . . To determine whether the organs of hearing were likewise still functioning, I twice shouted the name 'Troer' in a loud voice into the ear of the unlucky head. . . and after each shout the now-closed eyes opened and turned in the direction whence the sound came, and at the same time the mouth opened. . . which some will interpret as an attempt to speak. . . . Now I touched the severed spinal cord with a pin, and the expressions on the beheaded's face were so remarkable that several of those present cried: 'This is life!'—and I myself burst out, fully convinced: 'If this isn't life and feeling, what is?' For when I irritated the spinal chord, he closed his eyes in a spasm, clenched his teeth, and the cheek muscles were drawn up with a jerk toward the lower eyelids."

The year after this report—written out and witnessed by several impartial medical men, and also by the honest merchant Herr Otto—all research of this type was forbidden in Germany.

But in France it continued.

In *Archives d'antropologie criminelle* one can find an experiment from 1905, concerning the beheaded M. Languille, performed and described by Dr. Beaurieux. It is clear, intelligible, and entirely meets the present-day requirements for observations laying claim to the rank of a phenomenon. Dr. Beaurieux writes:

"The head fell down, landing on the cut-off neck surface. . . . The accident helped me with the observations I wished to make.

". . . . The eyelids and lips of the guillotined man moved in irregular jerks for around five or six seconds. This phenomenon has been observed by all who have pursued, under the same conditions as I, what happens after the severing of the neck. . . . I waited a few seconds. The spasmodic twitches stopped. The face became calm, the eyelids closed halfway. . . .

"Then I shouted in a loud, sharp voice: '*Languille!*' I saw how the eyes slowly opened, without any spasmodic contraction—this fact I intentionally underscore—but with a calm, perfectly clear and normal movement, such as one experiences every day when people are awakened from sleep or from their own thoughts. At the same time Languille's eyes fixed very decidedly on my own, and the pupils contracted. It wasn't a vague, expressionless look I met, the kind one recognizes in the dying when one talks to them; those were undoubtedly living eyes which looked at me.

"After a few seconds the eyes closed again, slowly and naturally, and the face took on the same expression as before I spoke to him.

"Then I shouted at him again, and again the eyes opened slowly and without jerking, and two eyes—which without a doubt were alive—stared fixedly at me, and even more piercingly than the first time. And again they closed, this time not all the way. I made a new attempt; there was no reaction; the eyes had the glassy expression with which one is familiar in the dead. . . . The whole process took between twenty-five and thirty seconds."

And so, ladies and gentlemen, we must reckon—that is to say: we must assume—that for awhile after the separation from the body the beheaded is still able to observe and understand his own gruesome state.

All this is part of the culture we live in—I would say the *Christian* culture, in symbiosis with the scientific.

Of course, there is an endless amount of far more drastic material written down about these things, not least from earlier times; but I have chosen to keep strictly to things which can be subjected to control by the experimental methods which we regard today as methodologically tenable—and also to avoid descriptions of a shocking and sensational nature.

From my personal viewpoint, that of the public executioner, none of these medical and scientific observations contains anything new; all these details are things which every headsman is familiar with from his own experience.

For many of us this eventually becomes a great strain on the nerves.

Of the other methods of dispatch practiced today, we should also mention the gas chamber, which is employed particularly in the U.S. It has its origin in the renowned Venetian "lead chambers"—but I shall bypass execution with gas here, because it awakens emotional side issues which don't pertain to the case, inasmuch as this method of execution has been burdened with the role of I. G. Farben Industries and the German National Socialist Party during the Teutonic golden age in the fourth and fifth decades of our own century.

Of greater immediate interest is the method which is widespread over great parts of the USA—electrocution, popularly known as execution by the "electric chair."

It must be regarded as the least reliable, the slowest, and certainly the most painful method of execution in common use today.

Technically the explanation lies in the following:

Nothing is easier than to dispatch a person instantaneously and painlessly with electric current; at a tension of
10,000 volts hardly any human creature will even know
what's happening. But 10,000 volts leave behind a charred,
stinking lump of flesh, and that isn't the intention.

What is desired—as befits a culture which is, above all,
hygienic—is pretty and well groomed, presentable corpses
after an electrocution; not least because of the journalists,
jurists, priests, and parish council members who are present.
Preferably no burn marks.

This isn't new. Ever since the abolition of public, aggravated capital punishment, *consideration for those present* has
been of great significance. The delinquent is also counted as
being among those present—and likewise society itself,
although the latter must be regarded as being present only in
spirit, represented by its pillars. Unnecessary evils, of both an
aesthetic and a moral nature, are to be avoided; this has
meant consideration for the person carrying out the death
sentence (the executioner), for the soon-to-be-departed's sur-
vivors, for the witnesses, and for society as a moral whole. In
German regions this was already fixed by law at the beginning of the previous century.

Consideration for the delinquent meant:

Certainty, speed, ease—in other words, not protracted
agony. We're familiar with this in practice.

For family and children:

That the sentence should be carried out without exces-
sive severity, and in a manner which was not unnecessarily
ignominious.

Consideration for the executioner:

That his position as an honorable citizen of the state
should not be tainted to an unnecessary degree.

Consideration for the witnesses:

That the execution should not have an unnecessarily
depressing effect, or by its harshness be harrowing to their
sensibilities; that the chosen means of dispatch should not be
immoral, or offend the witnesses' feelings.

Consideration for the invisibly present State:

That the execution—especially in countries ennobled by Christianity—should eschew forms of punishment which could seem like acts of revenge rather than the exercise of justice; therefore mutilations were to be avoided. The corpse must—in Christianity's domains—look as *beautiful* as possible.

This is the problem with the electric chair: to produce a well-groomed, soigné corpse, without visible traces of the slaughter.

This requirement places the American executioner, the "State Electrician," in a professional situation of boundless difficulty, because a well-groomed corpse—in other words, not a burned-up, stinking pork roast—presupposes that the subject has been dispatched by minimal current.

However, each person's power of resistance to the current is of an amazingly *individual* sort.

So you begin with a relatively low voltage, and if that doesn't suffice, you increase it. If that doesn't suffice, the voltage is increased again and again, until consciousness is gone, and thereafter until death has occurred. Frying must be avoided at any cost.

The autopsy takes place immediately, in order to avoid awakening on the part of the dead.

You usually start with a tension of about 1700 volts. Generally speaking, people faint from that—or at any rate many lose consciousness at a current of this strength.

The electric chair is, as you know, an American invention, and is therefore preferred for nationalistic reasons. Because of the procedure's uncertainty, painfulness, and long duration, practically no other country has adopted it. Formosa is almost the only one. In many states in the U.S. they've retained hanging for humane reasons—despite the fact that one of the reasons for constructing a new, national apparatus for taking lives was that so many executioners could no longer stand to carry out a hanging.

The State Electrician's dreadful task is to determine a voltage which will have a swiftly numbing effect, and thereafter a

lower tension which will kill slowly—since above all the delinquent mustn't catch fire and die of self-ignition. There's a tendency to start with too low a voltage.

From a purely technical standpoint electrocution is monstrously simple; the criminal (or more correctly: the *condemned*;
time has shown that just in recent decades a disconcerting
number of innocent persons have been executed)—the condemned is placed in a wooden chair and carefully bound fast
to it with leather straps around his chest, stomach, neck, arms,
and legs. His crown is shaven, and one electrode is fastened to
his head, the other to one of his ankles—both electrodes moist-
ened with salt water to insure good contact and the lowest possible resistance, and to hinder combustion. A leather mask is
now drawn over the delinquent's head, to prevent the witnesses from observing his face during the execution.

Now that the moment of truth has arrived, the current is
turned on and off at varying strengths until death has occurred.
This is repeated until the attendant physician can ascertain with
his stethoscope that the heart has stopped beating.

When the switch is turned on, the body immediately
arches as if to burst the leather straps which hold it fast.
Under the leather helmet—or mask—smoke issues from the
electrode which is in contact with the scalp. This is accompanied by a faint odor of burnt meat. The hands first become
red, then white, and the tendons and muscles and veins in the
neck stand out like steel wires. This is an American executioner's description of a successful normal execution.

The subject doesn't catch fire—but the length of time
before death occurs is highly variable. The same applies to
the point at which consciousness is lost. That this is a significant burden on the electrician's nerves goes without saying.
As executioner he knows that the physiological power of
resistance is much greater in some persons than in others.

Thus the method reminds one very much of the original
French electro-interrogation method, except that the electrodes
are placed differently—not in the sex organs, but around the
ankle and on the crown. Of course the purpose is different,

and the voltage is different; besides, an American electric treatment will seldom be of the same duration as a French one—although today, of course, the Americans have taken over the French method of interrogating political dissenters.

By way of introduction I've mentioned a perfectly successful electrocution—of the ideal type, where the frying doesn't take more than from six or seven to ca. thirty minutes.

As an example of the opposite—*"aller Anfang ist schwer"*— we can mention the very first execution in the chair, which was carried out in New York at the end of the last century. The murderer was named William Kemmler. The reactions produced by both witnesses and photographs of the execution were almost enough to abolish electrocution. It proved to be almost impossible to finish Kemmler off.

We're even better informed about the execution of the murderer White. They sat him in the chair and turned on 1150 volts. That didn't work at all, and White's heart beat at its usual speed. They repeated the experiment with increased voltage. Still with no result. In his despair, the executioner now set the tension up to almost 4000 volts, with the result that White caught fire. Flames arose from all over his body, and the room was filled with the loathsome stink of seared meat. Only several minutes later did the executioner dare to turn off the current. By then White was dead not of electric shock, but of the heat. They could just as well have roasted him on a spit.

The odor—and everyone agrees on this—the odor of all executions of this kind is reminiscent of roast pork.

In U.S. criminal jargon, in fact, they just use the word "burn": you're going to *burn*.

It's also true that, even without visible burning or combustion, the body temperature rises enormously; in the brains of the electrocuted, temperatures have been measured at over 140 F. There was an odd case in Texas in 1938, where the power failed after the delinquent had taken his place in the chair. For three hours he stood and watched while they tried to repair the apparatus, but it wasn't until several days later that he could take his place anew. This time to everyone's satisfaction.

Far more frequent than technical surprises are the physiological deviations in the delinquents—some have a preternatural power of resistance to electric current, which the State Electrician naturally can't know about in advance. (There he is handicapped in comparison with the Hangman.)

A peculiar example can be taken from the Ohio State Penitentiary in the year 1904, where we meet the murderer Michael Skiller.

Skiller was placed in the chair and received a current of 1700 volts through him for several seconds; he seemed numbed at first, but then he emitted a series of horrible shrieks of pain. He was now fully conscious.

While he waited in the chair for the next treatment, they raised the current to 1900 volts—which had exactly the same effect on Skiller: he again emitted the same wild screams of pain, until the executioner shut off the current. When it proved to be impossible to drive the tension higher than 1900 volts, they turned it on for the third time, and this time they left the current on for fully fifteen minutes—that is, right up until Skiller no longer either screamed nor breathed.

Possibly even more astonishing was the execution of a certain Mrs. Judd. She made her entrance among priests, journalists, doctors, lawyers, and prison folk, trying to look unconcerned by smiling a sincerely meant, "brave" smile. The smile is supposed to have had a dreadful effect on the onlookers, who saw only a deathly scared grimace. She wanted to say a few words, but only brought forth a wild shriek of terror. When she had been securely buckled in and they were pulling the black cap over her head, she cried with all her strength a long, despairing "Mother!"

When they turned on the current, she raised herself with superhuman strength halfway up in the chair, as she was tossed back and forth by the current raging through her body. She didn't lose consciousness for a moment.

The poor executioner now increased the current all the way to 2000 volts, but without producing any other effect than the first time. This now lasted for several minutes, but even a full 2000 volts raging through her wasn't enough to render her unconscious. Much less kill her.

She was then—after many, many minutes' electrocution—unharnessed and taken back to her cell.

Only after the technicians had worked for over an hour to raise the voltage—but not by so much as to risk a complete grilling, with the attendant self-ignition—only then was the woman dragged back to the chair. This time she is supposed to have put up a direct resistance against the prison guards, and also to have used improper language.

Even now, with this greatly increased voltage, it took several minutes before death occurred.

Of another electrocuted person, a certain "Fred," it is recorded that when they opened him for the autopsy he woke up, and his heart was still beating, so they brought the opened corpse back to the chair and executed the corpse anew.

Otherwise the American regulations are very logical: in the morgue—the next room—the executed must be opened immediately, and to such a degree that "it prevents any return to life."

Thus the doctors become the real public executioners.

Messieurs and mesdames, mesdemoiselles!

Finally, I would like to mention—to bring the executioner's viewpoint sufficiently into the picture—that in our profession, as in all other fields, we have our *occupational diseases.* Our occupational diseases are mental illness and suicide. *No other job category in the world has such a high suicide rate as we public executioners.*

I would ask you to think about that. I would ask you to think about the fate of our dynasties, to think about a certain Anatole Deibler who tried to flee from his family's fate. This professional fate of ours includes every disintegration of the human mind, from almost harmless psychoneuroses to psychoses and to the suicide which is the end of everything.

I can mention a colleague I myself esteemed highly, who always surrounded himself with a cloud of unbearably strong perfume of a certain brand—because he could never get rid of the smell of blood, this piercing and inescapable odor which produces nausea, vomiting, and other digestive troubles. I can also name my poor French colleague, Louis Deibler—of the Deibler dynasty, of course—who during an unlucky execution was drenched with a jet of blood six feet high, a veritable fountain of blood, which hit him with full force. He subsequently became possessed by a washing mania which never again left him any peace: he walked around his own home in despair, begging his wife and children to assure him that the blood spots weren't visible on his hands. The well-known, able public executioner in Munich, Herr Scheller, died incurably insane. The same goes for his Russian colleague Pilipiev.

Even the darling of Vienna, the eminent and popular Josef Lang, known as "Pepi," executed himself in 1936—despite his harmonious, benevolent, and cheerful disposition. The same "Pepi" who was pursued by almost all the women in Vienna, from prostitutes to judges' wives, from criminals to noblewomen and young ladies from the highest strata of society— even Josef Lang killed himself.

The unfortunate "State Electrician" Hilbert in New York was also a man with the very best of nerves, a powerful, healthy person—who finally went berserk in the execution room and started throwing the high-voltage electrodes around; who gradually became prey to terrible depressions; who refused to follow the prison director's orders; and who, in addition, showed the paranoid trait that he constantly believed he was being poisoned by his enemies. His doctor strongly advised him not to continue in his job, but he was unable to do anything else or to adjust to any other milieu, nor could he resist the terrible attraction of his profession as electrician. He returned to death row and the electrodes—he followed his fate—and he drained the cup to the bottom. Before one of his last electrocutions this big, strong man completely collapsed physically and was seized in the execution room itself with the most violent attack of rage. But still he continued to perform his work, until a certain day when nine men were sitting and waiting for their last hour; *nine men* were sitting on death row and waiting for Hilbert. Suddenly Hilbert took his leave, left the condemned sitting there, and went home to his own house and shot himself in the cellar.

The English public executioner Billington also broke with his profession one day, and killed first his whole family—and then himself.

The German executioner Julius Krautz slew his assistant one day, was sentenced to the penitentiary, and killed himself in prison.

The despairing, unhappy Paul Späthe spent the last part of his life burning a wax candle for every soul he had dispatched—after which he himself died by his own hand.

The dreadful, macabre, and unsuccessful hanging of Mrs. Thompson in England led the famous executioner John Ellis—a barber by trade—to make an unsuccessful suicide attempt shortly after the woman's grotesque dispatch; and somewhat later he carried the suicide through, by cutting his throat with his razor. The poor German executioner Schweitz shot himself in Breslau.

Just as one could prolong the list of unsuccessful executions, so one could likewise endlessly prolong the list of public executioners who fell by their own hand. Here I've only mentioned relatively well-known names—names of outstanding, able, and great executioners.

I beg you to think about this.

Who has made us suicides, ladies and gentlemen?

I beg you in God's name to understand that even the public executioner deserves the same compassion as any other suffering and unhappy human being.

I beg you to understand that we are installed in our offices by kings and by princes, by popes, cardinals, bishops, and princes of the church; we are installed in our offices by city councils, by governments, and by members of parliament; we are installed by ministers of justice, we receive our commissions from politicians and ministers of justice—and we are paid by you who pay the taxes for the state's exercise of its sovereign power. For what does the word "sovereign" mean in its full and complete meaning? That a state is "sovereign" means that it has the power to take lives.

So I beg you, I entreat you, to understand one single thing: We, the public executioners, we are humankind's deputies. We stand in the penitent's cape before the incomprehensible universe. We, executioners and suicides, have borne the burden of the whole human race's guilt and sin—the guilt for the permanent witchhunt.

And we bear this guilt until we go to our deaths with it.

It's not just the lowest functions of society we've had to perform, in earlier times as "night-men"—as the sanitation workers who rid the cities of their physical excrement, the stinking contents of their bellies.

We've also been the great deliverers who relieved society of its own stinking spiritual essence—relieved the state of the stinking moral content of its soul, worse than any excrement from any bowel. We've taken over society's rotten conscience.

We—the few hundred members of Europe's executioner-dynasties—we stand guilty on everyone's behalf, on behalf of the human race, guilty before God. We are guilty by proxy. That blood is on our heads. Burdened with all humanity's brutality and heartlessness, all its boundless evil and sin, we stand before an either/or: before the empty, lifeless cosmos—or before God, who must judge us.

I've already said the following: People think of the judge, they think of the jurors, they think of the relatives, of the priest, of the doctor, they think of society—and they even think of the condemned.

Who thinks of the executioner?

It isn't my task to bring up for discussion the question of the death penalty's function, or the function of punishment in general. I belong to society's executive organs, not to its legislative ones: *you* belong to the latter, ladies and gentlemen, not I.

So I want, in all simplicity, without drawing any conclusions, without the slightest attempt to answer the questions which a causerie of this type may have awakened in thoughtful persons—I want to do something entirely different in conclusion.

I want—like the previous speaker—simply to stress the fact that we live here, on a (relatively speaking) infinitely thin crust of green and moist earth, filled with peaches, stinging nettles, animals, and people; we live on this thin, thin crust—with liquid, seething minerals right under us and with the dead, deathly cold, lifeless universe, meaninglessly idiotic in every way, above us. The fire under us, the cold of death above us.

And on this beautiful, fruitful, moist green crust which is given to us to live on, we've slaughtered, massacred, and tortured each other for so long as history can tell.

Why in God's name do we *hate* each other so terribly?

Here my own thoughts stop, and likewise here ends this little talk: why in hell do we have a consciousness with the power to comprehend this?

✧✧✧

Lacroix seemed very tired when he left the lectern—but still he walked surely and confidently down to his seat, got his black hat, and with his few notes in his aged brown hand, left the hall.

I too went out immediately, down to the grapes and tomatoes in my garden.

It was a warm evening, and the hall with its many people had been overheated.

CHRISTINE

After the terrific heat in the assembly hall it was a relief to get down to the garden, among the ants, the tomatoes, the bats, and the blessed darkness. I took off my clothes and sat down naked on the stone table, like a stout and heavy and aging Pan; but the *rifrescamento* which hung in the air beneath the coal-black, clear starry sky wasn't potent enough. The cooling had no effect. The sweat went right on pouring from my face and neck, armpits and chest. It all ran down between my heavy chest muscles and over my navel and collected in the dark locks where the belly ends. I got wetter and wetter, and suddenly I pulled myself together, walked over to the brook and crept down into the water, which is no longer so cool now as it was only a few days ago. But it still had the right effect: as soon as I'd put my feet in the water I began to feel better already, and when I sat down on the rocky bottom— the brook is no more than two or three feet deep—I felt it like a cold shock around my chest and shoulders. The water isn't deep enough to swim in, but you can lie there and make like a flounder or a frog or some kind of water lily among the crayfish. There's nothing evil or bad in them; they don't bite, it's only we who boil them alive.

I got up out of the water, but after only a few minutes I felt the heat getting the upper hand again, and crept down into the brook once more; I sat down in a hollow, with water up to my armpits and my chin resting on my knees. After a while I was really freezing and clambered out again and went back to the garden. This time I was sufficiently refreshed: now I felt the night only as warm and soft and living around me, comfortably lukewarm, full of life, full of mating and lewdness, full of odors and of the faint night sounds which tell of the life which exists on this accursed, leprous, spiritually gonorrheal globe which is our little green home and which I love so indescribably, so full of lust, so full of thought, so full of cruelty, and so full of beauty. The sky was black as tar and the stars shone insanely, thick as thick, everywhere, all over the whole sky. In the enormous leafy treetops in the park there was a rustle of a faint, faint breeze, all too subtle to be called a wind.

I brought out the white wine, the black bread, bacon fat, the stinking, reeking, antibiotic cheese, and I sat stark naked at the stone table and smeared fat on the pumpernickel while I drank of the cold wine.

Cold?

Since I don't have electricity in my house (only the little direct-current line which powers the alarm bell), I naturally don't have a refrigerator either. But people have lived before there were refrigerators, and I've solved the problem in my own way. The world is plagued with plastic bags. But I—in my omniscience and my enormous cunning—I collect them. (After all, we can't leave them all on the moon, containing excrement from Mao, Nixon, Brezhnev, Franco, Tito, Salazar, and Castro—as proofs of the highest which mankind has so far produced.) No, I use my plastic bags in a wholly different way: I put butter, cheese, cream, salami, trout, boiled, crayfish, and all God's gifts into the bags; then I suck the air out of them—not in order to create a vacuum, but to avoid air bladders which will prevent the bags and their contents from sinking into the water. Into these quasi-vacuum bags I put everything that tastes good, and sink it down in the brook. Even today it didn't have a temperature of at any rate more than sixty degrees. In a week it will be more difficult; then I'll have to put the white wine, the butter, and many other things in the well outside my palisade. There the temperature never gets above forty-five or so.

That was—as Lacroix says—a digression.

But I sat there naked in the warm night with the stars over me and with the rye bread and the white wine inside me—and I felt good in the good temperature, and I didn't think about the fire under me or the deathly cold above me. I was happy that little Christine was coming, and every time I thought of her I could feel the blood streaming to my central masculine organ, which would stir slightly.

All at once something entirely different happened, which stunned me.

I had forgotten to put out milk for the hedgehog, and now the little black thirsty lump was coming across the terrace. It came out of the darkness, as if it were loneliness itself, forlorn Creation itself—slowly, soundlessly, sniffing after moisture. It walked across the terrace turning its snout in all directions, all the way over to my feet. When I'm alone it has no fear. It will drink water or milk from a saucer even while I'm holding it in my hand.

I took my shirt and got up, put the shirt carefully around the hedgehog and lifted it up onto the table. While it stood there, I got the saucer of milk and served it. The hedgehog looked at me with its small black eyes. Then it drank.

For awhile we drank together. I've tried, but it doesn't like white wine; it wants water or milk. So we drank each our own. When it was finished, I put my shirt around it again and set it carefully back down on the ground. Then it went about its business, lonesome, soundless, into the darkness. In among the tomatoes, the nettles, and the grapes.

The frogs were singing down in the brook now.

I was fully aware that Christine had a lot to do and would hardly get here in less than an hour, and at the same time I felt a terror of death. It wasn't just terror, it was despair at knowing that one must die and leave everything. That one must leave all this, all this which I love so inconceivably: the sight of the stars, the smell of feces, the chorus in Beethoven's

Ninth, green tomatoes, the taste of milk or peaches, the smell
of piss, the sight of the sunrise. . . . Never to see the sunrise
again, never again to see the flowers close against the
evening, never again to see the little black lump, the hedgehog out sniffing after water. . . never again to see the apple
trees in bloom, or the blossoms on the peach trees. . . never
again to see the tomatoes growing. . . . It's this which is the
despair of death: never again to see the countless things one
loves so beyond all reason. Never again to see Michelangelo's
Pietàs—the long, thin, deformed one in Milan, the mutilated
one in Florence, the perfect one in Rome. . . never again to
see a Roman bust, or Donatello's great *Horseman*. But above
all: never again to know the smell of night. Or of seed.

In some way or another this is extremely important to me:
to see the flowers close against the night.

But also the castles in France. I'm not thinking of the
Loire. No, I belong in other places!

I'm thinking of Chantilly, when it's mirrored in the water.
Of the tapestries in the Musée de Cluny, of the manuscripts
in the sacristies. I'm thinking above all else of Les Saintes
Maries de la Mer, and above all else on earth I think of
Tarascon, of the castle which stands like the God Yahweh by
the beach, a hard, strong, brutal, and French God, heavy, mil-
itant, and terrible. Perhaps more beautiful than any other
building, if one leaves those of the Arabs out of account. And
I think of Les Baux, where the Church exterminated the
Huguenots, where thousands and tens of thousands were
slaughtered in a way which turns the SS butcheries of whole
villages several centuries later into innocent bagatelles. I also
think of the trout in the river above Tivoli outside Rome.

And I think of the smell of small children, and of turnips,
and milk. Of the smell of women, when they've become wet
in front.

Should I never see, hear, smell, never feel all this again?
Nevermore?

I sat there thinking of this people, this land—of winegrowers, electro-torturers, great painters, poets, and professional

Arab-murderers. Of professional revolutionaries, execution-ers, and judges—the last in common with all other countries.

But there's something else about France, about Gaul. Something which is found only in this land where the national soul has been incarnated in the wine labels and in the cuisine. There's something which *isn't* Marat, not Danton, and not Robespierre. There exists an eternal France, which isn't even the Seine or Molière. There exists a France which isn't Monsieur de Paris or Monsieur de France.

If I were to name this dreadful and mighty nation in two words, those words would be Cézanne and Rodin.

This unbelievable nation, which through one man, through one sculptor, through one single sculpture, had its whole enormous intellectual vitality, its unbelievable old-man's strength of inner power, translated into one single image—the land's intellectual vitality and strength trans-formed into muscular power: into Rodin's *The Thinker*, into a citadel of immortal bones and muscles, gathered into one sin-gle colossus of concentrated tension: *The thought!*—a leviathan of intellectual power.

Who doesn't know the photograph of Rodin in his vine-yard—a winegrower himself, like all his countrymen?

His big, flat, broad feet, his heavy legs and the volumi-nous swelling around his thighs, hips, and belly. Then his stomach and midriff—it all gets broader and broader the higher you go—up to his chest, which resembles a weightlifter's, his shoulders, as broad and heavy as if they were made of stone from Notre Dame; the nape of his neck, his heavy beard, his short, round, powerful skull, and the broad, heavy nose continuing the line from his low, broad forehead. Look at him beside the muscles in the shoulders of *Le Penseur*! Look at them both: they're both monstrosities of heavy bones, muscles and thought!

And then the *other* one: Paul Cézanne, man of private means, petit bourgeois and amateur painter, a man who ran away from the war against the Prussians, who ran away from the Commune, who didn't give a damn for France, for freedom or the revolution—who sat among his apple trees and his wonderful faraway blue mountains, which he painted again and again. The old *rentier* and amateur painter. An old, old fool, who thought he was a painter, who sat among his flower pots, his greenhouses and his big, blue mountains, who moved to the south of France—solely because the seasons were more stable there, and his observations could continue under unchanged conditions month after month. The old village idiot, Paul Cézanne—no, he had no relation to the revolution of '71: he didn't eat rats and he wasn't a sharpshooter. He was no revolutionary—at any rate not at that moment; he ate his cheese and drank his red wine, as every decent petit bourgeois in this fantastic brutal land of the Guillotine has always done, without letting himself be bothered by the smell of blood from the scaffold.

He just painted—like the old, crazy amateur he was, picture after picture—he often took months to plan one or two brush strokes. He was an old *rentier*, an old bourgeois who thought he was a painter. And in the meantime the revolution passed by. The old *rentier* and amateur went on painting.

Slowly, surely, and quietly he changed our image of the world. Our whole world looked different after Paul Cézanne had painted it. Systematically and from the bottom up he reconstructed our whole image of the world into a new image, with cubes, circles, ellipses, and cylinders, and using his materials in a way that no one in world history has seen the like of: he made white lead, cobalt blue, siccative, linseed oil, and turpentine unite in a surface which was more beautiful than any gem, lovelier and truer than any enamel.

But the most important thing was: he *rebuilt* our image of the world.

After Paul Cézanne the world was different from before.

What did his contemporaries achieve in Paris during the Commune? Not a little! Their names live, and we love these names. But who *changed* the world? The old *rentier* and petit bourgeois, with his little house and his bank account—*he* rebuilt the world.

There is no opposition in this, only clarity. Only *clarity!*

One day a very old man, an old *rentier* and idiot who thought he was a painter, went out once more to paint from nature, the way *he* saw it. Not as others had thought it or felt it or seen it.

He painted—as a faithful naturalist and witness to the truth—his own picture of the world, and it has become ours. Then came the rain, and the old man packed up his painting gear, and the wind was strong and the rain was violent, and the next day they found a very old *rentier* and amateur painter lying beside the road—still with his paintbox under his arm.

He still needed three days to die. So strong was the old man.

What is left today of the Paris Commune of that time, aside from a couple of plays about it, good but never altogether true? I don't know, but it isn't much.

What remains of the petit bourgeois with the bank account? What remains of Paul Cézanne—of his thick, blue-black beard and his bald crown?

What he left behind is a changed world.

One can ask oneself: who was the *great* revolutionary? Was it the pistoleers in Paris (*no* evil shall be said of them!)? Or *was* it the little petit bourgeois in Provence, Paul Cézanne, with his bit of cheese, his red wine and his paintbrushes carefully rinsed in turpentine?

The heavy, humorless, square, strong, bearded, and bald Paul the Great stands beside Rodin—for me—as France.

I heard steps beside me in the dark. It was the little nurse Christine, who had finally come. She too is France.

Christine was tired after being on duty and was likewise bothered by the heat. She had already undressed completely and was wearing only the white smock. She was sweating, and I gave her some white wine; but the sweating continued, and after a few minutes we went down to the brook and bathed. She sat down on the rocky bottom, where it was about a foot deep, and I washed her with cold, dark water until I saw that she was coming to herself again. I even poured water over her hair.

Then we went up to the terrace and sat down at the table, as wet and naked as human beings can be.

"Do you want to bring out the lamp?" she said.

I got out the kerosene lamp and lit it, and now I noticed a letter lying on the stone table. The envelope was sealed, and I went inside for a knife. Christine sat utterly still and naked, with her feet on the table.

I read the letter aloud:

"*Ma chère petite Christine, mon cher vieil enculé Jean:* I know exactly what you're up to tonight; I know what you're going to do, and I wish you a good time. God bless you both! Have talked with Paris, and am taking the big Citroën tonight and sleeping in it, while Pasqualino drives. The whole family of that loathsome legionnaire and parachutist was burningly interested in the proposal concerning a death certificate which doesn't point to suicide. Be good, both of you, and take—along with Harun-al-Rashid—good care of La Poudrière! (Who the devil was it who killed the Hungarian idiot: you, al Assadun, Ilya, Fontaine, *le général,* or old Lacroix? Or was it *I?*) Take good care of La Poudrière; into your hands I commend my soul.

Avec fellatio and cunnilingus from

good old Lefèvre."

Christine laughed heartily.

"Never," said she, "I've never met a doctor at any other hospital who is so loyal to his patients. He loves them. Lefèvre is the good shepherd, he'd give his life for every single one of them."

In the light of the kerosene lamp I sat looking at her; she's a feminine type which is only produced in Alsace and in North Italy—the thin limbs, the slender waist, the square shoulders, and the somewhat angular pelvis. The narrow small of the back. In the half-light she could just as well have been a fifteen-year-old boy.

"When did you meet al Assadun?" she asked suddenly. "You certainly knew each other long before you came to La Poudrière."

I told her how it was, but the whole time I sat looking at her body.

I met al Assadun at a public bath in Africa, during a very brief stay some time after the war. I had been inside the damp steam room and had been washed afterwards; then followed the Arab massage which is ten times better than any European one; the muscles don't get kneaded, they get stretched. The treatment can be extremely painful, because the masseur uses all his body weight and all his muscular strength to twist and stretch the musculature; your sore, stiff European muscles get stretched and twisted, until you feel as if you're twelve years old again. After the massage and yet another washing I was, as always among the Arabs, laid out on a sort of platform, packed into blankets, with a pillow under my head, and served a cigarette and a cup of green tea with sugar, lemon, and peppermint. I lay perfectly still and rested. A few feet away lay another man, somewhat younger than I, and we greeted each other politely. After a while we got into a conversation, and he said that he worked at the University, where he taught Arabic language and poetry, but also German, French, and English literature.

"But," he added after a bit, "by profession I'm a doctor of medicine—from the Sorbonne."

He said that he wasn't practicing as a doctor for the time being, but preferred to teach something other than his real specialty. The war had been unpleasant, highly anatomical, and repulsive, and he felt better teaching in a humanistic field.

Thus we got acquainted, and al Assadun was a specialist in Hölderlin, who wasn't unknown to me either. It was raining outside. After the bath he drove me back to my hotel in his little old Renault 4 and even accompanied me into the bar, where—while I drank my aperitif—he emptied a whole glass of orange juice; believer that he is, he never touches alcohol.

As I was telling this, I sat and looked at Christine—then I broke off the narrative:

"Christine," I said, "now we're going to bed."

"Isn't it too warm inside?" she rejoined.

"Yes," I said, "but I'll bring out the blanket. Then we can lie on the terrace."

She smiled.

"But I make one condition," she said. "You shall be utterly passive, and do only what I tell you."

I nodded:

"Into your hands I commend my body."

"A promise is a promise," said Christine. "Go get the blanket."

I went in and got the blanket off the bed and came out with it over my arm.

"Christine!" I said. "I make my conditions too. You shall answer a question first."

"Yes?"

"What in hell is going on at La Poudrière now? I mean between the patients and the ambassador's wife and the American general?"

"Nothing except that the patients are freezing them out. They don't want to have anything to do with them."

"That's terrible," I said. "At a place like La Poudrière nobody should be frozen out. We're equally great criminals, all of us. Nobody should feel that he's better than the others— not even better than those two damned Russian-American idiots. Before God we're all Americans!"

"It isn't a *moral* thing," said Christine after a little thought; "it's because both of them—the ambassador's wife and the general—have been going around saying that today the world can only be ruled by the genuine superpowers, all other countries must give up their sovereignty and resign themselves to being satellite states without their own foreign, military, or economic policies. Small independent states are an anachronism from earlier centuries. According to Adolf Hitler, the small independent states were already finished for good in the thirties. And furthermore they claim that the U.S. and Russia have been chosen by God to rule the world."

"By God?"

"Well," answered Christine, "he says *God*, and the

ambassador's wife says *History*, which is God to her."

"They go around talking about this?"

"There have been wild discussions about it. And now *le général* is just as hated by everybody as Dr. Báthory was before somebody killed him. Hardly anyone talks about anything but Russia's and America's world empire."

"The Frenchmen must really be enchanted?"

"Nobody's especially delighted. And both the ambassador's wife and the general have been kind enough to exhort everybody to think of what happened to the Czechs and the Greeks when they rose up against their masters."

Christine sat down on the blanket and folded her arms around her knees.

"That isn't so stupid," I replied. "The only thing which can save the world now is a revolution in Russia and a civil war in the U.S. But the tiresome thing is that the rulers will try to prevent the civil war and the revolution by starting wars against other countries. In other words, they'll follow the old method of solving their internal problems by creating a so-called external enemy. For the time being they have the Chinese as witches—and in a while the Great Dread will begin anew. After new assaults on outer space the Dread will come again—the dread of the fire under us, and of the dead, meaningless, idiotic space above us. We'll be privileged to see the permanent witchhunt reach heights as never before in history. Changes in the image of the world entail changes in the life on this little green crust of ours—and it's these changes we fear most of all. Never has humanity been so full of terror as today."

"I don't feel any fear," said Christine. "I believe in what I see, and in what I feel. And right now I feel that I'm sticky-wet between my legs. Lie down!"

"Wait a bit," I said; "so now they're going around up there hating each other like wolves?"

Christine nodded.

"The worst thing is old Lacroix saying that in a long life in his special trade he's seen a lot, but that until now he had believed that at least there was one thing he'd been spared:

the sight of the naked human soul. But, he says, now that he's looked the little killer of blacks from the Pentagon in the eyes, he knows that he hasn't been spared that either."

"Who do you think killed Báthory?" I said.

"I don't know," she replied, "and I'm not especially curious, either. I'm much more curious about who'll be next."

I bet they could hear my laughter all the way up at the clinic.

"Now we have more serious things afoot," said Christine. "Lie down and lie perfectly still. Don't touch me. Leave everything to me, and just do what I say. You've promised."

I lay down.

No one—no one in the whole world—could complain with reason that the little nurse Christine lacked knowledge of anatomy. And she knew what to do with it. She hardly used anything but her fingers and mouth and tongue, and every time she noticed that the rhythmic muscle spasms were beginning, she slackened the tempo or went over to something else. She kept it up like that for nearly an hour. And I was unremittingly on the brink of collapse the whole time.

Then she decided to let it happen, and she achieved it with her mouth. Just as the liquid spurted out with full force, she bowed her head slightly and received the moisture with her eyes, nose, face, and lips. The next jets she permitted to spout up over my stomach and chest. Then she laid her head and face down against my belly and rubbed the seed all over me.

Finally she raised her head and looked at me. Her face was gleaming wet. Then she lay down with her head on my shoulder and her arm across my chest.

The smell of semen came from both her face and from my own chest. It was strong and distinct and stood out from the other odors in the warm, dark night.

She lay there smiling for awhile.

"This smell," she said, "this smell of seed is found in only one single place in the whole universe—on this little green crust of ours. It's absolutely the best thing I know in the world, and now I've rubbed millions of germs of life all over both you and myself. Isn't that a teeny weeny bit remarkable?"

She lay still again, just sniffing at me and herself, then she continued: "Isn't this just as remarkable as that idiotic and absurd madhouse of yours, as you call outer space?"

I think she went to sleep almost as soon as she'd said this, and her breathing was deep and regular, right next to my ear. I lay there with this sleeping child in my arms and gazed up at the sky, which was sown all over with glittering stars. At the same time I was still aware of the odor which sat on her face and hair.

I heard something rustling almost soundlessly nearby, and raised my head. A dark lump was moving across the terrace, visible in the gleam of the lamp.

It was the hedgehog out sniffing after water.

LEFÈVRE

Thermidor 8, the year 176

Is there any more to tell?

Yes. Everything abides. There is no end. It's not true that there's the consolation in it all that it won't last forever. In reality everything goes on. Everything lasts forever. There is no end to anything. Today again the hospital cat piddled on an eminent humanist and statesman—the newspaper was lying outside on the stone table, and had Brezhnev's portrait on the front page. His felonious visage had turned yellow and wrinkled from the cat piss.

Puss received half a can of sardines from me.

And it has also rained—a long, heavy summer rain. The air is light and clear, and La Poudrière lies newly washed and glittering with freshness—the garden, the park, the trees, the vineyards—all, all of it is moist and green and juicy, an insane explosion of wild fertility in the sunshine.

The little nurse Christine comes to me often, and she always brings something with her—wine, cheese, and one time *foie gras*. It must have cost her a week's salary. She never behaves in exactly the same way; she's a new girl from one time to the next. Only the friendliness is always the same. She is like people were before the Fall.

Our little Belgian, M. Fontaine, visits me now and then. Now he's writing his private bestiary, his *vita sexualis*, his *via dolorosa*.

Le général and the ambassador's wife haven't shown their faces—but a couple of times she's howled again in the night. Those long, wild, plaintive wolf howls, her Siberian loneliness, are the human thing about her.

It is her real voice: the human voice.

Sometimes Christine comes down just to see the picture of the young Yugoslav partisan over my little desk where I write down the records as best I may. In a strange way his position—with his legs planted firmly some distance apart, his hands clenched above his head, and his peaceful, almost virginal face with the thin German wire around his neck—seems almost like an act of cruelty in contrast to the grinning officers who are going to execute him.

They didn't succeed in conquering him—and they are to be pitied.

Christine stands looking at the picture for a long time, then she nods and goes up toward La Poudrière again.

Partway across the lawn she turns and waves at me.

Once I took an evening off with al Assadun and smoked hash up in the music room at Lefèvre's. It was the same thing again: seeing the music turn to metal and glittering jewels, seeing the music like a mountain of diamonds, and at the same time seeing the burning candles turn to stars, transforming al Assadun's face into gold.

While we were eating afterwards, with all the appetite which hashish gives, we had a conversation.

I asked him again what he thought of a solar system which just repeats itself over and over in eternal, meaningless, feebleminded ellipses and circles. And he answered that for him it wasn't meaningless, even if only Allah and Mary understood the meaning.

"Jochanaan," he said, "I have a religion which is compatible with both the empty, dead space—with the deathly cold above us—and with the sea of flame under us. My religion is compatible with nature."

"What do you mean?" I said.

"I mean that we have only Allah—we have no intermediaries, no church, no priests, no dogmas—and consequently no *theology* either. It's not *God*—not Allah—who is incompatible with reality. It's *theology* which is incompatible with *intellectual honesty*—to use your compatriot Nietzsche's term. It's *theology, dogma*, which can't tolerate reality."

We've talked about this a lot. al Assadun is at his very best now; he's happy as a mother over his little French-Arab son, and over the fact that his wife has come home from the maternity ward. Of course he's also very pleased that the spiritually worm-eaten, state-salaried Arab-murderer of a Hungarian has kicked the bucket, and that now we've probably set an example proving that it's permitted to break the necks of paratroopers, foreign legionnaires, and telephone operators. If the permission could be broadened to include Russian ambassadors and American generals as well, he maintains, then even Europe would be on the way back to culture.

He doesn't think that this has anything to do with witch-hunting; it's a matter of garbage removal, which ought to be left to private initiative.

al Assadun gets a special pleasure out of the fact that it's Dr. Báthory's French family which is bribing the police to hush up the fact that it was a suicide when it *wasn't* a suicide, so that the shame of this non-suicide can be confined to the familial high-finance circles.

"I hope you broke his neck in a slow and painful manner," I said, "the way a *sal arabe* ought to dispatch foreign legionnaires."

Harun-al-Rashid smiled quietly.

"Only Allah and Mary—and *one* other—know who performed the execution."

"What do you really think of the brothers Goncourt?" I said.

"I've thought quite a bit about one of their theories lately," replied al Assadun. "They maintain that one can only write the truth about the things one hasn't experienced oneself. That's true. But on the other hand the famous gringo Hemingway maintains that one can only write the truth about

the things one *has* experienced oneself. That is also correct.
The funny thing is that as you approach the truth, there's no
longer any contradiction between opposites. One thing is
true—and at the same time the direct opposite is also true."

"Oh yes," I said, "and I know that Mohammed was born of
a man, and that that's why you crawl around in the desert bug-
gering each other—in anticipation of the next male parturition.
How Arabs get pregnant at all is a mystery to gynecology."

"Not to us," he said. "You should never forget that Plato
as well as Aristotle came to Europe in our translations at a
time when the shitty overfucked frog-eaters in Gaul could neither read nor write. I won't even mention the Goths or you
Eskimos."

Ilya has been in too, and as usual he lifted me up in the air
and kissed me on the cheek.

"Little Ivan!" he said: "You man from Greenland!"

But he was angry, depressed, furious. He has always
despised Russia, and now the ambassador's wife with her
American-style *Herrenvolk* act has blown life into his loathing
for it all.

I tried to console him:

"Everything passes, Ilya, everything passes away. A while
ago the Teutons were the master race, and you see how
things are going with them. Now they sit there counting their
money—they're thinking about deflation, that's all; they have
no future and no vitality. They can't even manage to roast
Jews anymore. Before them it was the English who were the
master race, and look what they're doing today: they live off
selling arms to your two-legged African brothers, so that they
can at least earn a few shillings on the massacres. Everything
passes away, Ilya. And there shall come a day—the greatest
and most beautiful day in history: there shall come a day
when there is neither any Soviet Union nor any United States
of America. Believe me."

But Ilya wouldn't be consoled.

"You know, Ivan," he said, "the Russians are the most

sadistic people on earth. There's no atrocity a Russian-speaking person can't commit. That was both described and proved long ago by Feodor Dostoevsky.

"If you had any idea, little Ivan, what I saw during the Civil War—and on both sides, mind you—then even you, who aren't totally lacking in experience of our two-legged friends—even *you* would be speechless. I don't believe that the French discovered electro-torture. I believe it was already in full use during the Lenin terror—not even to mention the logical mathematical consequence of Lenin's philosophy, not even to mention the Stalin period and the present period of so-called 'neo-Stalinism.' Do you know the truth? There *isn't* any 'Stalinism'—there are only *Russians;* there is only Russia—Holy Russia.

"You should have experienced what I went through in the Russian countryside, in the years I was a fugitive from Lenin's executioners—logically enough because I belonged to the group which wanted to combine socialism with freedom, the same group which was being persecuted in the U.S. at the same time as in the USSR: the anarchists, the only libertarian communists, and therefore the *only* ones who were dangerous to the power-hungry. Little Ivan, you should have seen rural Russia during the *samagonka* period! There's hardly anyone today who knows what samagonka is. I'll tell you. Actually 'samagonka' just means a poisonous, sometimes lethal, home-brewed substitute for vodka, containing a quantity of the higher alcohols, and sometimes other, paralyzing toxins as well.

"No one who hasn't experienced it can imagine the decadence in the countryside, and in the villages—which in Russia are often quite big. You should have seen the cruelty, the inhumanity, Ivan! People talk about *Lenin*! Have you reread Lenin's works—as an adult?"

"Yes, Ilya, I have."

"Were you greatly impressed on second meeting?"

"No. Not much impressed at all."

"Well. Well. It *isn't* all Lenin's fault: Lenin was a damned ordinary—very intelligent—Tartar. There are hundreds of thousands of them. He was intelligent, but not *great enough* to be to blame for the whole hell. It's only the villagers who blame the *Vlasti*—but it isn't the *Vlasti*, it isn't the *government*, which is to blame. The blame rests with the individual Russian. That's the truth: the Russians' cruelty is surpassed only by their *cowardice*.

"A typical Russian execution, during the period when the Czar had abolished the death penalty, was to make the condemned run the gauntlet between his friends in the corps or company, and make him run until he died of it. Thus he wasn't *executed*, but unfortunately died while being punished. Russia had no death penalty at the time. But every Russian soldier would happily help flog a comrade to death.

"That's Russia.

"I've seen Russian peasants pack little children in bread dough before putting them into the oven alive. I've seen them rub sick people with tar to make them die faster—or hitch them to the plough and whip them until they dropped dead, in order to be rid of them. During the *samagonka* period it was common to dispatch chickens, dogs, pigs, and cats by burying them alive. It was done for no reason, just for the sake of amusement. You should have seen Russian peasants killing thieves by dragging them after a cart for hours, until they were flayed alive. You had one big error in your lecture, where you gave the impression that the Soviet state chiefly used the sleep method—i.e. depriving the suspect of sleep for several weeks—to force confessions. Nothing is more erroneous: the method is effective, and it was much used, but the interrogators also had at their disposal instruments of the most exquisite sort. They were fully on a level with the Christian church—with both Protestants and Catholics. They had their pincers, their spikes, their methods of hoisting up—and judging from everything, their electro-method as well.

"It wasn't *Lenin*! It was the *people*!

"Of course nothing good can be said about him. Absolutely not one single good word. He was a swine—as you said, on a level with Luther, Paul, and Thomas Aquinas. He

was a conscious intellectual traitor to the revolution and to all
of Marxist thought.

"To *combine* Marx with Lenin!

"To talk about Marxism-Leninism, that's like talking about
the Grand Inquisitor Torquemada in the same breath as
Christ. It's like mixing oil and water: Marxism *can't* be mixed
with Leninism.

"What did Lenin do? He twisted Marxism into its absolute
opposite.

"Marx was an *opponent* of the state, he saw the dissolution
of the centralized state as communism's final goal. Lenin was
a *worshiper* of the state and of centralized, monolithic state
power. He created the expressions—as you pointed out yourself—'democratic centralism' and 'the theory of the elite', the
total dictatorship of the Party—the opposite of the dictatorship of the proletariat, of the propertyless. Lenin destroyed
the soviets and made them into puppets of the Party clique,
into instruments of the police state. Marx stood firmly on the
foundation of the classic revolutionary ideal: Marx was an
advocate of the hard-won, bourgeois freedoms of information, expression, and movement. Marx was a *libertarian*.
Lenin used all his rhetoric—at which he was a near-genius—to
scoff at and mock and ridicule the 'bourgeois' freedoms.
Nobody has ever hated freedom more than Lenin. Not even
the Teutons' Adolphe le Grand.

"Marx was fully aware of the intellectuals' enormous stake
in the struggle to free the proletariat, in the struggle for the
workers' human dignity. Lenin created a *hatred* of the intellectuals—who had endured prison and torture and had sacrificed
their lives for the oppressed: as a demagogue he whipped
mistrust of these intellectuals into his own ignorant masses,
whom he himself was now to oppress.

"Lenin did this because he knew that the intellectuals,
writers, philosophers, scholars—wearing their pince-nez—had
fought on the barricades and sacrificed lives and children for
the cause; from these rebellious intellectuals Lenin could
never expect full obedience and submission, he could never

make them into the dogs he needed to surround himself with.

"The whole myth of the intellectuals' unreliability—which has colored all labor parties, including social democracy (with only the anarchists as an exception)—was consciously created by Lenin, and sustained by police terror, censorship, and torture—by mass exterminations and terrorism.

"Marx was an opponent of terrorism and regarded the terror during the Commune as a result of the bourgeois fellow-travelers' eagerness to show their 'revolutionary' spirit.

"In the same year that you, little Ivan, were born, Lenin wrote the manifesto of terrorism itself—of 'dehumanization of the person' (to use Bukharin's words) as a necessity within the so-called Soviet state: *Terrorism and Revolution*. Rosa Luxemburg was right: Lenin's terrorist medicine was worse than the disease it was supposed to cure. Lenin wrote the Theology of Terror.

"Therefore he's a sacred cow in every country whose regime rests on terror, police and violence. He's the great antithesis of Marx—and while Marx was a genius of creative thought, Lenin had a genius for destruction—above all of Marxism.

"'Marxism-Leninism' is an idiotic concept which can only be used by idiots."

"There's an excuse for Lenin too," I said.

"What do you mean?" said Ilya, eyeing me mistrustfully.

"I mean, of course, his celebrated syphilis. It isn't discussed in Soviet textbooks, and it isn't included in the study of Leninism—despite the fact that it's the only thing which makes Leninism comprehensible. As you know, Lenin didn't die of a gunshot wound or of a cerebral hemorrhage either, but purely and simply of his good old faithful syphilis—in a blossoming paralysis. And as you also know, syphilis has a remarkable ability to break down all moral inhibitions once it has reached its final paralytic stage. How many honest old men have been convicted and punished for indecencies toward minors because of an act which wasn't lewd, but the result of a classic syndrome? What happened to Lenin resulted in his total abrogation of all political morality: his whole centralism, his theory of the elite along with his conversion to terrorism, and likewise of course his putting the terror into practice, are exclusively symptoms of the paralysis. Only by beginning with syphilis can one understand Leninism and evaluate it correctly. It isn't Lenin's fault that his terrorist theology has been accepted by the rest of us, who don't carry around an equally advanced syph."

Ilya nodded.

"No, no," he said. "The misfortune isn't *Lenin's* fault. What's happened is due to the inconceivable cowardice and cruelty which is Russia's national soul. There's only one country in the world which has maltreatment of animals as a popular sport, for example burning cats alive: and that's Holy Russia."

"Ilya," I said, "we all want to believe that the people we ourselves know best are the most inhuman. As you know, Russians, Italians, Germans, Frenchmen, etc., etc., have always been constitutional sadists. But I can tell you that the little countries, the small nations which have always bragged so hypocritically about their humaneness—Denmark, Holland, Belgium, etc., etc., Albania or what you will—Ilya, they do exactly the same thing when they get a chance.

"Our little two-legged friends are the same everywhere.

"All over this green, temperate, moist surface of a planet on an insane journey through space, people commit the very same acts, over and over again. We Eskimos, too, do the same as you. It's that which is the phenomenon.

"It's *that*, Ilya, which is interesting!"

"That damned hellish shitty nymphomaniac of a lying ambassador's wife," said Ilya, "she knows everything. She's seen everything close up, and still she screams about how we've pissed on Lenin. I only wish I'd had the chance. Although neither Lenin nor Stalin is the main thing; the main thing is the people, the rabble, the mob. . . *vox dei*. . . the holy people. . . *they're* the murderers! What would that odious little puritan Robespierre have been without that howling sea of good, simple, honest people? *Nothing!*"

✧

Lord be praised! Glory be to God, Jesus, Allah, and Mary! Our good old frivolous Lefèvre is back again. He's more foul-mouthed than ever. His cigarette hangs vertically under his mustache as always, and with his old, sad look he's more cheering than ever.

He came via Lyons, and he didn't need to say a word about how the matter of the sadistic Hungarian parachutist and his thoroughly mendacious French family had turned out. He just smiled at me. Then he almost killed me with a clap on the shoulder:

"Jean, *bon vieil enculé!*"

He came to my garden with a bottle of Napoléon, and drank almost all of it himself. In the evening he gave a lecture.

Lefèvre's lecture bore the title:

THE CULTURE OF THE STAKE

DEAR FRIENDS, LADIES AND GENTLEMEN:

I'm very, very glad to be back at La Poudrière again. As a sort of chief physician, as a friend, and—like most everybody who has experienced the mortal dread of our time, also as a fellow patient—I would like to express my pleasure at seeing you again.

With that I shall return to the topic.

No psychiatrist should be allowed to practice unless he possesses a certain knowledge of church history—not of the official, falsified, and mendacious church history, consciously twisted and distorted (and not just by theologians and church politicians of both main confessions)—but of the *real*, the *true* church history, which shows such a dreadful picture of man that even truth-seeking secular, anticlerical, or even atheist historians have contributed to the falsification, quite simply because for psychiatrically understandable reasons they couldn't *bear* to reproduce the picture of human nature which church history has etched into reality.

This must be a matter for the historians' own conscience: carrying on the falsification, silencing the truth—in other words, furthering the *lie.*

For psychiatry, on the other hand, a knowledge of the real, the true church history is *absolutely indispensable professional reading*—because it shows better and more nakedly than any other field what people are capable of doing to other human beings.

Without this insight—which doesn't make one happy—we psychiatrists are not equal to our work or our task; without church history we don't know what dwells in a human being.

Political history is also indispensable reading for the psychiatrist.

These areas show us *what* a human being is. And I want to define this question more precisely, this question which is of such burning interest to all of us who are gathered here: *"What is a human being?"*—by juxtaposing it with the other questions which form the basis of our life here at La Poudrière:

The fire—the flaming hell of fluid metal and fluid minerals under us—and the deathly cold, empty, dead space with its minus 459.7 degrees above us: in other words, our life in this endlessly beautiful, moist, green, and luxuriant garden of paradise on a thin, thin crust of temperate earth, the juicy blessedness of fecundity and produce we live on—and the permanent witchhunt which has continued without cease.

So to the question: *is* this mathematical, pedantic, macrocosmic watchmaker's shop of timetables and necessity, all this terrible precision in the dead cold space—*is* it the madhouse it must be if it has no meaning? This idiotic, absurd, and above all totally meaningless, inconceivably vast universe, if it is without meaning, then it should cease to exist. *Shouldn't the cosmos stop functioning in its idiocy as soon as possible?*

The third question is: *Why have we treated each other so on this microcosmic crust—this thin layer of mould and organic life, decay, consciousness, and bestiality?*

✧

Without the faintest hope of an answer (where the answers begin, so does the bestiality!), without *hope*—I simply want to express the wish, like the previous speakers, that I may pose the question more precisely—since, although I'm not criticizing anyone, and have only appreciation for their contributions, I think that the statement of the problem needs some supplementation.

Just as every statement of a problem at times needs to be amplified.

Being a Frenchman, and having a relatively thorough knowledge of French history, I want to state that decisive Christian atrocities have taken place oftener in France than in any other country. They began in Trier, where the Christians, because of Christological and theological disagreements, had already begun killing each other in the fourth century.

Since then it has continued.

In hardly any other land has the Church waded in blood as in France; here the same mass murders in the name of Jesus's love have left a trail of blood through history which is without parallel.

I shall limit myself mainly to the Christian Church's total extermination of the Albigensians and the Cathari—to the Church's never wholly successful physical annihilation of the Waldensians, and to the massacres, not one hundred per cent successful either, of the Huguenots.

The witch trials we've gotten a picture of, albeit simplified and by no means adequate in its representation of the extent of the massacres. During the church's period of power this permanent bloodbath, this permanent witchhunt aimed at those who think differently, attained an extent and a bestiality which undoubtedly surpasses the activities of our Russian, American, and German brothers in our own time. It's impossible today to cite exact figures—Voltaire calculated the victims of the Christian Church at ca. nine million, but his calculations are most certainly based on a fragment of what really happened.

If to the Church's and the Christians' delight in killing, their indescribable and, to us patients, inconceivable lust for

blood—if to this you add all the wars—besides the total anni-
hilations, the genocide in whole regions within France and
other countries, and the Church's bloody persecutions of the
Jews; if you also count the wars which the Church has
brought about directly, such as the Crusades and the Thirty
Years' War, the massacres in Poland and in other countries;
and if we add to this some of the wars which the church has
supported and approved, if you also count the persecutions
and bloodbaths involving Arabs, Turks, and the extermination of, for example, the entire aboriginal Cuban
population—then we're approaching figures which are utterly
without parallel in world history: we must conclude that
Christ's teachings about love, equality, and brotherhood—
about turning the other cheek—have been the greatest misfortune in human history to date. And if in addition we take into
account the way in which the Christian churches have almost
without exception enthusiastically supported the modern crusade against communism—supported Hitler, Mussolini,
Franco, Salazar, etc., etc.—then we get up into numerical concepts which we simply can't comprehend.

But even *without* those bloodbaths in which the Church
has only assisted, only been an accomplice—if we restrict ourselves to the slaughters for which the Church alone is responsible, we'll find that Christ's teachings have caused several
hundred million deaths. Far more than Stalinism and
Hitlerism put together. No religion, no impulse in the whole
history of the world has made Satan's dominion over the
earth possible to such a high degree as the four little Gospels
have done. "Christ's teachings" have a minimum of three
hundred million deaths as their fruit. Never has the world
seen such an incarnation of evil as the Christian Church.

All this is suppressed by church history, and here the confessions have abetted each other by mutual agreement,
Catholic and Protestant church histories have supported each
other with falsifications, deceptions, and concealments—hush-
ing up each other's crimes. The murderers have conspired to
conceal each other's actions.

They still stick together, and increasingly so, because the total end of every form of Christian church is approaching.

It is deplorable—deplorable in the extreme—that secular, "honest historical research" has contributed to this suppression.

The Christian Church's methods of slaughter are not unknown.

We know that they burned three-year-old children because of their lewd association with the devil, and the same time as they burned one-hundred-year-old women for the same shameful deeds. But what people don't know is that Christ's deputies on earth—here in our beautiful, fertile France—burned whole cities with the sick, the aged, women, men, and newborn children. Even pregnant women were dragged into the flames amid the singing of pious hymns. There were whole regions where every living person was burned—or quartered, broken on the wheel, had the intestines drawn, tongue torn out, and sex organs torn off. There's a description of a certain besieged city where all the male corpses lay with their own sex organs—their cut-off penises—in their mouths, as if they were smoking cigars. This, my friends—*this*, and *nothing* else, is the Christian Church!

It involves extremely interesting psychological phenomena, which have to do not so much with the Gospels as with the effect they've had on people.

Where the Church is concerned, this is not the past. Not so long ago we were told through the entire world press that the American murder of children in a distant continent was a "highly Christian war"—the words were uttered by a certain Cardinal Spellman. The expression has been repudiated by the Vatican—and we see daily, hear daily, read daily about priests, about divines speaking out in favor of freedom and humanity, against suppression, etc., etc.—"for" the poor people!

Against the background of the Church's history this can only be described as conscious hypocrisy and deception. The churches have always supported the strongest and the richest side—and when "leftist-radical" or even "revolutionary" clerics step forward today, we must assume that the churches are taking security measures: what counts is to be friends with the rulers, if the revolutionaries should turn out to be victorious in country after country.

The Cathari and the Albigensians were pious, unworldly people without any aggression against the Church. They just wanted to live their own lives in prayer and asceticism. The same goes for the Waldensians. They were butchered by the hundreds of thousands, and *here*, ladies and gentlemen, *here* we come to the heart of the matter, and to the reasons why I have called this little psychiatric causerie "The Culture of the Stake." These people entered the torture chambers and the red-hot coals without complaint, without dread, often with little children in their arms. It is precisely *here*, precisely at this point that world history turns, that it shows its other side: persons who could have escaped torture, mutilation, being roasted alive—just by changing their opinions. Just by renouncing their own thinking and their own will.

The Christian Church claims to have hundreds of thousands of martyrs. That's a deliberate lie. The Christian Church has a handful of proven martyrs—but it has made millions and millions of those who thought differently into martyrs.

The Church has waded in blood—that's true. But not in its *own*. It has waded in the blood of others to a degree which our fantasy refuses to imagine. Only exact historical research of the future will produce a true picture.

But it isn't the murderers, not Hitler, not the priests, not the executioners, not Stalin, not the popes and cardinals and the other butchers who interest us. What will occupy us this evening, and just for a little while—is the martyrs, the true (not the Church's!) martyrs: those who died for their own free thought and conscience.

Here we're face to face with a far more powerful and more incomprehensible problem than that which was raised earlier—when I say *incomprehensible*, I use the word in accordance with my own modest understanding of what a human heart is.

Thousands and thousands have given their lives for freedom of human thought, for freedom of conscience, and for the freedom of future generations—this freedom which we treat so badly today.

The bloodbaths aren't the main thing; the main thing is the *heretic.*

What is it that gives a person such strength?

Greater than the problem of evil is the problem of good.

Once again I would like to begin with the meaninglessness of outer space, the insane fire under us, and the deathly cold above us. On this green crust of vegetation, excrement, fertilization, life, there are still people who don't let themselves be crushed by being physically torn to pieces; they are invincible. They sit in prisons all over the world, they're abused and maimed by the vassals of the heads of state—today we know the details of the concrete methods all too well for me to need to mention them. We're all a bit nervous here at La Poudrière.

But there are people who don't let themselves be crushed.

It is this which is the miracle—and taking as my starting point the fire under us and the outer space above us, I want to say that if this whole mad watchmaker's workshop is insane and meaningless, then so is everything else totally meaningless.

In that case it's idiotic not to bow to the Church, the Party, or the lackeys they have at their command. Those who sit in prison, who withstand all the tortures which a sick theological or military brain can think up; which a policeman's, jurist's, or officer's stunted little brain can devise—and that is no little: in that case these invincibles aren't martyrs, they're *idiots.*

I shall mention one of these idiots, one who is so well known that I need only mention his name—Giordano Bruno—to turn everything upside down.

Why in the name of hell didn't he concede that Satan's— i.e. the Church's—servants were right? Why did he enter the flames of his own free will? Even while the executioner was kindling the first flame he could have changed his mind and acknowledged that the Church was right in its teaching about the solar system—and thereby escaped being roasted alive.

Instead he just turned his face away when one of Satan's servants, a Christian priest, held the cross up before him. He died without making a sound—and according to eyewitnesses, with signs of contempt and loathing.

The secret is that Giordano had withstood the Church's most extreme means of coercion year after year; he had been tortured by every conceivable method to persuade him to retract his doctrine, and had withstood every torment. He no longer feared the fire.

When the executioner's assistants lighted the bonfire on the 17th of February in the year 1600, at that same moment Giordano Bruno crushed the Church.

At this stake the Church was burned, not Bruno. But it took time to understand that.

This little idiot, thin and emaciated, pale, exhausted—who calmly mounted the pyre, and there with full consciousness crushed the Church and placed it for all time on the dungheap of human ordure where it belongs; this little idiot, born in the city of Nola, south of Naples—a deeply religious man who had entered the Dominican order at the age of only fourteen; this little idiot showed yet another sign of good sense in that he unmasked Calvinism, the sickest, spiritually most perverse Christian subspecies which has been produced, apart from Luther's devil-worship.

It's possible that Calvin was an even greater swine—I mean an even more stunted, hunchbacked spiritual syphilitic than Luther was. Bruno remained a believer until his in many ways extremely uncomfortable and perhaps slightly premature demise, but one may assume that he had lost some of his original sympathy for the Church after seven years of torture. Note: torture without result.

Here, in addition to our other questions, it may be possible to ask how (and why in hell???!!!) our crumb of consciousness has arisen.

How is it possible that we—in the midst of all this meaninglessness—go around being conscious of everything that's happened? How can we know about this lifeless cosmos which the believing Bruno unveiled?

In this connection, of course, one can also mention Hus, a deeply believing Christian, who was likewise roasted by the Christians.

That happened around two hundred years earlier, and also for purely Christological reasons. He didn't die soundlessly: he sang a hymn as he stood in the flames.

We have a less well-known, but all the more jolly, picture of the roasting of Michael Servetus, which took place in Geneva the 27th of October 1553. He neither remained silent nor sang during the burning—on the contrary, he shrieked like a madman and heightened the people's *joie de vivre* and their religious feeling. It was one of the really great folk festivals in Calvin's perverse city.

Michael Servetus was a Spaniard, a deeply religious person, but also highly gifted scientifically. He was a doctor and conquered new territory in exploring the circulation of the blood.

However, he thought that the doctrine of the Trinity, which indeed survives to this very day, was a mockery of God (3 = 1), in that it is an insult to human reason—which of course it still is. For this reason he fled to Geneva, to escape being burned by the Catholics.

Calvin didn't share his view of the Trinity; Calvin was of the firm, intelligent opinion that 3 = 1.

Servetus was an intelligent man, but not a courageous one—not by *nature*, that is. He was now imprisoned—in Geneva.

Calvin resorted to every possible means to explain to Michael Servetus that 3 = 1. But there Servetus was inflexible. He screamed and cried, he carried on like a madman during the interrogations, he howled and sobbed—and the very thought of the forthcoming bonfire made him throw himself on the floor and embrace the great Calvin's feet, begging to be spared the fire. Only on one point was Servetus absolutely inflexible: weeping and howling with physical dread he refused to acknowledge the obvious logical syllogism that 3 = 1.

When they led him to the stake one beautiful clear
autumn day, he cried the whole time—while a clerical mathe-
matician versed in the doctrine of the Trinity walked beside
him and explained to him that he could escape the whole
roasting if he would admit that $3 = 1$. But Servetus refused.
The wind was brisk, and Servetus wasn't disturbed by smoke
or the like; he screamed so it could be heard all over Geneva;
but he never admitted that $3 = 1$.

He died, roasted alive and very slowly, because of his con-
viction that $3 = 3$ and $1 = 1$. Mathematics and human reason
were no bad joke to him. Actually, Michael Servetus died for
neither religious nor ideological reasons, but purely and simply in honor of the little multiplication table (a table which,
naturally enough, has always been a great nuisance to the theologians). He was no hero, he pled for his life and he begged
for mercy; but *one* price he wouldn't pay: conceding that
human reason is nonsense.

That isn't so easy to understand fully.

These are three examples; in the heretic and witch trials
one can find thousands. In Lenin's and Hitler's torture chambers as well.

I shall remind you of the American anarchists who were
hanged during a popular orgy of blood after the Haymarket
"trial" in Chicago—a trial fully on a level with a Lutheran,
Calvinist, or Catholic trial. Judicially it revolved around the
fact that everyone knew that the condemned were innocent
of the sharp-witted charge, which was that even if they
demonstrably hadn't thrown the bomb, still they had thrown
it anyway.

Here I'll quote a few of their last words from the scaffold
before the disgusting, protracted, and unsuccessful hangings
took place:

George Engel: *"Hurrah for anarchism!"*

August Spiess: *"There will come a time when our silence will
speak louder than your voices!"*

Adolph Fischer: *"This is the happiest moment of my life!"*

Those are words for the American people to live by.

I want to call to mind an old Hebrew legend: that as long as there are still thirty-seven righteous people in the world, so long can this world exist.

Of course a causerie of this sort can't possibly end with any form of conclusion. Only with facts. In every age people have *also* been like that.

Must we set up the innocent, mutilated, tortured, hanged, or burned victims against the empty, literally godforsaken outer space? In all its dreadful, agonizing meaninglessness—must we set up the living, bleeding, tortured remains of a person not yet executed, or the charred remains of a three-year-old child burned to a crisp by President Nixon's napalm against the dead, empty, totally meaningless, American, and lunatic outer space?

Yes, we must.

We won't get off with less.

Of course I have no answer—and any answer would be facile, cheap, and theological (or Leninistic) to the point of being comical.

We here at La Poudrière would be ashamed of such an answer. But we aren't ashamed to pose the question in all its sharpness and clarity. And now I thank you for your attention.

Once again I walked alone through the dark summer night down to my grape and tomato arbor. The stars were very clear against the sky. I sat down by the stone table with a piece of bread, a bottle of red wine, and a piece of coarse liver paste.

There was a rustling up by my garden gate, and something large and heavy came walking in.

It was Lefèvre.

He sat down, and I gave him bread and wine.

Neither of us said anything.

He chewed slowly and thoroughly before he put his cigarette back in place under his huge mustache.

"Do you know who killed that Hungarian shit?" I said.

It was great to hear Lefèvre laugh again, with his carefree, powerful, joyous laughter.

"As a doctor and curator of souls I have a duty to remain silent!" he replied. But he didn't stop laughing.

"Who'll be next?" I said.

Lefèvre laughed again.

"One single record-keeper can ask more than ten angels can answer!" he said. "Do you have any more wine?"

"Of course."

I went in and got a half-gallon bottle of ordinary local red wine.

"You old sodomite, you old sodomite!" said Lefèvre. "Have you had a good time with little Christine?"

"Yes," I said, "when it comes to angels she's the only one I've had to do with lately."

We sat silent for a long time, then he spoke again:

"Tell something," he said. "Tell me a story."

"It would have to be about Puss and Christine," I said.

"Has something happened to Puss?"

Lefèvre's voice sounded anxious.

"Puss was pregnant when you left," I replied. "You're certainly a fine doctor!"

"That I didn't know," he said, looking at me with concern. "Did the birth go well?"

"Just as splendidly as with your little Arab from the boys' brothel in Algeria."

He sighed with relief.

"But of course the kittens had to be dispatched, and they weren't burned—they were dispatched in the usual manner, by drowning, and it was little Christine's task to bury them afterwards. Which she did. But when she was walking past the burial mound a couple of hours later, there was something which said 'Meow!' And out of the grave came the resurrected Pussykins in person."

"That was a lovely story," said Lefèvre. "So it survived both drowning and burial."

"Gloriously."

"And then what happened?"

"It got drowned again, and if it still survives, then we'll just have to continue, as with other executions—until death occurs. Why should it have things so much better than other people?"

"Just over and over again?"

I pondered a bit over the answer, then I said:

"It will doubtless gradually get used to it. The daily drowning and burial will become a habit, and Pussykins will accept that well, that's the way life is. That it's a part of it all."

We sat there in total silence for awhile, then Lefèvre pointed at the eastern sky:

"There's Saturn!" he said.

"Yes," I said, "so?"

"No, no," he said. "Only the sun is perfect."

Something rustled over the terrace, something black and quiet and lonesome.

"What's that?" said Lefèvre.

"It's just a hedgehog out sniffing for water," I said. Then I got up and went in after a saucer of milk for the hedgehog. It drank for a long time, and I thought of a boy in Africa and a girl in Sicily.